PRAISE FOR GRIDIRON GIRL

"A fast-paced, character-driven novel about a girl going her own way." — *Kirkus Reviews*

"*Gridiron Girl* is an engaging story about an elite athlete and her journey to step away from her role as the captain of a state bound volleyball team to pursue her true passion and earn the spot as the football team's starting quarterback. Julia's timely story of sports, family, determination, and romance will inspire readers to stay true to themselves, especially those who have ever considered redefining themselves."
—Kimberly Gabriel, award-winning author of *Every Stolen Breath*

"*Gridiron Girl* is an uplifting read packed with tons of girl power, delightful banter, and a whole lot of heart! I can't get enough of Julia's strength and her take-no-prisoners attitude! Definitely a must read!"
—Molly E. Lee, author of *Ember of Night*

"Inspiring and entertaining, Tamara Girardi's *Gridiron Girl* expertly balances sporty-action, depth, and humor as she speeds us through the challenges and rewards of a teen who rises above expectations to accomplish a dream."
—Nova McBee, author of the *Calculated series*

"*Gridiron Girl* is the book my football-obsessed heart has been craving. Give me a girl who knows how to go after her dreams even when the world is set against her, mix that with all of the epic sports-movie feels while also showing young women that they can do anything they set their mind to, and top it all off with phenomenal writing and edge-of-your-seat action, and you've got a story destined to become a young adult classic. Every teen girl needs to read this book."
—Chelsea Bobulski, author of the *All I Want for Christmas* series

ULTIMATE TAKEDOWN

IRON VALLEY SERIES

TAMARA GIRARDI

 WISE WOLF BOOKS LAS VEGAS

WISE WOLF
BOOKS

This is a work of fiction. All of the characters, organizations, publications, and events portrayed in this novel are either products of the author's imagination or are used fictitiously.

ULTIMATE TAKEDOWN

IRON VALLEY SERIES

For my children—
Frank, Clara, Gabriella, and Domenick
If you work through life's challenges with the tenacity
and grit of a wrestler, you can accomplish anything.
All my love.

"THE KNOWLEDGE THAT EVERYTHING GOOD CAN BE TAKEN AWAY AT ANY SECOND IS WHAT MAKES ME WORK SO HARD."
—RONDA ROUSEY

CHAPTER 1

THE BOUT NUMBER ON THE SIGN AT MAT 42 READ
3009—three matches before mine. With my headgear positioned
tightly over my braids, I stretched my neck and ran through the steps
of my go to throw. *I'll lock my hands on her hip bone. Pull her in tight
and wrap my leg around hers. She won't be able to escape.*

Between the mat and the encroaching crowd—slightly smaller
than usual since it was preseason—I warmed up with five standing
tuck jumps.

The sign flashed number 3012.

"Annalise Fiori," I said, checking in with the man running the
head table.

"Red," he said.

I scooped the red strap from the mat and retreated into a corner to
secure the velcro around my ankle, mentally running my technique
over and over.

"You got this, Annalise," Coach Law called. "Like we practiced.
Wrestle smart."

I nodded and approached the ref and my opponent at the center
of the mat. I didn't know her name, but her first initial, according to
the board, was a "J".

"Shake hands," the ref said.

We did.

The chaos of noise—fans cheering, coaches and teammates yelling moves, children playing, referees blowing whistles—faded. Since I'd been a kid on the mat, I'd loved that sound void, the way my headgear silenced the rest of the world. Isolated me. Turning the team sport into an individual challenge. Adrenaline alive in my veins, a rush that couldn't be contained.

On the mat, I had myself. My training. My technique. My strength.

Win or lose, the outcome was mine to own.

J's hips and legs rushed into focus. She protected herself, but that was easy to do before the whistle. Once we were live, she'd reach or leave a leg unprotected. Her vulnerability would be my opportunity. I'd take it, and with it, take her down.

At the whistle, we burst into motion. Low in our stances, circling on the mat. Her knees revealed the rhythm of her movements. I lowered my level and took a shot, reaching for her legs. She quickly reacted by throwing her hips down in a sprawl. I lost my grip, but as she circled up, I wrapped my arms around her waist. I locked my hands and adjusted while she squirmed. I aimed for the tip of her hip bone, but she pushed at my lock and tried to get away. I tugged harder, locking my hands again. I felt the rush of the moment.

I had her.

Pushing with my hips and pulling at her body, I triggered the leverage to flip her over my shoulders, landing her on the mat in a textbook suplex. Adrenaline exploded through my body at the sound of her thumping against the mat under my complete control.

"Good, Annalise!" Coach Law yelled. "On your toes. Run your gut wrench."

Following my coach's advice, I moved into position to score two more points, but the ref tapped my shoulder before I could turn her.

"Blood," the official said calmly.

Red smeared J's face and dripped through her fingers, which were cupped under her nose. We retreated to our respective corners, and the trainers descended on her.

"Annalise, you have blood on your arm," Coach Law said.

That was the first I'd noticed it. "What happened?"

"On the takedown, she smacked her nose off the mat," Coach Law said, cleaning my skin with disinfectant wipes.

The score read 5-0.

"Your work on that suplex is paying off."

"Thanks, Coach," I said, knowing my success had everything to do with him.

Coach Law owned the Keystone Club, a private wrestling club in our hometown. It was where everyone who was serious about wrestling spent their evenings, after practicing in the afternoons with their school teams. I'd been toiling on his worn blue mats for years.

I had to in this sport if I wanted to compete against boys. And that's exactly what I did. Competed against girls in tournaments through the club and against boys through my high school team— all in the name of earning a scholarship to wrestle in college. I had a few prospects, but I didn't only want to wrestle. I wanted to study art. It might not have made sense to everyone, but for me, the sport and art complemented each other.

Wrestling was a swirl of motion like a brush across a canvas. The blur of color, and the burst of emotion. Every match a blank canvas, full of possibility. Like an artist could choose any composition, a wrestler could choose any moves. Step by step, both the masterpiece and the match evolved.

Finding the perfect college left little margin for error.

Kind of like competing for two teams in one day—also something I happened to be doing.

I glanced at my phone face up next to Coach Law's knee. Across the River's Edge Sports Complex, my high school teammates—all guys—huddled around video games and listened to music. Chilling. Prepping. Not exhausting themselves in two different brackets like I was. My bout would be called on the boys' mat soon. My best friend and teammate, Dom, had promised to give me a ten-minute warning.

"Let's go," the ref called when J had stopped bleeding.

In the neutral position, we faced off again. She left her leg exposed, so I shot for it.

And watched her nose plug, red with blood, drop to the mat.

Another time out.

The wiping, plugging, pinching, wiping, plugging, pinching of her nose. Took. Forever!

I bounced on my toes, checking my phone screen every few seconds. Finally, the trainers plugged her nose and held the plug in with athletic tape stretched across each side of her face.

Points for creativity, and let's go!

Back on the mat, we circled again, adrenaline coursing through me to end this before I'd have to forfeit my boys' match and miss the chance to finally beat Trevor Jacoby, the boy I was set to wrestle next who had beaten me every match, every year.

With her makeshift nose plug, my opponent stalled. The ref warned her to get into the action. She'd lean forward and hand fight me with a few swings and weak collar ties before stepping backward and out of my reach until the time ticked away, and the period ended.

Heading into the second, my phone lit up with a message from Dom. I had the length of two matches, so about twelve minutes to get back over there. I could make it. Even if we had to stop for blood again, I'd make it.

The ref signaled the start of the period, and I went hard and tried to set up a duck under to put myself in position for another suplex. I got behind J, but this time she immediately dropped her weight forward, to the ground. Her fall fed me two more points. Better for her to give up two than get thrown over my head again and lose five points to end the match. Back on the mat, I was in position for a turn. Pushing with my toes, I held her legs tightly crossed together and rolled.

Once. Two points.

"Again, Annalise," Coach Law shouted.

She fought against me.

"Give it all you got!"

On my toes again, I pushed. I needed one more.

The ref stopped me. What? No.

The trainers stormed the mat. Blood. Again!

They taped her nose plugs back into position while I bounced on my toes and thought about the boys' mat. Maybe the ref would be kind enough to wait. I'd text Dom the second I was on my way. But to walk right onto that mat after finishing on this one, I'd be tired and at a disadvantage.

I should have never wrestled the girls' match first. If my mom had been there, she wouldn't have let me.

Why did I think I could make it?

"Let's go!" the ref called.

I jogged to the center circle, waiting for the signal, and immediately took a shot off the whistle, taking my opponent down once more and earning enough points to lead by ten and win the match. I shook her hand and waited for the ref to raise mine before rushing to her coach and then my own.

"I have to be on the boys' mat, Coach."

"Go. We'll talk later."

I nodded, scooped my phone and ran. I voiced a text to Dom that I was on my way, but it barely went through by the time I got to my team. The scoreboard read the weight above mine.

"Dom!"

He patted my back. "I'm sorry, Lise. The two matches before yours were quick pins."

I slumped onto the mat. "No…"

"What took you so long over there?"

"I suplexed her onto her face, and blood spurted everywhere."

His eyes widened. "Wow. Okay. That's kind of awesome, though. Not the blood, but you've been trying to get a suplex forever."

I'd also wanted to beat Trevor Jacoby forever.

"Trevor looked relieved. I don't think he wanted to face you again."

Shocker. I found him in the crowd, smirking. Relaxing. Snacking on carbs. Listening to his headphones. He waved, wiggling his fingers in a taunt. Someday, Trevor Jacoby.

Someday.

A few years earlier, he'd beaten me soundly, pinning me in the first period. After a few matches against each other, though, I'd fought back. First getting pinned in the third, then going the whole three periods with him, then even scoring on him despite losing by a regular decision.

"Last time he beat me, he cried," I said.

"I remember," Dom said, shaking his head. "Because you scored points on him. Can you imagine what he would have done if you'd actually beaten him?"

I so wanted to find out. While I'd worked my best skills and techniques against J, Trevor had walked onto the boys' mat and gotten a win for no other reason than bad scheduling.

Utter crap.

Not that I should have been surprised. I'd competed in this world long enough. Even the breakdown of the River's Edge Sports Complex demonstrated the inequality in painful clarity.

The high school boys wrestled in the wide open basketball court room. The space bustled with two rows of mats, parents in pop-up chairs, spreads of healthy snacks and electronics on picnic blankets, and even the occasional toddler in a playpen. The middle school and elementary boys competed on the equally massive turf section of the facility with similar scenes of family, friends, and food.

The boys had two rooms.

The girls had two mats.

Despite years of everyone telling me girls' wrestling was the fastest growing sport in the country, it still wasn't a sanctioned high school sport in the state of Pennsylvania. That meant wrestling only boys at school, unless out of sheer luck, another school had a girl on their team that happened to wrestle my weight class.

You might hit the lottery once in your life, but you didn't hit every week.

"After you wrestle, I'm heading back to the girls' mat. I didn't even talk with Coach Law after the match."

"Thanks for sticking around."

"Of course," I said and meant it. Dom Roppolo had been kind to me from the moment we'd met as kids. The memory went something like this:

> *Me to a boy with a sideways smirk and a name I won't mention: Do you want to be my partner?*
> *Boy: No.*
> *Me: Oh. Why not?*
> *Boy laughed, spraying me in the face with spit in the process.*
> *Me: Gross.*
> *Boy: Maybe girls don't belong here.*
> *Me…dropped Boy to the mat with a thud: Maybe you*

don't belong here.

Dom stepped between us and offered to be my partner. After that practice, the other boys didn't mess with me when Dom was around. I improved by wrestling someone bigger than me. And the boy-who-must-not-be-named stopped wrestling a couple years later.

Leaving Dom and me in our peaceful best friendship ever since.

"You ready?" I asked, bringing my attention back to Dom's match.

"Yeah. I think I have Nick Walsh."

I rolled my eyes. "From Forest Run. Any of his other pals here?"

"You fishing for news about Sebastian Love?"

I scowled at Dom and studied our opponents around the mat.

"He could be here, but I haven't seen him."

Good. Nick Walsh was one thing. Sebastian I couldn't take. Not today. I slumped against Dom's duffel bag with my mini sketchbook on my lap. My pencil moved while my mind wandered to thoughts of the Forest Run High School wrestlers.

Not that I would admit it aloud. Like to anyone. Ever. But in middle school, Sebastian had been the cutest boy I'd ever seen. With short black curls spiked messily to the side and captivating eyes that sometimes looked as blue as my favorite Gatorade and other times as green as the emerald of my birthstone, he'd floated around the wrestling mat with confidence, shooting at the right moment, extending his arms and legs to leverage his body weight and strength. Every tournament, his name appeared as the victor in each round of the bracket, even the championship matches. Every duals competition, he beat opponent after opponent.

In other words, he'd made eighth grade me swoon and twelfth grade me sketch his likeness. I scratched out his face and flipped to the page of my sketchbook. No more Sebastian drawings. He didn't have power over me anymore. I'd been thirteen and hadn't crushed on many boys in my few years of existence. If I had, maybe the outcome of the whole Sebastian experience would have been different.

Maybe.

CHAPTER 2

DOM AND NICK FACED OFF IN AN EPIC BATTLE AT THE 160-pound weight class. I hadn't seen two wrestlers more well-suited in a long time. The match attracted the attention of fans around the room, even if they weren't anywhere near our mat. After two and a half periods of struggle, Nick turned Dom onto his back, but Dom refused to be pinned. He pushed out of it with a strong bridge, reversed control, and earned the points he needed to win the match.

I smacked his shoulder when he came off the mat. "That was epic! Congratulations!"

"Thanks," he said with a grin. "A little too epic for preseason."

"Hey, Annalise."

Ugh. Nick Walsh. Fabulous.

At least he was alone. Sebastian usually wrestled a lower weight class than Nick. Since that match had already ended, I hoped that meant Sebastian wasn't there. Not that I was about to ask Nick and give Sebastian the satisfaction to know I thought about him. Ever.

"Hey," I said, stiff from confusion at why he would even speak to me. It had been years, and our last words hadn't been kind ones.

Nick shook Dom's hand again. "That was one of the best matches I've had in a while."

"Me too," Dom said.

"If you ever want to train together, let me know."

"Sounds good. Thanks."

Nick walked away with his family.

"Was that weird?" I asked.

"No. It was kind of cool, actually. He's wicked strong. I'd like to know his regimen."

"Don't ask me to tag along and be friendly with Nick and his pal."

"Wouldn't dream of it," Dom said.

"Congrats again. I'll be back for our next match." Which wouldn't be nearly as tough as wrestling Trevor. "Gotta go see Coach Law."

He waved, and I hustled to the girls' mats.

Younger competitors in their pigtail braids and tiny singlets practiced moves on the two girls' mats before the next match. I found my coach with a handful of my teammates all hydrating and snacking in the corner of the turf. I checked in with a few of them to see how they'd done after I'd rushed away. Most of them had won, setting us up for possibly advancing through the bracket to the girls' team championship later in the day.

"Hey, Annalise," Coach Law said. "How did the match you were rushing to go?"

"I missed it."

He shook his head. "I'm sorry. If it's any consolation, your moves were great."

"Thanks, Coach."

"Coach Lawton!" a voice boomed from behind us.

"Sally," Coach said with a smile as if he were greeting an old friend. I guess he was.

"Is this Annalise Fiori?" the silver-haired woman wearing an official duals shirt and badge asked, shaking my coach's hand.

"Yes it is. Annalise, this is Sally Errico. She organized the event."

She? A woman organized this entire event. I didn't know women had that opportunity with wrestling.

"Sal's also an advocate for girls' wrestling at the state level," Coach added.

"We were glad to see you in the bracket," Mrs. Errico said. "You're quite the competitor. Having wrestlers like you here elevates the sport."

"Thank you," I said to be polite, but my mind wandered to all the ways adults in power could elevate the sport without putting that task on the shoulders of high school wrestlers.

"It also communicates to the state that girls are here to stay when it comes to wrestling. The more we can show that, the better chance we have of a sanctioned high school sport in Pennsylvania."

"Great," I said. "These girls deserve it."

"You do," Mrs. Errico said.

She chatted and smiled in all the right ways to show she was a genuinely nice person, but a question teased the edge of my thoughts and wouldn't go away. "Mrs. Errico?"

"Yes." she said, tucking her arms behind her back and turning her full attention to me.

"What other ways are you working to elevate the sport?"

She raised her eyebrows and smiled. "Great question. I've been working with the state athletic committees to convince them to officially sanction girls' wrestling. We hope it will happen soon, and when it does, it means more opportunity for girls across the state."

I could appreciate her enthusiasm, but her promises weren't new. Maybe it was the frustration from missing my match fueling me, but I couldn't stop myself. "I've heard for years that girls' wrestling is the fastest growing high school sport in the country with an increase in numbers year after year for decades. If that's the case, why hasn't the state already sanctioned the sport?"

Mrs. Errico looked at me as if I were the most entertaining puzzle she'd ever seen. "You're right. The state wants at least one hundred high schools to have a program before they sanction girls' wrestling. High schools want the state to sanction the sport before they invest in a program. The classic catch-twenty-two."

I wondered if our athletic director at Iron Valley would create a girls' wrestling team.

"I saw your match," Mrs. Errico continued. "Impressive win."

"Thank you."

"Have you ever thought about speaking up for the sport?"

"I'm not a spokesperson," I said.

"But you could be. You're a great wrestler with prospects. People would listen to you."

I wasn't sure that was true, but I didn't have time to think about it, let alone act on her suggestions. "I spend most of my time training. I have to get stronger to compete with the boys, which is something I have to do since there aren't many girls' teams. I also have to train in two different styles, which is something my male opponents don't have to do. I don't have time to be a voice for the sport."

The classic problem with the human race. The people who might have something important to say don't have time because they're spending every waking moment in a system that doesn't work for them.

Mrs. Errico nodded, thoughtfully. "You make good points. Thanks for sharing them. I'll take that back to my colleagues and see if there is something we can do to help."

"Thank you."

"If you ever change your mind, here's my card. It could mean anything from giving interviews about your wrestling experiences to spearheading an effort to develop a team at your school."

I tucked her card into my bag.

"I have to check on a few things. Annalise, it was a pleasure. Coach Lawton, good to see you."

Mrs. Errico weaved her way through the crowd, and Coach Law nudged me. "You seem fired up."

The weight of the day pushed too hard on my shoulders. I slumped onto the ground next to him. "I can't believe I missed my boys' match. I…"

"What?"

"I get up before most of my male teammates. I work out more than them. I lift more than they do, and while they're over there snuggled up on the mats, playing games on their phones, I'm rushing over here to compete in another match. It's…"

"Frustrating? Unfair? Infuriating?" Coach suggested.

I sighed. "Yes. That and more."

"Look, Annalise. If I've learned anything coaching this brutal sport for the past twenty years, it's that mental toughness is more important than anything else. Anything. Your mental toughness," he tapped gently at my temple, "I don't want to throw anyone under the bus, but it's tougher than any of the boys I coach."

"Thanks, Coach."

"Whether you want to help Sal with her mission for girls' wrestling or not is up to you, but I have no doubt you can do whatever you set your mind to."

That made one of us, but Coach Law's opinion held some weight, so it still sparked good vibes. Only time would tell if they were good enough.

***

THREE HOURS LATER, DOM AND I FINISHED FOR THE day. I'd won all three of my girls' freestyle matchups. Two teams had forfeited since they hadn't had anyone in my weight class. Had I attended duals only in the girls' bracket, I'd have paid for the full day and come away with three matches, only one of which was actually competitive. On the boys' mat, I'd wrestled six matches and won half—the ones I'd expected to win. Tired and cranky, the fact I'd lost my opportunity to wrestle Trevor weighed on me like an unrelenting collar tie.

On the way out the door, I grabbed Dom's arm and pulled him into the line for chicken nuggets.

"You're not going to eat that."

"Yes. I am," I said.

"You're stress eating."

"So," I said and ordered an eight pack and a Gatorade. "You want anything?"

"Nope. I'll eat yours when you decide you don't want them."

"You should get your own," I said.

He crossed his arms. Fine. I paid and collected my greasy goodness. Fried food was not on my nutritionist-approved meal plan. I popped the first nugget in my mouth and groaned at the explosion of salt. By the time I chewed through the chicken, though, it didn't taste as good.

Dom held out his hand.

"I hate you," I said and turned over the bag of nuggets.

He tossed one in his mouth. "I can deal with that."

On the drive home, we talked about school, our families, and our sport. For years, everyone we knew had told us we'd get together someday. That it was inevitable. Two people—gasp, a straight boy and a straight girl in high school—couldn't spend the time together we did, enjoy each other's company like we did, and not end up rapturously in love.

We disagreed. Senior year, and still no sparks.

Wow. Senior year.

When I'd started in the sport, senior year had seemed so far away with all of its possibility and promise. My childish hopes and dreams about what the sport could become some day had hit a deadline. For me, change was too late. The canvas didn't feel blank with possibility anymore. Instead, the painting awaited finishing touches, not major changes or new visions.

Now that my final high school season had arrived, nothing could be clearer.

CHAPTER 3

DOM SLOWED HIS TRUCK IN OUR LONG DRIVEWAY TO avoid hitting three deer who had wandered across with little more than a look in our direction.

"For living in suburbia, you have this country feel going on."

"Tell me about it," I said. "Wait until spring when all the critters emerge."

"I'll pass," he said. "Are you painting tonight?"

"Nah. I have to get to Ashley's playoff game. Thanks for the ride." He tipped an imaginary hat and waved.

I dropped my keys into the tray on the counter with a clatter that contrasted with the otherwise quiet house. Mom had planned to meet me at the game after running a string of errands, and my sister had left on the bus hours earlier. Keeping an eye on the clock, I showered and changed before running back out the door and jumping into my cold, hand-me-down sedan. Too cold. I started the engine and hustled back inside to grab a peanut butter sandwich, apple slices, and carrots—the dinner of wrestling champions everywhere.

In the garage, the painting I'd been working on the night before caught my eye. A pumpkin patch landscape with a sky that was more late night than twilight. Maybe a little purple would lighten it and even contrast the orange of the pumpkins. I squirted a dot of purple onto a paint pallet and brushed it across the sky, swishing and blending until I caught the shade I'd envisioned. With a dot of white paint, I blended to gradually lighten the background to create more of a silhouette. I stood back. Yes. Much better. Maybe it would be the look to score me a spot in the local gallery's art show. With two months until the application deadline, I'd have to make a lot of progress and fast.

I studied my creation with a critical eye. Once it dried, I'd need a few stars. Only the brightest ones that could be seen in a twilight sky.

"I'm going to get into this art show," I said aloud. If positive affirmations could work before a wrestling match, hopefully they could work for art, too.

My sister always said—no! My sister!

I dropped my brush into the garage sink and hit the door opener. Exhaust poured from my car into the cold night air. I'd painted for twenty minutes! The inside of the car burned with the heat on full blast. The gas gauge read half a tank. Thankfully. How embarrassing would it have been to run out of gas in my own driveway.

I calculated travel math. About thirty minutes to the game. More with traffic, hopefully not too much. One hour until the game started. I could make warmups.

I *would.*

Positive affirmations.

Or not. Traffic hated me. The parking lot laughed at my attempt to find a spot closer than a mile from the building. Stepping inside made it clear why. Fans packed the gym, a canvas of colored dots that reminded me of the pointillism technique I'd studied that summer at art camp. The first of the two semi-final matches to be played there that night would end soon according to the scoreboard. With the second game following it, fans from four different schools flooded the space. The first match between our volleyball rival Pacific High and my personal rival Forest Run was in the fourth game with a tie score. If Forest Run beat Pacific, they'd go to five games. I waved across the bleachers to my sister sitting with her team in a huddle of Iron Valley purple jerseys.

Ashley pointed to the scoreboard. The day before, she'd told me she'd be shocked if Forest Run could play with Pacific, let alone beat them. The morning had reminded me—with sports all things were possible.

My stomach growled. I'd never grabbed the dinner of champions from my kitchen. Oh, but that twilight sky. Gorgeous! I backtracked to the concession stand in the lobby and stood behind the hordes of people waiting to order.

The options disappointed. I still had a couple pounds to lose for the season. Concession stand fare wasn't about to help, and Dom wasn't there to eat my discarded junk food. I usually had a stash of jerky and nuts in my car, too, but Dom and I had crushed that. I mentally calculated the distance to the nearest fast-food restaurant that served salads. By the time I'd walk across the packed parking lot to my car, drive through the Saturday evening traffic, and get to the front of the line, I'd miss my sister's game, or more importantly warmups. Since she didn't start varsity, if I missed warmups, I'd likely miss her playing altogether. And, since the state championship tournament would be the same day I was at a wrestling tournament on the other side of the state, the night was my last chance that season to see her play.

I scanned the menu one more time, hopeful to find a stray mention of fruit, jerky, or even pretzels.

No luck.

"Annalise Fiori?" a familiar voice said from over my shoulder, and my body froze.

Sebastian. Definitely no luck. None in the world. I glanced in his direction without actually setting my eyes on him. "Do I know you?"

"Cute," he said.

Cute. There was that word again—the word that had brought me a world of pain and embarrassment as a naive middle-schooler.

"Not even gonna say hi?"

"Hi," I said without turning around.

He stepped forward, so I couldn't continue ignoring him and pointed to the concession stand menu. "Makes it difficult for people like us, huh? M&Ms. Hot dogs. Loaded fries."

"Please don't group you and me into an 'us.'"

The kids in front of me ordered, and I moved into their previous space with gratitude.

"A friend of mine bought out the produce section at the local grocery store." He pointed to a cluster of Forest Run guys, including Nick, across the lobby holding a bag of oranges, three bushels of bananas, and a massive veggie tray.

My stomach grumbled. "I'm not hungry."

"You sure? We have plenty to share."

"I said I'm good. Thanks." More grumbling. Two hours. Two hours until the games would end, and I could eat.

I could make it.

Somehow.

"Your team start practicing yet?" Sebastian asked.

I ignored him, hoping he would get the hint. He didn't.

"You don't have to be rude."

"Actually, I do."

He sighed. "Good to see you, too."

The people in front of me picked up their food and stepped aside. I moved forward, away from the slimy Sebastian air.

"What can I get you, hon?" the woman behind the counter asked.

"Can I have a bottle of water, please?"

"Is that all?"

Sebastian snickered.

"Yes. Please."

He'd stopped chatting but kept breathing right behind me. Like a wild animal ready to pounce. Or a serial killer filling every neuron in your body with fear of your impending doom. Or, you know, Sebastian being Sebastian.

Forest Run on the ticket should have warned me like a billboard utilizing only the boldest colors that he'd be there. He probably dated one of the girls on the team. I wondered what he stood to gain from that relationship—the question a painful reminder of what he'd planned to gain from ours. Not that you could call what we'd had—or did—or whatever a relationship.

Did he have to breathe like such a dragon?

I exchanged a dollar for the water and pushed my way through the crowd of pleasant fans. Their happiness contrasted with my itchiness. I twisted the cap of the bottle, grateful for the cool rush on my tongue. Not food, but something. Maybe enough to take the edge off my irritation. I could have starred in a Snickers commercial.

Snickers? Yum.

I glanced back toward the concession stand, but instead of candy I saw Sebastian. And my hunger for chocolate faded to more itchiness. Maybe I was allergic to him. That would explain a lot.

Poking my head back into the gym, I caught Ashley's eye. She waved me over. I climbed the bleachers and hugged her.

"Sit," she said.

I glanced at Coach Medina not wanting to be accused of distracting the volleyball team before their big match.

"It's fine," my sister said. "I already checked with her. The game will be over in a minute, and we don't need these." She opened a cooler behind her, revealing a feast of fruit and veggies.

My stomach grumbled louder than when I'd thought about Snickers. "Seriously?"

"Coach's sons used to wrestle. She gets it."

The beauty of the inside of that cooler demanded to be painted. Apples, oranges, bananas, broccoli, blueberries, and grapes. A rainbow of heaven. The artwork would be a masterpiece. A magnum opus. I reached in and peeled a banana. I bit off more than I could chew, and asked my sister between bites, "Who do you want to win?"

"Forest Run," answered Ally Malone, the team's setter, and another senior I'd had classes with since kindergarten.

The banana tasted beyond delicious. Changing my eating habits—cutting processed foods and sugars, to make weight—always reminded me how flavorful healthy food could be. I had my eye on an apple next. Until my sister said something that turned my stomach.

"Is that Sebastian Love?"

I lowered my head and groaned.

"It is," Ashley said. "He's looking right at us."

Sebastian and his friends climbed the bleacher steps closest to where we were sitting. The other Forest Run guys peeled off into a semi-empty row, but Sebastian kept coming. I would not look at him. Or his messy, yet perfectly styled hair. Or his forearms.

Definitely not his forearms.

"He can't take a hint to save his life," I muttered.

"Ashley! Hey!" he said.

"Sebastian," she said, not giving away any emotion in her voice. I appreciated that she wasn't too friendly, the loyal sister that she was. "You're a blast from the past."

Maybe he could blast right back there. I made a point of turning my entire body away from him.

"You playing in the next game?" he asked.

"My team is," Ashley said.

I caught the subtlety in her answer and wished she'd be playing. Nearly a foot taller than my five-feet-four-inches, Ashley competed as a middle hitter on the volleyball team, but the seniors on Iron Valley's team dominated, especially at middle. As a junior, Ashley had only seen varsity playing time a few minutes here and there when the team had led by huge margins. Since tonight was a regional semi-final, I expected the game to be too close for her to get on the court. We both did.

"I hear good things about you girls," Sebastian said, and I rolled my eyes at his attempt to charm. "I couldn't make it to the match when you played at our place earlier in the season. I was away at a wrestling camp."

"Good for you."

Oops. Did I say that out loud?

Ashley elbowed me in the side.

"Right," Sebastian said. "Good luck, Ashley."

He ambled back to his seat, not that I watched or anything.

"Who was that?" Molly Mattola asked in a voice that suggested she was way too interested in the answer.

"A wrestler from Forest Run," Ashley said.

Molly sighed. "Why couldn't our schools have merged this year instead of next? I wouldn't mind seeing him in the halls."

I would. "The merger isn't happening, is it?"

For years, people had chattered about Forest Run merging with another district, maybe ours, but it all felt like chatter. Until about a week earlier when rumors that the deal was nearly done poured out from behind closed doors.

"My aunt's on the school board," Molly said. "And she said it's happening. Forest Run is too small. The fact they're in the semi-final of the playoffs is a miracle. Most of the teams don't even have enough players to compete."

I imagined the Forest Run players on the court—the ones giving the powerhouse Pacific High School such a challenge—merging with our team. Taking our varsity spots. Or more specifically, Ashley's. She'd worked too hard for too long not to start her senior year.

"So they'll bus them to all of our schools?" Ashley asked, seemingly unfazed by the possibility of competing for the position that should have easily been hers.

"It's not that far," Molly argued. "Besides, I think some of their buildings are new and could be used for elementary schools. It's the junior high and high school kids that will merge with Iron Valley and come to us."

Selfishly, I was glad I'd graduate before it happened. Seeing Sebastian at wrestling tournaments a few times a year tortured me enough. Seeing him every day?

Gross.

Dom and Nick competed in the same weight class. If we'd merged this year, they would have had to wrestle each other for the starting spot in their weight class. What if I'd have to wrestle Sebastian for mine?

No. One more year.

Nothing but gratitude for that.

Pacific led Forest Run in the final game of the five-game series, 10-8. The first one to fifteen would be the winner.

"Let's go stretch, girls," Coach Medina called, and the bleachers around me cleared. "Annalise, help yourself to the food."

"Thanks, Coach."

"Any time. Please drop the cooler at our bench when you're done."

"Sure thing."

Ashley and her teammates squeezed into a corner of the gym beside the bleachers to stretch for their game. My stomach jumbled with the same jitters I felt before every one of my wrestling matches. Over the years, I'd made friends with a lot of the girls on the team, especially Chandra and Melanie, Ashley's closest friends. After a tumultuous start to the season, I wanted this for them like I wanted pins in my wrestling matches.

Forest Run pulled off the upset defeating Pacific, 15-13. Sebastian and his friends stormed the court to celebrate with the team until security ushered them away for the purple shirts of the Iron Valley Vikings to take their place for warmups. I settled in, wanting to watch every move Ashley made in case it was the last time I saw her play.

"Hey, Lise!" Julia Medina slid into the spot next to me with a couple carloads of football players behind her.

I hugged her. "Jules! Congrats on your season."

"Thanks. We feel good about having another game on Friday."

"You should," I said.

"How's wrestling going?"

I held up the apple.

"I don't know how you do it."

Ashley dove for a hit and made a great play. "Yes!" I cheered and turned my attention back to Julia. "Which part?"

"Competing against guys. Eating so healthy."

"You know a thing or two about competing against guys. Speaking of that, I haven't seen Owen around wrestling open gym yet. Maybe you're keeping him busy?"

She raised an eyebrow at me. "Digging for the sordid details?"

"Maybe."

"Tough," she said and laughed. "And as for the whole competing against boys thing…" She glanced at her teammates who were more interested in the girls on the court than our conversation. "It hasn't been easy. To be honest, I'm not sure I'd want to do it for years of my life like you have."

"But it's been worth it?"

She grinned. "Totally worth it."

The volleyball team shifted to serving practice. Ashley had been working on a jump serve.

"C'mon, Ash," I whispered.

As if she'd heard me, she glanced my way and waved before taking a deep breath, tossing the ball high, and crushing it deep into the court.

"Her jump serve looks good," Julia said.

"I know. I'm so proud of her."

"Who's that down there waving?" Julia asked.

"Black hair? Eyes you can't pick a color for?"

"Yes, and yes. Gorgeous, too."

"Never mind. I thought you meant Sebastian Love, an annoying wrestler from Forest Run who enjoys torturing me with his games."

"He's pretty adamant about getting your attention."

I lifted my hand in an unkind gesture without taking my eyes off Ashley.

"Annalise Fiori!" My mother's voice said. "Did you flip me off?"

Oh crap.

"I'm so sorry, Mom. That was meant for Sebastian."

She spun around. "Oh, darling Sebastian? Is he here?"

Julia patted my shoulder.

"One of his games is winning the heart of my mother, so she doesn't believe me when I tell her what a jerk he is."

"Mrs. Fiori, so good to see you," Sebastian said. "I was trying to get your attention before I left."

Making a conscious decision against giving Sebastian my attention or anything else, I scooped up the cooler and headed for the Iron Valley bench.

CHAPTER 4

I DROPPED THE COOLER BEHIND THE FIRST CHAIR, grabbed another apple, and nibbled on it while Ashley practiced hitting. Sebastian chatted up my mom like an old friend.

He was like a weed that kept growing back.

Over.

And over.

And over.

No amount of weed kill could get the job done.

Memories of him flooded my mind like artworks of the past. A watercolor painting of a wrestling tournament in eighth grade, when my coach had knelt in front of me, reminding me of our game plan. Over the purple of his Iron Valley wrestling hat, three boys had sat across the mat, wearing Forest Run team hoodies and cheering for my opponent.

Sebastian had glanced at me, our eyes locking and setting off a sparkle inside me that I'd never felt before. He'd smiled and nodded, not like responding to a question in the affirmative. It was "the nod". Followed by a curl in his lip and the death of my innocence.

Seconds later, I'd felt Sebastian's gaze on me again. When I'd caught his eye, he'd made no point of looking away. I could sketch that memory for days and never fully master that look of shameless interest on his face.

Or evoke the feelings in my audience that I'd felt.

In my memories, my Forest Run opponent and I had shaken hands and started the match. I'd pegged him in seconds. Boys had two speeds when they wrestled girls—fast and furious or tentative. I had moved for wrist control and shot my sweep single, taking him down and proving my theory—he'd been the tentative type. I'd wrapped my right arm tightly around his waist while securing an arm bar with my left, getting a tilt on him and earning back points before he'd rolled out of the position. I wouldn't let him get a reversal on me or break free to earn a point.

I'd held him down on his stomach and worked to see what turn I could set up next, but he'd brought his knees up under him and tried to use my pressure to push himself upright. I lifted his ankle like an emergency brake to stop his upward movement, bringing him back to the mat before the ref blew the whistle signaling the end of the period.

The second period hadn't lasted. Right off the whistle, I'd taken him down again. I could still sense his fear and hesitation and capitalized. With another arm bar, instead of tilting him, I'd ran the bar. I could feel him trying to brace. He hadn't fought it well.

I'd ran the bar right over for a pin.

The ref had blown the whistle, and I'd released my grip. As we stood to go back to the center of the mat and shake hands, he'd pushed me as hard as he could. The ref had put his hands out to stop my fall and levied a one-point penalty on the Forest Run team.

The penalty point had only pissed him off more. On his way off the mat, he'd slammed his head gear. Another one-point penalty for Forest Run.

Their coach had shaken my hand and apologized for his wrestler's behavior. His teammates had tried to shake some sense into him, but tears had scarred his red cheeks.

He'd lost to a girl.

Utter devastation.

Our dual with Forest Run had ended with us on top by two points.

"Guess that kid shouldn't have thrown his head gear," Dom had said with a smirk.

His loss. Literally.

After the match, I'd gotten in line for the concession stand alone, an immovable smile still on my face from our win.

"Can I have a banana, a veggie plate, and a Gatorade, please?" I'd asked when it had been my turn to order.

"Hey," Sebastian had said, creeping up beside me.

Frozen, I'd gotten lost in those confusing eyes.

"You wrestled great."

"Thanks."

He'd smiled.

"What?"

Pink had flushed across his cheeks. "Nothing."

"Okay," I'd said, not even close to believing him. I'd known that look. He'd had something to say, probably about me being a girl, but I didn't want to hear it. "Well, see ya."

Before I could take a few steps, he'd jumped in front of me. "I'm sorry. I wanted to talk to you, but now that I'm here, I don't know what else to say."

"Why did you want to talk to me?"

He'd laughed and ruffled his already messy hair. "I…thought you were cute."

My heart had stopped. Coach would have to revive me for my next match. No, seriously. I'd hoped there was a defibrillator nearby.

"Cute? Me?"

"I heard your school had a girl wrestler, and I thought...I mean I never imagined…I'm not saying this right."

I hadn't thought so either, but he'd made one thing clear. The super cute Sebastian Love had thought I, Annalise Fiori, was cute, too.

"Bash!" someone had called from the gym doorway.

"I gotta go. My friend's match is about to start."

"Good luck to your friend."

With a grin, he'd responded a simple, "Thanks."

That grin. It'd captured me in that moment, leaving me to lean against the brick wall in the hallway, stunned.

Shaking away the memory, I refocused on my sister moving around the court with her team. I envied their dynamic. Ashley had friends from the team over the house all the time. Playing a sport together had strengthened their friendship. Dom was great, but I didn't have that closeness with any girls on my team because there were none. Hopefully, Mrs. Errico would succeed sooner rather than later, so another generation of girls couldn't say the same.

***

BACK AT HOME, GRABBED A YOGURT BEFORE CHANG-ing into shorts and a tank top and heading to the basement. My birthday present from four years earlier sat in the corner of the family room without a speck of dust. I settled into the well-worn, sliding seat, gripped the handles and stretched my neck and shoulders before pulling. I rowed slowly at first to warm up, but after a couple minutes, I pulled harder. Faster.

The rowing machine faced floating shelves meant to inspire me. Trophies from big tournaments lined the top shelf. Underneath, five pegs overflowed with medals. For fun, I'd organized them by color. Red. Blue. Purple. Gold. Green. Surprisingly, few tournaments awarded purple medals, but those were my favorite. From the bottom shelf, three pictures stared back at me. One of me and my mom both wearing singlets and wrestling at the Keystone Club when I'd first discovered the sport. One of my dad and me in front of Monet's Water Lilies painting at the art museum. One of Ashley and me on the paths in the woods by our house. In the photo, we'd been six and seven years old. We'd named the paths and installed signs, so we could navigate them. Love and pride poured from the photo as we squeezed each other in an intense hug.

My people.

I rowed harder, and the time passed.

Ten minutes. Fifteen. Twenty.

Sweat dripped into my eyes. With the morning's disappointment still weighing on me, too many stories played in the back of my mind. The time I had to forfeit a match because a boy was too embarrassed to wrestle me, and the tournament organizers didn't have the intelligence or the guts to do the right thing. The time in middle school my team did a sumo wrestling drill, and the shock when I'd beaten everyone. The direct messages from idiots who had had something stupid to say and felt brave enough to say it behind the guise of the internet. More times than I could count that my hair had been pulled or my face pushed into the mat after the whistle by some boy whose ego I'd bruised.

"How long have you been at this?" my mom interrupted my thoughts. She looked over my shoulder and saw the forty-three minutes and twelve seconds time on the display. "That's enough, Lise."

I let the momentum of the machine slow to a stop. "I didn't even realize."

"I know you get lost in it. You should set a timer."

I nodded.

"Is this about seeing Sebastian today?" She handed me a towel. I dabbed at my face and neck.

"No," I said, drawing out the word.

"I know you had a crush on him in middle school, and the hand gesture suggests that maybe you weren't happy to run into him."

"Sebastian irritates me. That's all."

She gave me the "mom look".

"Mom."

She shook her head. "Nothing. Nothing at all."

It was never nothing. Mom always took on the work of two parents. That included everything from the cooking, cleaning, volunteering at school, attending our sporting events, and the list went on. She and my dad had split years earlier, and they managed a co-parenting strategy well. Sort of. A private contractor, my dad traveled a lot in foreign countries for months each trip. When he came home, he spent a lot of time with us and brought the best presents, especially art treasures for me. When he was away, he emailed and called when he could, which wasn't often.

But mom was always there. Always watching. And always making assumptions.

I kissed her on the cheek. "Good night, Mom."

I left her behind in the basement. Her and all her innuendos about Sebastian. That canvas had been painted a long time ago, and the result hadn't been pretty.

CHAPTER 5

"FOREST RUN HIGH SCHOOL WON'T BE ABLE TO COM-pete with anyone this year," Dom said at after-school wrestling practice later that week. "I have a cousin who goes there. She said they can barely field a team."

They'd been the team to beat when we were little kids, but I guess things changed. My mom said the school board hired a terrible superintendent, and over the years, everything in the district went south. Families moved away or sent their kids to cyber or private school. The drop in enrollment meant a drop in their sports classification, too. We hadn't competed directly against them in years.

Lucky for me.

"Molly Mattola's aunt is on the school board. She said we're merging with them next year," I reiterated the gossip from the game the other night.

"Go," Coach yelled, and we both climbed into the plank position. We were in the mat room, our school's auxiliary gym that gave us enough space to practice, but little room for much else. We even ran our warmups and conditioning through the high school hallways.

"I don't think they have a choice anymore," Dom said.

"At least it will be next year." After I graduated. After Sebastian graduated. The hovering embarrassment every time I thought about more people learning about what happened between us threatened me like an ultimate takedown. Being around Sebastian felt like stomping across thin ice. He held the power to reveal the most embarrassing moment of my life.

Best to stay far away.

"Down," Coach said.

Dom crumbled against the mat, but I sat up, unfazed. I'd been doing planks every morning and night for months. I actually held them at home longer than Coach asked us to at practice.

"You good on your weight?" Dom asked.

"Getting there." I had two pounds to lose to feel comfortable in my weight class but losing four would put me in the best possible position. "You?"

"I tried, but how is it fair to start wrestling practice right after Halloween? In October, peanut butter cups are like a main food group for me."

I got his point. I watched Ashley eat as much as she wanted with all the aerobic workouts she did for volleyball. While she had ice cream, I ate carrots—bonus—dipped in ranch dressing. When season started and even if I hit my goal weight, I limited sugar as much as possible. Splurging meant indulging in carbs, but sugar could mess with my performance, and I wanted every possible advantage I could get.

"You can come to my house and use the rowing machine if you want," I suggested.

"I may have to. Will Ashley's hot volleyball friends be there? There's an outside hitter I have my eye on."

"Have your eye on her somewhere else. My house is not your dating network."

"Ruthless, Fiori," he said with a laugh as Coach called us back into more reps.

After planks, squats, and bridges, Coach told us to start drilling. Dom and I partnered up and practiced hand fighting and our shots. Later in practice, we wrestled live, doing our best to crush our partners. Coach moved us around, matching us up with different wrestlers for varied reactions and experiences. The only opponents I lost to were significantly heavier than me. My teammates slapped my back when I beat them. They congratulated me. They even cheered for me. It had taken years, but I was at home on the team.

"What are you smiling about?" Dom asked.

"Nothing," I said.

"No seriously? You have a crush on someone I don't know about."

"I don't do crushes—not in that sense. I'll crush you on the mat though."

He rolled his head back and fake snored.

I pushed him sideways, and he fell.

"Gotta work on those abs," I teased.

"Okay, wrestlers," Coach called. "Bring it in."

We huddled around Coach Joseph, a cloud of stench hovering around us.

"Good work today. I'm proud of you. I can see the strength in this team. You support each other. Work together. Push your teammates to be better. That's going to take us far."

I glanced at my teammates and nodded. They were the best.

"It's because of how hard you work together that I know what I'm about to say is going to be well-received."

Huh? Dom nudged me, but I swatted his hand away. What could Coach say that he'd have to prep us for?

"Our friends at Forest Run have not been able to field a team this year, and their coaching staff resigned yesterday. Our school officials reached an agreement last night for their wrestlers to join us a year earlier than expected."

My knees didn't work anymore. Neither did my heart or my lungs. I stared at Coach's lips, focusing on the shapes they were making, but they weren't words. At least they didn't seem like any words I knew.

"Coach," I said.

His lips stopped moving, and everyone looked at me.

"Yes, Annalise?"

"I'm sorry. I didn't mean to interrupt. I…" I what? Hallucinated? Heard what you said entirely wrong?

"I know this is an adjustment for everyone."

"Forest Run wrestlers are on our team now?" I managed.

"They are," Coach said. "Six of them. And I'm sure we all understand what it feels like to be left out or treated less than. We aren't going to do that to our new teammates. We are going to welcome them with enthusiasm. I expect tomorrow's practice to go exactly how today's went. Does everyone understand?"

My teammates muttered agreement.

"Does everyone understand?" he repeated with more force.

"Yes, Coach."

"Good. I'll see you tomorrow."

He would not. I quit. I could not come tomorrow. The chaos in my mind teleported me back to that first day Sebastian and I ever spoke. After he'd headed for the mat for his next match, I stood in the middle of the walkway. Confused. Surprised. Sebastian had thought I was cute. I'd repeated it to myself over and over, but it still felt more fiction than fact.

No boy had ever wanted to talk to me about something other than school or wrestling. If he tried to talk to me again, what would I say? That first day, I'd sat with Ashley in the stands and watched Sebastian warm up with his coach. When it was time for his match, he'd stepped up to the line, shook his opponent's hand, and in less than a minute, the match had ended with a quick pin from Sebastian. When the ref raised his arm in victory, I'd jumped up and cheered.

"Friend of yours?" Mom had asked.

"Yeah, Lise?" my sister said, studying me with her nosy, little sister gaze.

"Yep," I said without making eye contact with either of them.

I made an excuse to leave the stands, but Ashley followed me.

"It's us now," she said. "Tell me the truth. Who's the cutie?"

Being Ashley's loyal sister, I told her everything. All good things *then*. Give it a few weeks, though, and the bad definitely outweighed the good. Thinking back, the memories were crystal in my mind. Clear and solid. No changing them.

I could not be on Sebastian's team. Or see him every day.

Or…be reminded of what he'd done to me.

I had my own bathroom at the school where I could hide under the guise of changing. Alone, I ducked my face into my hoodie and pulled the string around my face tight. Maybe I could quit the high school team and compete at open tournaments. College coaches would still see me that way. I'd catch their attention.

And they'd ask why I didn't wrestle for my high school.

I couldn't exactly answer that a boy had embarrassed me in middle school, and I couldn't bear to be on the same team as him.

Besides, this was my team. I loosened the hoodie and re-emerged. I wasn't quitting over a boy. I'd seen it too many times. Friends who wrestled years ago bullied out of the sport by boys refusing to wrestle against them at tournaments because they were girls, dads of opponents embarrassing everyone in the room when their sons lost to a girl, and the sexual remarks—the sexual remarks were a different beast altogether. They released an inner monster in me. That inner monster had never lost a match.

I changed my clothes and closed my locker. Catching my expression in the mirror, I reminded myself of something my mother always said: I was fierce.

I wasn't going anywhere.

***

THAT NIGHT, I STORMED THROUGH ASHLEY'S BEDROOM doorway unannounced and collapsed onto her bed. Fierce, indeed.

"What's up, sis?" she asked from her desk.

"Sister sleepover."

She dropped her pencil and spun in the swivel chair. "On a school night? This has to be intense."

I sat tall in her bed and found my safe breathing stance.

"Oh boy. What is it?"

"Forest Run wrestlers."

Her eyes widened as I took another deep breath.

"Are joining the Iron Valley team as a co-op."

"Shut. Up."

Unable to sit upright anymore, I collapsed against the pillow again. Ashley snuggled next to me and nestled her head against my shoulder. "Oh, Lise."

"I've spent years avoiding him, and now he's going to be on my team."

"Maybe you won't have to spend much time together."

"He's close to my weight," I said. "I'll be lucky if Coach doesn't partner us in practices."

"Yuck."

Yeah. Yuck.

"Definite sister sleepover," Ashley said.

For the first time since I'd heard the news about Forest Run wrestlers joining our team, a few pounds of the overwhelming weight dissolved. I might have a fragmented team, but I had the perfect sister.

CHAPTER 6

IN MY FIVE-A.M. WORKOUT THE NEXT DAY, MY TRAINER scolded me three times for being distracted. I tapped the toes of my fuzzy winter boots through classes and stared at the clocks in every room—long enough to realize most of them needed a serious cleaning. By fifth period, I considered standing on a desk with a duster to clean them myself.

Even the dissection of a frog in biology couldn't sway my attention. All I thought about was the impending moment when the Forest Run wrestlers would walk into our gym that afternoon and transform my senior season into something I wouldn't recognize.

My teammates hustled to the locker room after the last bell of the day and changed. Back in the wrestling room, we stretched and glanced at the door every few seconds.

"Anyone know them?" Dom asked.

Justin Chan, a junior who wrestled the 138-pound weight class, said he did. "I worked out with them at Reversal for the last couple months. They're cool guys. Competitive."

The Reversal Wrestling Club was a private gym like the Keystone Club, but closer to Forest Run. I'd heard rumors that it had been struggling for business, too.

"Yeah, but how competitive?" asked Wesley Donovan, a senior

who wrestled at 189 pounds. "Let's get real. Some of them are going to slide into our weight classes."

"I'm already good for 189," Owen Malone boasted. Wesley raised an eyebrow at him. The two wrestled each other hard and would compete tough for the weight, unless one of them cut a few pounds to a lower weight class.

"You wish," Wesley threw back. "The point is we're not only wrestling against ourselves for the roster anymore. I think it's bullshit."

A few nods and grunts around the room demonstrated agreement.

"But we won't have to forfeit any weight classes," Justin offered.

"Who said we'd have to forfeit without them?" Wesley asked.

Owen shrugged. "We're a little light this year. We'd have to move some people around or forfeit a couple. Probably why the coaches agreed to co-op so quickly."

That made sense. Unfortunately. And knowing Nick and Sebastian's skill level, Iron Valley could practically guarantee regular victories in at least two weight classes because of them.

"We don't know what to expect," I said, trying to bring a positive spin to the fears circulating among my teammates. "The best we can do is keep working hard and helping each other get better."

The door creaked, and six boys wearing green and white athletic jackets came through it. They took a few steps inside and stood next to each other, staggered and intense like a photo shoot for some teen television drama. With his shoulder length wavy brown hair under a backwards hat and his height of at least six feet, Nick stood out as one of the larger wrestlers in the group, except for a new guy I didn't recognize that bested two hundred pounds, easy. About half his size was the red-headed boy I'd wrestled and beaten four years earlier—the one who'd handed me two points for his bad behavior after losing to a girl. Even smaller than him, though, was a boy with dark hair and eyes and a friendly smile. A blond similar in size to Dom rounded out the group with none other than the black-haired boy I'd hoped to avoid the rest of my life. Not that I looked at him directly.

My teammates stood, too. On the middle of the mat, we all wore black and purple Iron Valley shirts and shorts.

The showdown.

Our coaches hustled to welcome the Forest Run wrestlers. I stayed with my team, moving with them across the gym behind our coaches, waiting to be introduced. I refused to search the huddle for those bright eyes I knew too well.

I blended.

Or better yet, maybe faded into the background.

Until the inevitable occurred. I found those eyes. Or maybe they found me. I looked away and refused to look back.

"Thank you all for being here," Coach said. "We welcome you. We have spots for you in the locker room and a welcome pack of Iron Valley clothes."

The Forest Run wrestlers exchanged glances.

"You're a part of this team now." Coach's voice was gentle, but he left no room for debate. "I understand how awkward that might be for you. It's an adjustment for all of us, but I don't want to see a color divide on those mats. Everyone wears purple and black. Understood?"

"Yes, Coach."

"Good. Take a few minutes to get changed, and we'll start practice."

After the Forest Run wrestlers played dress up, Coach led us to the center mat for ice breakers. The bane of teens everywhere. We sat in a circle and shared our names, grades, and how long we'd been wrestling.

When it was my turn, I made eye contact with all of the new wrestlers. "I'm Annalise Fiori," I said, wanting to add *Don't try to intimidate me or bring drama.* "I'm a senior, and I wrestle the 126-pound weight class."

Nick caught Sebastian's eye, and they communicated something in a boy language I didn't speak. It definitely meant drama, though.

The rest of the guys introduced themselves while I pretended to be as nonchalant as someone binge watching on a Saturday afternoon.

Coach sent us off to run a couple laps around the school and welcomed us back to the gym with extra intensity and enthusiasm.

"Excellent," Coach Joseph said, rubbing his hands together. "Now for the good stuff. Circuits!"

The Iron Valley originals hustled around the room to one of the circuits the coaches had set up for our workout. The Forest Run newcomers followed along, occasionally at the guidance of one of my teammates.

"Split the groups," Coach called. "Let's get to know each other!"

I headed for the pull up bar. When I was nearly there, I made eye contact with Sebastian. He'd been on his way to the same circuit. No denying it. No turning around without explaining myself and my unwillingness to "get to know him better."

"Love," I said by way of a greeting.

He squinted at me. "Are you using my last name or happy to see me?"

"I'm ever happy to see you."

He laughed.

"Don't flirt with me, either."

His red-headed friend—Grant I'd learned during our ice break-ers—joined us. I hoped Grant didn't remember our middle school experience as vividly as I did. Not that that was likely.

"Who's first?" I asked.

"Ladies," Grant said.

"So is that you?" I countered.

"Okay. Let's soften those edges, Lise," Dom said from over my shoulder. "Looks like we'll be the group of four this time."

I took a deep breath. "I'm not a lady, Grant. I'm your teammate."

Grant headed for the pull up bar. "Whatever. I was trying to be polite. I could care less that you're a girl."

If only I could believe him.

"Forget it. I'll go first." Grant jumped for the bar, positioned his hands, and pulled off six reps with ease. By eight, his arms started shaking, and I couldn't stop the grin spreading across my face. So much so my best friend raised his eyebrows at me and shook his head. Grant dropped after twelve, the last one being quite the struggle. He smirked at me.

"Great job," I said, not wanting to give away that I was about to destroy him. "Next?"

Sebastian took his turn. He pumped out more than his teammate had. When he passed twelve, he counted loudly, poking fun at Grant.

When Sebastian hit seventeen, Grant said, "Now you're showing off."

He pulled himself up once more and dropped. "Wouldn't want to show off."

I would.

Dom went next, matching Sebastian's eighteen by struggling through the last two.

"Your turn, princess," Grant said.

Dom scowled at Grant. "Show 'em, Lise."

CHAPTER 7

I JUMPED AND GRABBED THE BAR, GIVING MYSELF AN
extra second to make sure my grip was solid. I started smooth, moving
through the first five without any struggle. With each rep, I breathed
deeper, letting the stress of life melt away with the exertion. By ten,
the metaphorical zone we talk about in sports surrounded me like a
bubble of strength and intensity.

At fifteen, fatigue crept in, but I managed three more before it
overwhelmed me. I'd tied Sebastian and Dom. One more. I breathed,
and pulled, squeezing my abs. Nineteen. Dom cheered. You control
your body, I thought, and pulled again, struggling through the rep.
It wasn't pretty, but my chin touched the bar a twentieth time. Dom
wasn't the only one cheering this time. A few of my teammates from
around the gym called my name and clapped.

I let my body hang for a few seconds, wanting one more. I
squeezed again and pulled, memories of the boys like Grant who
thought they were so funny dominating the burn in my muscles.
Coach blew the whistle. I didn't stop. My arms shuddered, but I
managed one more, an exclamation point on my reps. I dropped from
the bar and rubbed my angry hands.

Dom nudged me with this hip. "Damn, girl."

"Impressive," Grant said.

"Thanks." I snuck a glimpse of Sebastian, hating myself for the curiosity swirling inside me, but I had to see his reaction. I probably shouldn't have.

With a half-smile on his lips, he gave me a nod.

A nod I'd seen before—after every match I'd won in eighth grade. It had been his way of congratulating me. It'd been dangerous then but felt even more dangerous now.

***

"GOOD WORK TODAY," COACH JOSEPH SAID AFTER END-less drills I'd managed to finish without interacting with Sebastian or Grant again. "All teams have adversity, and we have to work through that adversity, so we can come together as one unit and face our opponents united. We are merging two schools. Two teams. Two identities and cultures. This will take some time. I want you to be patient with me and yourselves. We'll figure it out together."

Patience was a wrestler's virtue. Rushing through the motions on the mat meant missing out on an opportunity to earn points and win.

"The coaches are bringing around worksheets for you. I know this isn't class, but you need to get to know each other. To respect each other. Each of you will have to talk with fourteen teammates and learn three things you didn't know about them. Forest Run students, your fourteen will be from Iron Valley. Iron Valley students, you will talk with your own schoolmates you know least and all of the newcomers from Forest Run. Is that understood?"

Everyone nodded. "Yes, Coach."

Were they nodding on the outside and groaning on the inside like me? Was it impossible to think we could be a team without having to sit down to tea and braid each other's hair?

"Excellent," Coach continued. "This may seem like a silly ice-breaker to some of you. Let me assure you—skipping it is not an option."

Or what? Extra workouts? Before-school running? Great. I'd take that over playing nice with Sebastian. It might even help me reach my goal weight faster. I folded the paper and laid my pencil over it.

Coach glanced my way. "I'm not registering anyone for competition until the forms are in my office."

I picked the paper up again and smiled at him. Sebastian took a step in my direction, so I grabbed another Forest Run wrestler first—Vinny Romano, I learned. This was Vinny's first year wrestling, and he was a 113-pounder. He enjoyed pasta and pizza from his family's restaurant where he worked as a dishwasher when he could, and he'd never wrestled a girl.

"Hope I don't ever have to either," Vinny said. "No offense."

I smiled at him, hoping we'd get to go live some day. I'd kick his…deep breath. Get to know them, Annalise, I scolded myself and hustled after Nick, finishing that interview as quickly as I could, too.

Grant Akins told me he'd never seen anyone do so many pull ups, and that softened me a little. He softened me a lot by adding that something else I might not know is when he'd lost to me in middle school it wasn't the first or the last time he'd lost to a girl, and in a way, he'd thought it was pretty cool that I was so tough. As long as I didn't kick his ass again—his words.

"Thanks, Grant. That's actually kind of cool."

"I'm sorry I was such a jerk when you beat me. My dad had me all…" His voice faded, and he shook his head. "No excuses. I'm sorry."

"Forgiven," I said with a smile and meant it.

Sebastian cleared his throat behind us. "Thanks, Grant. All good here." I walked away without acknowledging Love hovering. Not sure why. I'd have to talk to him at some point. Or maybe I could make something up. Oh! Or I could see what Dom wrote about him and copy his answers!

But what if Coach Joseph found out?

I finished interviewing all of my teammates but one and stretched my legs on the mat. I'd wait for Sebastian to finish his interviews with everyone else.

Then, I'd talk. To. Him.

Yuck.

I spun the pencil in my fingers, but after a couple minutes, the spinning transformed into sketching. On the back of Coach's chart, I sketched the room. The mats. The Iron Valley logo on them. I added some shimmering around the pull up bar, remembering my performance there earlier in the practice.

Lost in my sketching, I barely noticed Sebastian sitting next to me, until his flame-throwing breathing caught my attention.

"If I didn't know better," he said with all the stupid charm he could muster, "I'd think you were avoiding me."

"Me? Avoiding you?"

"Okay," he said, nodding in that arrogant way of his. "Let's get to know each other. Even though we've *known* each other for a long time."

I scowled at him. Was that some sort of innuendo? About that singular, stupid, weakness-of-the-century moment when we'd *known* each other?

"Unfortunately," I managed.

He smiled. "You make a pretty good show of hating me."

"Who says it's a show?"

"Look, Lise—"

"My name is Annalise. My friends call me Lise."

He sighed and lifted his pencil. "I'll start there. Name is Annalise, but friends call her Lise."

Great. On our way to finishing this torture. "And what about you? We can keep it simple like what's your favorite color or favorite food?"

"Two for one. Color is purple."

"That's not true."

"No," he insisted. "It is. I think a guy who can rock purple has a special kind of confidence, don't you?"

I thought he had a special kind of something that was better not to say. I recorded his answer. "Your favorite food?"

"Chicken marsala."

A scoff sort of slipped out.

"What's wrong with chicken marsala?"

"Nothing," I said. "It's delicious. Most people would choose pizza, cheeseburger, or maybe even ice cream, but no. Sebastian Love goes with the exquisite chicken marsala."

"Maybe I'm an exquisite person."

Eye roll. I was never eating chicken marsala again.

"Your turn," he said. "Give me something."

"I like black."

His eyebrows perked up, but he wrote the answer down.

"And I wear a special anklet under my socks during matches. My grandparents gave it to me, and it's my good luck charm."

His pencil hovered over the paper, and I busied myself checking my list of Forest Run players, as if I didn't know Sebastian was the last of my new teammates to mark off. Nobody knew about the anklet. I always wore high socks to cover it, afraid a ref might make me remove it.

"I'm going to write that you have a secret good luck charm," he said. "In case Coach doesn't want you wearing jewelry while competing."

"Thanks," I muttered. Why would he do that? It was actually kind. What was he up to? "I, um, need one more for you."

"Bash. My friends call me Bash."

I knew that already, but I still wrote it down. Fair was fair. Three details, and we were done. I stood and hustled toward the locker room, eager to create as much distance as possible between me and Sebastian.

CHAPTER 8

SHOWERED FROM PRACTICE, I STOMPED—ACCORDING to Ashley—to the garage. The chill of winter had gripped our little part of the world, making me grateful for the industrial space heaters my dad had scored second-hand for my otherwise non-climate-controlled painting studio. "Studio" stretched reality a bit. I painted in a corner of the garage and hoped none of the lawn equipment fell from the fragile hooks in the ceiling while I did it. Maybe if I secured a spot in the gallery exhibit I could lobby for a better painting space in the house. Or even a shed in the woods on our property. I'd seen way too many online and had fantasized quite an extravagant studio with floor-to-ceiling windows overlooking the snowy landscape while I mastered my art.

In reality, I'd be lucky to submit the application for the winter show by the deadline. A small voice whispering that I'd done my absolute best to ignore told me not to waste my time trying. I'd applied the past two years and received standard rejections. On one of them, the gallery owner had even misspelled my name. An extravagant studio in the woods wouldn't make me a better painter. It'd only give me a space I could privately lament my shortcomings.

The heaters clicked on with a thunk-thunk-thunk. The twilight pumpkin patch I'd touched up the night of Ashley's game had dried brilliantly. Dusted with a few stars, the painting watched me in all its perfection, while I stared down a blank sixteen-by-twenty-inch canvas, wondering if I could ever paint another thing.

I tapped my brush on the table, dripping paint I'd forgotten was on the bristles.

My mind fluttered through the vault of my memories to the weekend after I first met Sebastian. I'd searched the tournament crowd of wrestlers and their fans for those blue-green eyes that had twisted my soul. And found them. A smile had spread across his face when he saw me. I'd tried to stop myself from doing the same, but my lips knew something I hadn't. His friends had headed for the gym, but he allowed himself to get swallowed by the crowd in the lobby, riding the wave of people moving in my direction.

I'd crashed into Ashley the moment Sebastian had found me.

"Oh," she'd said. "I didn't realize…"

"I'm Sebastian."

"Ashley. I'm Annalise's sister."

"You wrestle, too?"

"I play volleyball. My sister is the tough one in the family. She'd kick your butt, you know?"

Sebastian had laughed, his mouth and cheeks creasing in a way that had made him even cuter, his beautiful eyes shimmering with humor.

Annalise Fiori. Total goner.

"I don't doubt it," Sebastian had said. "Lucky for me we aren't the same weight."

He'd looked at me, and my breath tripped on itself. "Hi."

"Hi," I'd managed.

The silence had fallen between us in a mix of awkward hope, like something epic was on the verge of being said, but the universe couldn't decide exactly what words either of us should use.

"I'll let you two catch up," Ashley had said with a grin. Behind him, she'd danced and made a kissy face. I'd pretended not to see.

"How's your bracket today?" he'd asked.

"It shouldn't give me too much trouble. How about you?"

"I like your confidence. I'm feeling pretty good about mine, too."

"You're from Forest Run, right? What grade are you in?"

"Eighth. You?"

"Same."

"I didn't lie earlier," Sebastian had said. "I'm glad you aren't in my weight class."

"Me too."

Boys always got weird when they had to wrestle me. I hadn't wanted Sebastian in that territory. Instead, he'd fallen into a different realm—the kind that had us sneaking under stairwells and behind rolled up wrestling mats to talk between matches. School. Family. Friends. Ambitions. Television. Music. Vacations. We'd talked about it all.

Week after week.

His dad had come up a lot. He'd get angry Sebastian didn't ace a test. He'd made Sebastian come to the tournament with a cold, and I should stay back. He'd tried to force wrestling on Sebastian's younger brother, Christopher, but the little guy had no interest in it. So, again, all the pressure fell on Sebastian to achieve perfection.

"My dad expects me to win everything every time. You know? And always with a pin," he'd said once.

"Sorry."

"What about your dad?"

"My dad travels a lot, but I see him sometimes. My mom used to wrestle. She wants me to work hard and have fun."

Sebastian's eyes widened. "Your mom wrestled?"

"Yep."

"Wicked."

Despite its depth, our friendship had existed in the wrestling world only. We hadn't message during the week, but I'd thought of him. All the time. At each tournament or duals on the weekends, I'd searched for him in the most nonchalant way I could manage, hoping if he saw me first, I wouldn't look like my mood for the entire day depended on his presence.

When my eyes had gotten what they wanted and found his face in the crowd, my chest did these flips it never did any other time in my life. Ever.

When Sebastian wasn't there, a heavy weight settled on me—no flips allowed.

At one tournament at the end of the season, Sebastian had found me first, pulling me to one of our favorite hiding spots at that school.

"I have to tell you something," he'd said, and my mind had wandered to all the things it could be: maybe he wanted me to be his official girlfriend. Or to meet his friends. Oh! He was going to ask me to go to his winter formal. Maybe he wanted my number so we could take our relationship outside of the wrestling bubble.

He'd taken a deep breath, leaving me to hold mine.

"I cut weight."

H*uh?*

"We're going to wrestle against each other today."

Not any of the things I had imagined. Much, much worse.

"I'm sorry, Lise. Part of me was hoping you wouldn't be here today, so we wouldn't have to compete against each other, but the other part of me…"

"What?"

He'd leaned closer. "Wanted to see you more."

Closer.

Closer.

Sebastian's adorable grin had appeared the moment before his lips pressed against mine.

"You okay, sweetie?"

I jumped at my mom's voice, ripping me from the memory of Sebastian's kiss.

"I'm sorry," she said. "I wasn't being quiet."

She loaded groceries into our garage fridge with crinkling bags and shifting thuds. Not quiet at all. My mind must have been buried deep.

"I heard mention of Rebecca Watterson's exhibit on the radio. Did you hear it opened at the gallery?"

"Yeah. I, mean, I knew, but I guess I also forgot."

I'd seen the newspaper article on the series. The local artist had taken a Jackson Pollock approach, placing her canvases on the floor, dipping her pets' paws in different colored paints, and then letting them walk over the pieces.

"You planning to go sometime?" she asked.

"Definitely."

If I could find someone to go with. Nobody in my family appreciated art like I did, except my dad, but he'd be traveling for work for a few months. My mom would go because—obvious—she was my mom. But then she'd look at all the paintings sideways until she was practically upside down as if connecting with art could only be achieved from awkward angles.

I'd wait until Ashley owed me big. Big enough to go with me *and* pretend it wasn't horrible.

"Are you okay?" Mom asked. "Your colors are angry."

I studied the canvas I'd been haphazardly swirling my paintbrush across. Unexpected black paint mixed with the orange color I'd intended. My mom was right. The colors screamed at me from the easel.

"I thought you were working on a fall series?"

"I am," I said, fumbling for an explanation that would cover up the fact I'd been thinking about Sebastian and subconsciously swooshing the darkest colors of the planet across my canvas. "This one is Halloween."

"Okay, honey. Good luck. Turkey sandwich and fruit salad soon?"

"Sure, Mom. Thanks."

She blew me a kiss and went inside, leaving me alone in the garage with my music and my paints. With swirls of black and orange in the background, I brushed the illusion of a jack-o-lantern in the foreground and created a border of various candy types, thinking of Dom when I painted the Reese's peanut butter cup.

The door to the kitchen burst open, making me jump like a true Halloween scare. Ashley plowed into the garage with Chandra.

"Come with us," Ashley said.

"Where?"

She sighed for dramatic effect. "It's Friday night. There's a party."

I rolled my eyes for equal dramatic effect. "I'm in season, which means I have a five-a.m. workout, and you literally have a championship volleyball game tomorrow."

"Lise, this is our last year together before you leave me and go away to college. We won't stay long. I promise. An hour or two."

I glanced back at my half-done painting.

"Please don't blow me off to paint Halloween when it's over."

"It's a fall series," I protested. And I was nowhere near ready to submit my art show application.

"Please," Ashley begged.

The two of them gave me puppy eyes, and I caved. "Fine, but I'm only coming to make sure you are out of there in two hours and in bed." And I was back in this garage to paint as soon as the layers dried.

"Yes!" Ashley said. "Get dressed. We leave in fifteen minutes."

"No. I need to eat first."

Ashley exaggerated a groan with a neck roll.

"It will take me five minutes."

Mom had turkey sandwiches waiting for all of us with lots of fresh fruit and veggies. After I hit my calorie mark, I picked out a pair of jeans and a short-sleeved crop top that showed the cut of my abs. I'd learned that showing my muscles scared guys away. If a little bit of muscle was enough to scare them away, they weren't worth sticking around.

Ashley came at me with a wet rag and a makeup bag. "You have paint in your hair." She tugged on my ends and then shaped my curly, blonde locks into a messy braid.

"I hope I find someone cute tonight," Chandra said. "As long as he has better hair than me. No shaved heads. I like hair between my fingertips." She closed her eyes and sighed.

Ashley scoffed. I almost did, too, but it was fun to watch Chandra gush over boys. I didn't have that with my guy friends.

"Okay, Miss I-can't-date-anyone-shorter-than-me," Chandra fired back at my sister.

"I'm a tall girl," Ashley protested then glanced at me. "Tall girls dating shorter guys is totally fine. Just not for me. Lise, tell her your boy rule."

"No," I said instantly.

"This is gonna be good," Chandra said.

"Tell her!"

"Fine. He has to be able to beat me at wrestling."

"No wonder you don't go out with anyone," Chandra said. "Nobody can beat you at wrestling."

"Not true. I lost last weekend."

"Was he cute?"

"Not even close."

"He has to beat her at wrestling and be cute, a small sampling of the population," Ashley teased.

Sad but true.

"Where are we going?" I asked.

Chandra opened her mouth to answer, but Ashley covered it. "Don't tell her. Let it be a surprise."

I hated surprises.

CHAPTER 9

ESPECIALLY THIS ONE.

"You did not bring me to a Forest Run party."

Ashley smiled. "No. I didn't. Chandra drove. Technically, she brought you to a Forest Run party."

I glared at her.

"Maybe he won't be here." As soon as my sister spoke the words, the spirits of the world that loved a good laugh settled in with popcorn.

"The Fiori sisters?"

The voice sparked a deeper, down to my core glare.

"Or maybe you're not that lucky," Ashley whispered. "Sebastian! How's it going?"

I forced a smile that probably looked more like I had something shoved sideways up my nose.

"Great. Celebrating our new wrestling team with friends." He pointed to the Forest Run wrestlers in the kitchen with my Iron Valley teammates Justin Chan, Logan Locaputo, and Ethan White. Thankfully, Dom wasn't there. I'd have killed him. Not that I could judge the team for attending Forest Run parties.

Obviously.

Nick saw us and stumbled our way. He didn't stop until his face was inches from Ashley's. "Who is this angel?"

"Ashley Fiori. Who are you?"

He slipped off his baseball cap and held it over his heart. When his hair fell wildly over his cheeks, I feared Chandra would appear from the crowd to run her fingers through it.

"I'm the love of your life," he slurred.

"I think I'll be the judge of that," Ashley said, but she popped her hip and sassily rested her hand against it. As her sister, I knew that move. She was interested. Too interested. "How about we start with you getting me a drink?"

"Done," Nick said. He took her hand and pulled her to the kitchen, leaving me alone with Sebastian.

We stood side by side glancing at each other every couple minutes until he caved. "This is painful. There has to be something we can talk about."

"The weather's always a fine topic. Or true crime documentaries."

He cringed. "True crime. Really?"

I shrugged.

"Would you like a drink?" he asked.

"I'm good." I pointed to his cup. "You drinking tonight?"

"Water. As usual."

"Trying to cut weight?"

"Make weight, more like. You?"

"A little," I said. "But my mom insists I work with a nutritionist and lose weight right. It's the only way she'll let me wrestle."

"Smart. I've had some older cousins that developed serious eating issues cutting weight."

The conversation felt too heavy for the headspace I allowed Sebastian to inhabit. I tried to think of a polite way to walk away, but I didn't know anyone else to talk to. Maybe a bathroom break.

"Seems like Nick has a thing for your sister." Sebastian nodded in their direction, and sure enough they were both smiling, laughing and standing way too close.

Not Nick Walsh. The same Nick Walsh who'd once asked in middle school if he could "wrestle" me off the mat since he was out of my weight class on it.

"Unless you're scared that I'm too…big…for you," he'd said and winked. I was pretty sure the "big" wasn't a reference to his weight. And now he wanted to hang out with my little sister.

"Nick's a good guy," Sebastian said.

"Says his best friend." His best friend that I didn't trust. "She's my little sister. Nobody's good enough for her."

"I get that."

"How, exactly? You don't have a little sister."

"Nick's little sister is in eighth grade. She's like a sister to me, too, and watching the older guys drool over the younger girls in school makes me want to take someone's legs out from under them thinking about senior guys doing that to her next year."

"The challenge of being a wrestler with the ability to take anyone down."

He laughed, and then I knew for sure we were outside of the safe headspace.

"Do you know where the bathroom is?"

"There's one under the basement steps and another across the hall at the top of the stairs. I'd go upstairs, though. The basement one doesn't lock."

Potential disaster. "Thanks for the tip."

I managed to slip away from Sebastian, but before I headed for the bathroom, I went to the kitchen to check on Ashley. She and Nick were huddled in the corner, kissing. I tapped her shoulder.

She pulled away. "Lise?"

"Why don't you grab me a bottle of water?"

"Annalise, c'mon," Nick said, but I nudged him away from Ashley.

She put her hands up in surrender. "Fine. Good luck, Nick." Ashley stomped toward the fridge, and I unhanded her hot date.

"Hiding in the corner with my little sister? Slobbering all over her when you've known her for five minutes?"

"It's been a pretty magical five minutes."

"I bet," I said. "See the problem is she's my little sister. She's a junior."

"So am I," he said.

Hmm. I'd missed that detail in our "get-to-know-each-other" adventure at practice. Still, it didn't matter.

"Your little sister is like six…two…wait." He looked at his fingers as if he were a kindergartener doing math. After a few seconds, he shook his head, surrendering to the complexity of the equation. "Not that many months younger than me," he finally managed.

"Maybe it's not about the age but about your misogynist nature."

He stepped back. "Wow. Okay. When I heard we were merging our teams, I had a feeling this would come up."

"Look at you predicting the future."

"You have a whole lot of snark, you know that?"

"Wonder why."

"I can't believe I'm having this conversation only half-sober. Let me give it a try." He took a deep breath. "I shouldn't have said those things to you when we were in middle school, and I'm not saying that because my parents grounded me, or my coach tortured me on the mat."

"Or because you want to get in my little sister's pants."

"She's wearing a skirt."

"You're an ass."

"Sorry. The truth is my baby sister wrestles, and she's in middle school, and guess what guys have said to her."

That must be the same baby sister Sebastian had mentioned.

"It makes me want to tear them apart, until I looked in the mirror and realize I used to be one of them."

"And you want to tear yourself apart?"

His face twisted up in confusion.

"Nevermind," I said, feeling my shell of anger cracking a sliver. "I know from experience that sucks."

"Yeah, it does. I am sorry, Annalise."

I didn't know how to respond. When you hold on to something so hard for so long, it's hard to let it go with a moment's notice, even for a good reason.

"I mean it, and honestly, I'm glad I got the chance to say it. It's been eating me up for years."

I knew the feeling.

"I do like your sister, but the boy you saw at wrestling tournaments four years ago grew up. At least a little bit."

"What are you two talking about?" Ashley said, handing me a water and twisting the cap off a bottle of lemonade iced tea for herself.

"Nothing," Nick said. He stepped toward Ashley and held her gently by her elbows. "It's been fun, but I know you're here to spend time with your sister." He kissed her on her cheek and whispered something to her.

"Maybe," she said, teasingly.

He laughed, and then waved to me.

"Those Forest Run wrestlers got even cuter over the last four years, don't you think?"

I hadn't noticed. Not with the wall I'd built between myself and them, but with Nick apologizing and Sebastian seemingly trying to be nice, I was afraid the stones might start to crumble, letting in all sorts of thoughts and observations.

"Do you still think about it?" Ashley asked.

"About what?"

"Don't do that with me."

"What do you want me to say?"

"The truth. Like we always promised each other." She looped her arm in mine. "I like Nick, but I'm not about to spend time with someone that hurts my sister."

I sighed. Ashley had always been loyal. The best sister. The kindest and sweetest and all the good words you could think of. I couldn't keep her away from someone she liked because he'd said something mean to me four years ago.

"Nick apologized for it tonight."

"A boy who can apologize is even hotter in my view."

"He said his little sister wrestles now and hears the same kind of crap. If I had to guess, maybe he has changed."

"And Sebastian?" Ashley asked.

"Definitely not."

CHAPTER 10

THE NEXT MORNING, I SLEPT IN UNTIL NINE, HIT THE gym for my weekend workout, and video chatted with my nutritionist. She gave me tips about high energy foods for my upcoming competitions, and I added a few items to the grocery list app my mom used. Not a bad start to the day before I jumped in my car and drove thirty minutes to my sister's regional championship volleyball game.

Nothing could take the smile off my face the whole drive. Not the driver who changed lanes without signaling. Not the icky, brown canvas of western Pennsylvania winter waiting to be painted with sparkling white. Not even thoughts of Sebastian Love. Or the fact he'd probably be there since it was his school we were playing.

I found my mom in the bleachers watching Iron Valley and Forest Run warm up. Across the gym, someone stood and waved, catching my attention. Sebastian. Obnoxious much? I waved back as politely as I could. Then promptly looked away. At least this time, a volleyball court separated us.

As we sat there on the bleachers, my world filled in around us in the same way a painting starts sparse but then builds to be something beautiful. Friends from school. Volleyball parents. My wrestling teammates. The football team. Julia. Dom.

Julia patted my shoulder. "They got this."

I nodded. And hoped so.

Ashley crushed her hits and killed her serves during warmups. Wild that someone with her skill was second-string. Still, she cheered for the seniors and Melanie with everything in her soul. My mom took my hand in hers, and we squeezed. And then the game began. Maybe it was the movement of the Forest Run players' green jerseys around the court, but a memory of boys in green singlets filled my mind.

Sebastian had surprised me, pressing his mouth against mine at the last wrestling tournament of eighth grade. I'd closed my eyes and held my breath against his soft mouth. I'd seen a million movie kisses, but none of them had prepared me. Should I have opened my mouth or even, wow, use my tongue?

No.

No tongue.

I'd cringed in fear that Sebastian might have tried to push his tongue at me.

Thinking it was the right thing to do, I'd rested my hands on his strong shoulders and felt his hands in the small of my back. He'd pulled his mouth away from mine but gently found it again, opening my lips the tiniest bit.

Kissing Sebastian Love?

Magic!

Until…

"What's this?" Nick had said.

At the sound of his friend's voice, Sebastian had jumped and pushed me away.

Grant had sung about K-I-S-S-I-N-G in a tree.

"Are you two hooking up?"

Sebastian had stepped even further from me. "No."

I'd stared at him. He hadn't exactly been lying. That had been our first kiss, but the tone of his voice had held a certain level of disgust that I wouldn't ever want addressed to me.

"She's his *girlfriend*," Grant had said.

"She's not my girlfriend."

"You know what?" I'd managed as if I'd held an ounce of dignity intact. "I'm gonna go."

"She's mad now," Grant had said, and I'd punched him in the gut. Dignity be damned.

"Good strategy, Bash. Soften her up to you, so you can beat her."

No. That wasn't what everything between us had been. Sebastian had actually liked me. Right?

"You know me," Sebastian had said. "Always thinking of ways to win."

A fire had burned inside of me hotter than I thought my anger ever could. Without thinking, I'd backtracked to Sebastian and his friends, Nick laughing, and Grant still hunched forward holding his stomach, pulled my arm back, and punched Sebastian in the face.

Blood had poured down his shirt, causing him to pinch the bridge of his nose. "Lise, c'mon!"

"My name is Annalise, and I promise you by the end of today, you'll never forget it."

I'd carried my anger through the next match, destroying my opponent with a quick pin. Coach had hugged me, and following our tradition, we'd watched my name appear on the electronic bracket. For the championship match.

Right next to the name, Sebastian Love.

We'd wrestle each other for first place.

"You can do this, Lise," Coach had said.

Yes, I could. No way would Sebastian beat me. I'd watched him wrestle enough to know his moves. Maybe his strategy had been to soften me up with flirtations and lies. My strategy would be to know him better than anyone.

Nick and Grant had kneeled on the mat before our match and waved to me. My response had been to ignore them. The refs had to work out something with the table, so Sebastian and I had had a few seconds on the mat. I'd paced back and forth, keeping my muscles warm, like I'd done before every match.

"Annalise, I'm sorry about before."

"I'm not," I'd said. "Leave me alone. You lied to me all this time."

"No," Sebastian had said. "I lied to them."

"Why? Because I'm a girl and I wrestle?"

"No. Because you're a girl. They don't get it. They don't have girlfriends."

"I am *not* your girlfriend."

"You're being a brat."

"You're being a jerk."

"Shake hands," the ref had said. We did, but I'd refused to let his touch have any effect on me.

At the whistle, we'd circled in our stances, neither of us engaging. The sounds of his friends' voices threatened my focus, so I'd pushed them away, reducing my world into the silence of my headgear and the task of destroying the boy in front of me.

The boy who'd humiliated me thinking that would gain him some kind of edge. He'd played me for vulnerable.

I'd show him I was no such thing.

Showing his frustration and impatience, Sebastian had taken a shot from too far away. He'd aimed for a double leg takedown, but I'd sprawled before he could reach behind my knees. With him fully extended, belly on the mat, I'd spun around him, earning two points. He'd made a mistake, and I'd made him pay.

Feeling confident, I'd thrown in legs and dropped my hips too far.

"No, Annalise!" Coach yelled, but before I could correct my aggressive move gone wrong, he'd reversed me, tying the score 2-2. We'd fought hard on the mat, neither of us gaining an advantage. At the end of the period, he'd relaxed his muscles, releasing his grip on me. I'd faced him and his red cheeks and angry eyes.

We'd both made a mistake. Any coach would say mistakes are part of learning. I believed it. You either win or you learn.

In this case, I'd like to win *and* learn, thank you very much.

To start the second period, I'd chosen bottom, knowing I could escape from him and take the lead by a point. Not much, but if we'd both wrestled as well as history had showed we could, that one point could mean the match. At the whistle, Sebastian had broken me down on my stomach, pushing his head low to my left side. Willing to take a risk, I'd draped my left hand around his neck, pulling it for a possible headlock at the same moment my coach admonished me.

"Don't reach back!"

Again, my confidence had proven to be my Achilles heel. A skilled wrestler, Sebastian had taken my gift, sinking me with a half nelson. I'd felt my shoulder hit the mat and knew the ref would be counting back points. I'd rolled to my stomach and fought back to my base.

The ref had stopped us then as the period ended, with me down 5-2.

And a scowl on my coach's face.

I'd held up my hands. "I know. I know."

No more mistakes. I'd wrestle smart. I could beat Sebastian Love. Yeah, he'd been good, but so was I. Going into the third period, he'd chosen down. At the whistle, I'd applied strong pressure, driving our bodies forward using my toes and squeezing my right arm around his waist. I'd chopped his left elbow, and the combination of the textbook moves had pushed Sebastian onto his stomach. My turn to drive a half. I'd tried to run it, but he'd wrestled smart, squeezing his obliques and bringing his right knee up to his chest to counter me.

I'd set him up, but he hadn't known it yet.

Switching to a cross face, I'd grabbed his right tricep and swept him into a cradle.

For the pin.

With the ref's slap at the mat, my whole body had exhaled with glory.

On the podium, I'd pulled myself up as tall as I could and looked into the cameras taking our photos. No smiles. Only glares.

Ferocious glares.

I'd finally gotten that old saying about a woman scorned. I thought it could apply to anyone scorned, but I was quickly learning people wanted to blame girls for everything. What they feel. What they don't feel. What they "make" the boys around them feel.

I'd take the blame for what I'd made Sebastian feel on the mat. Hopefully it had been the kind of pain and embarrassment I'd felt in the lobby before the match. If that meant I was scorned and resentful, then I'd keep this trophy next to my bed for the rest of eternity to remind myself that sometimes resentful is a perfectly acceptable thing to be.

"Good match, Annalise," Sebastian had said when the cameras had finished their business. He'd reached for my hand.

I'd glanced at it and huffed a laugh before turning and stomping away, grateful the season was over. When we'd gotten home that day, I'd dusted off the nightstand next to my bed, moving a picture of my family to my dresser instead. In its place, I'd nestled my first-place trophy where it had been ever since.

That had been the end of my story with Sebastian.

Until now.

CHAPTER 11

MY FRIENDS RUSHED THE COURT AFTER THE VOLLEY- ball game. Nick hugged Ashley so tight I thought she might stop breathing. Sebastian nodded at me. Ashley introduced Nick to my mom, and Chandra tried to swipe a feel of his hair when he wasn't looking.

"You're terrible," I whispered, but she laughed.

Dom cornered me.

"Time to party!" Dom said.

"No," I groaned. "I went to a party last night." I gave my best friend a pointed look. "Tonight, we go to Rebecca Watterson's gallery exhibit."

"Lise…" he objected.

My index finger found its way toward his face. "Best friend code." The winter gallery exhibit application on my desk taunted me from afar. I had to finish my work, and I needed inspiration to do it. I prayed Rebecca's exhibit could give me that.

"Come to the party," Dom pleaded. "I'll go see Rebecca's exhibit with you another day."

It was the last weekend I had free from a wrestling tournament, meet, clinic, or camp forever, but something told me if I went home and sat in front of my canvases, that would be the only productivity

I'd have. Sitting. Maybe the party could give me inspiration.

Long shot.

"You promise you'll go with me another time?"

"Promise," Dom said.

"Any time I choose? I call and that's it. You're there in ten minutes?"

"It takes a little longer than ten minutes to get there."

"Dom!"

"Yes. Any other time. I hereby promise."

Chandra draped her arm around my shoulders and shouted to the crowd of Iron Valley Vikings. "Party tonight to celebrate this beastly volleyball team. I expect to see you all there!"

***

HOURS LATER, STANDING IN THE MIDST OF THE PARTY chaos, dressed in black leather pants and a tight, off-the-shoulder shirt, I realized I'd need more than a nap to get through the night.

Chandra was on the hunt for a guy with great hair. Dom played pool with Nick since my best friend had invited his new wrestling pal and said pal's whole crew to the party. My sister shadowed Nick with love in her eyes, and next to them, a gorgeous blonde draped her arm around Sebastian's neck. He caught my eye and waved. I waved back and moved in the opposite direction. After doing a loop of the packed house without any interest in pushing into anyone's conversation or—ew—makeout session, I slipped outside into the cold of the balcony.

My breath puffed a cloud that transformed into a sliver before fading completely. The expanse was dull and brown, blending into the dark night under the house's spotlights. I curled up on the outdoor furniture, squealing when the cold fabric touched my clothes. I unfolded a blanket hanging on the back of the chair and wrapped it around me. Slowly my body heated the little nest.

I hadn't explored brown as a color of fall. Maybe I could add more browns to my fall canvases to make the yellows, oranges, and reds pop. I could paint a night scene, too. I hadn't done that. Maybe some stars sparkling in the sky. I could even experiment with glitter.

I pulled a mini sketchbook and pencil out of my purse. My pencil moved over the soft white paper. Pumpkins. Pumpkin patches. Leaves falling from trees. Children jumping in piles of leaves. Carving pumpkins. Hmm. I'd painted mostly landscapes because I usually failed at painting people, but maybe I could try one or two. Children especially. I could capture the adorableness of those big, childish eyes.

I shifted to sketching faces, working to balance the symmetry of the features. No face was perfectly symmetrical, but more so than I usually drew them. I watched the faces take shape.

Until one took a familiar shape. With familiar eyes. And a face that sent my insides into the most contradictory of emotions.

I closed my eyes and sighed. Why, subconscious? Why?

The music from the party blared in a muffled way, until the balcony door opened, and Sebastian appeared, bringing the loud with him. I slapped the sketchbook closed and shoved it into my purse, as low as it could possibly go.

"What are you doing out here?" I asked, unable to hide the annoyance in my voice.

"Getting some fresh air." He rubbed his arms and hopped a few times. "You wanna share that blanket with me?"

I actually snorted.

"What are *you* doing out here?" he asked.

"Trying to get away from the party."

"Then I'm trying to get away from the party, too?"

"Why?"

"Why not?" he countered.

"Because you have a pretty hot date inside."

He grinned. "Jealous?"

I shifted on my chair. "Hardly."

"You noticed her."

"She was draped around you like a necklace when you waved to me. Kind of hard to miss."

"If you don't want me to bring a date somewhere, you can say so."

"Why would I care if you brought a date?"

"I think we both know the answer to that."

I threw the blanket at him and stood. "You know what, the party is sounding a lot better than the balcony right now."

"Don't be like that."

"Like what, exactly? Here's the thing, Sebastian. Either you're playing some stupid game like you did years ago, which I definitely want to avoid, or you're hitting on me when you have a date inside this house. Also kind of makes me want to avoid you."

"I get what you're saying."

"Good." I pushed past him and opened the door.

"But none of that has anything to do with not actually liking me." He reached for my shoulder. I got wrist control on him and snapped him down to the ground. He groaned and rolled onto his side.

"Does that make it more clear?"

"Crystal," he managed.

"Great. Don't freeze to death."

"See. You do care."

I hoped the door slamming in his face communicated otherwise. I huffed a deep breath. Why did he make me so irritated? And itchy? And just, ugh?

Back inside, I waved to a few people I knew from school, but before Sebastian could slip back inside and head for the pool table, making it look like I was following him, I side-stepped through the crowd on my way to the table myself. Nick and my sister came into view. Full-blown canoodling.

Ashley tossed her head back in laughter. Her face actually glowed. In that moment, I knew I'd give Nick a pass for anything he'd ever done if he made my sister that happy.

Ashley caught my eye and shouted, "Annalise! Where have you been?"

"Nowhere. Can I get the next game?"

Nick handed me his cue. "You can have this one, actually. I'd rather spend time with this fine girl right here."

Ashley kissed his cheek, and he blushed. Cuteness overload.

"Who am I playing?" I asked.

"Me," Sebastian's date said, very, very, very perkily.

I forced a smile wondering what external forces were at work in my life lately. And what kind of sense of humor they had. "Excellent. I'm Annalise."

"I've heard so much about you. The kick ass wrestler, right?"

Her kindness caught me off guard. I'd been primed to face off against pretty girls I didn't know, but she disarmed me with her smile and compliments.

"Thanks."

"I can't wait to come to one of your matches. I wish I had the guts to wrestle. I admire you."

Wow. "Um, thanks, again."

"Oh, I'm Elizabeth, by the way."

"Nice to meet you."

"You too. And I'm sorry, but I'm going to kick your ass."

I laughed at her bluntness.

"No seriously."

"Have at it," I said, and she totally did.

While Sebastian hunched over in a nearby chair and glared. Not that I was paying any attention to him.

CHAPTER 12

"WELCOME TO A NEW WEEK, EVERYONE," COACH SAID
Monday at practice.

I stretched my neck and shoulders. A new week. A fresh start. A chance for me to move forward with wrestling, my art show application, and my life in general without Sebastian getting under my skin. Or anywhere near my skin.

"It's our first full week together as a team. I read your getting-to-know-you papers last week. Good work. If we're going to compete as a team, we need to keep learning about each other and respecting each other. To help with that, I'm shuffling the groups."

My group had always been Cory Davis and Kurt Wynn, two wrestlers from Iron Valley, obviously. Shuffling for the purpose of getting to know our new teammates could only mean one thing—they'd be in our groups now.

I would not give Sebastian the satisfaction of glancing in his direction.

Coach listed the groups. Each one had at least one Forest Run wrestler. Nick was tall and significantly bigger than me, so he was in a group with Dom and our heavier wrestlers. With obnoxious smiles on their faces, Nick and Dom shook hands and bumped shoulders, their bromance growing.

The Forest Run wrestler who was closest in weight to me was, yep, Sebastian.

He rubbed his hands together. "Let's get to know each other better."

I glared at him.

"Coach's orders."

The two other wrestlers in our group were Cory and Kurt. They took one look at me and Sebastian and paired up, leaving us with no choice but to work together. I scowled at them. Kurt had the decency to look away, but Cory smiled, enjoying the entertainment.

So much for ignoring Sebastian and moving on with my life.

"Let's jog!" Coach called and blew the whistle.

I took off through the mat room, leading Sebastian by a few steps into the hallway and around the first floor of the school.

"I'm sorry about the other night," he said. "You were right. I shouldn't have said those things to you."

"Okay. By the way, your girlfriend's great."

"She's not my girlfriend."

"Makes sense. She is cooler than you."

After a few more steps, he said, "You don't make it easy."

"Make what easy?"

"Being nice to you."

"Why should I make that easy? That suggests I care if you're nice to me. I lost the ability to care how you treated me four years ago."

"About that—"

"I don't want to talk about it."

"But—"

"No. I'm here to get better, not to immerse myself in drama." Even as I said it, I realized I hadn't fully committed to the no-drama vision. I'd work on it. "You're my teammate. You should want that for me, too."

"I do."

"Great. Then focus on wrestling, and if it doesn't have anything to do with that, don't say it."

"Deal," he said.

I wondered how long that would last.

"Your school's nice," he said.

So not long. I grunted and ran faster. His footsteps sped up, too. We looped through the mat room again and back into the hallway, right into a group of girls from the swim team. Wearing their swimsuits.

Sebastian practically tripped over himself. "*Really* nice."

Boys. So predictable. He wasn't alone. Most of my teammates slowed their pace to stay in that hallway as long as possible. I shook my head and pushed myself. After another lap around the school, we stopped in the gym and stretched while everyone caught up.

Coach called us into lines for sprints, bear crawls, lunges, and the usual warm-up exercises.

"Good hustle, everyone," he praised us when we'd finished. "Let's do some hand fighting. Get with your partner."

I bounced on my toes and squared up to Sebastian.

"Ready?" he asked.

"Always."

He smirked, and we went for it.

I swung my arm, gripping the back of his neck in a collar tie and pushing his head downward. Before he caught himself, I moved in for an ankle pick and grabbed a little too hard. He stumbled and went down.

"Hand fighting, Annalise!" Coach called.

I did my best to hide my smile. "Sorry, Coach."

With the kind of intensity I'd seen in the eyes of too many boys before him, Sebastian came at me, securing a collar tie, but he didn't move my head downward. Probably too afraid to give it one hundred percent against a girl. I defended with a slide by, moving his elbow up and off my neck. I didn't push him as hard this time, but I did move behind him, making it clear I could have gotten a strong position on him if we'd been live.

He straightened and stretched his shoulders.

"Switch partners," Coach called.

I moved to Kurt, and Sebastian picked up with Cory.

"You gonna be as vicious with me as you were with Bash?" Kurt asked.

"I don't know what you're talking about," I said.

He scoffed. "Yeah. Okay."

We moved through the group, practicing our hand fighting and set-ups, then moving on to duck unders, takedowns, and sprawls. Sebastian demonstrated flawless technique on double leg takedowns, even walking through the steps for Kurt when they partnered up. I stuck to the ankle pick and added the single leg takedown when I couldn't get a good grip on the pick.

"Do you want to try a double?" Sebastian asked. "I can walk you through the technique."

"I know the technique. Thanks."

"Okay. Just trying to help."

"I don't need your help."

"We're teammates, Annalise. Helping each other is what we do."

"Get a drink," Coach yelled.

Perfect timing. The last thing I wanted to admit to Sebastian was that my strength came from technique, not physical power. An ankle pick bought me an advantage, but a double leg takedown was sometimes impossible if my opponent had more muscle than me.

I hustled to my water bottle, which was next to Dom's.

"You gonna ease up on Bash or what?"

"I don't know what you're talking about."

He gave me a bullshit face. "Lise."

"We're supposed to push each other to get better."

"We're not live. Lighten up, or Coach will make him your permanent partner out of spite."

He was probably right about that.

Dom took another swig of water. "You don't always have to prove yourself. You've kicked Bash's ass before. He's not likely to forget it."

Yeah, but that had been years earlier. My insides itched to establish that I'd gotten better over the years and could still take him.

"You look cozy with Nick."

"He's really good. Drilling with him is going to make me a ton better this year."

"Great," I said, and meant it.

Coach called us into a huddle to talk about the situational wrestling moves we'd work on next. "The whizzer kick can be defensive or offensive. But even if you don't complete the move, practicing the balancing strategy involved can help you in a number of wrestling positions. That's why we'll practice these several times each week. Dom, help me demonstrate."

Dom stepped forward and locked arms with Coach, side by side.

"You want to interlock at the waist or in an overhook. Doesn't matter. Change your positions as you move through the drill with different partners to get better practice." Coach demonstrated how to shift your feet, so one leg was between your opponents' legs, and your other foot was close to theirs to give you enough power to gain leverage. The goal was to kick your opponent's leg back, and then hop a couple of times.

Since the drill was one of Dom's favorites, I'd had a lot of experience with the move. Of course, practicing it meant pressing the back of my thigh between Sebastian's legs and hooking my leg around his. Not able to resist, I glanced his way and caught him blushing.

"Kurt," I said. "We're together next."

He nodded. "Sure."

The other guys on the team were comfortable wrestling me. I didn't care if they accidentally grazed my ass, and they didn't either. Or at least they acted like it. Maybe if I put Sebastian off to last, Coach would move us into another drill.

No such luck. After working with Kurt and Cory for a few minutes each, Coach yelled for us to move to our last partner.

"You can go first," I said.

"Okay."

We locked arms at the waist, and Sebastian moved with power, hooking my leg and nearly pulling me off balance. I recovered and hopped next to him three times. Maybe working with the other guys had settled him into the drill.

"Nice," I said.

"Thanks. Your turn."

I went for an overhook, but as soon as I pressed my body against his, he jumped back.

"Sorry." He took a deep breath and shook it off. "Go ahead."

I got into position again with an overhook. When I pressed my leg between his and hooked, he jolted backward. The force of my kick pushed him off balance, and without meaning to, I took him down.

"Stop the drill with the hop, Annalise!" Coach yelled. "Let's go."

I sighed. "Look. If you can't handle my thigh pressed against your crotch, then you might want to try another sport."

His face reddened all the way down to his neck. "How is this so easy for you?"

"I wrestle guys all the time. My body is strong and powerful. Not everything is sexual."

He rubbed his face but didn't say anything.

"Look, I need you to get over this," I said. "It took me years to earn enough respect with these guys that they treated me like a teammate instead of a girl. I don't have years with you. If we're going to be partners, you have to figure this out and find a way to be comfortable with it. And look at it this way, if you have to wrestle a girl from another school, you'll be ready for it."

"Okay," he said quietly.

"Okay," I said. "It's your turn again."

Sebastian moved into position. He back stepped and hooked my leg perfectly. We hopped a few times, and then released each other. Without speaking, we both knew it was my turn. I moved into position, this time locking at the waist. His shirt crept up with the contact, and my fingers gripped bare skin. He jerked his body, and I released him.

"Want to tuck your shirt in?"

"Sure. Thanks," he said.

When he was ready, I grabbed his waist again, and this time managed to back step tight enough next to him to kick my leg back and pull his with me. We hopped twice before he lost his balance, but I didn't let him fall to keep Coach from yelling at me again.

We repped the drill until Coach transitioned us into takedown situations. I worked my go-to takedown, an ankle pick. With the explosive power of his drive, Sebastian got repetitions of his double-leg takedown. Coach worked with every group individually to give defensive strategies to counter moves. When Sebastian countered my ankle pick, I switched to a single-leg takedown.

"Can I ask you something?" he said after we repositioned.

"Sure."

"Why don't you want to try a double?"

"It's not my strength," I said.

"But what if it could be? If you could work a double in when your pick falls apart, that would be tough to beat. Your opponent could be off balance enough from fighting off the pick that you'd have an advantage."

Or, I could get tied up in a way that *gave* them the advantage. The double left me vulnerable. I didn't do vulnerable. "Thanks. I'll think about it."

His pursed lips announced he didn't believe me. Good thinking.

But he didn't give up. The next practice during situational wrestling, he raised the point again.

"Your ankle pick would be even stronger if you could follow it with a double," Sebastian said.

"Do I have a strange sense of deja vu?"

"Seriously, though. It's like this low-hanging fruit. You have to give it a try."

"I don't need to," I said. "That's the beauty of the ankle pick. If my opponent gets free and I can't wrap up a single, then I move back into my stance. It's a low stakes-high reward move."

"But if you miss the ankle, you can drive forward on a double. Your attack would go from possible success to nearly impossible failure."

I stopped the drill and stood upright. "Why do you want to help me?"

"Because we're teammates."

I waited, not convinced that was the reason.

"And my best friend likes your sister. We should at least be able to get along."

That felt a little closer to the truth, but not the whole truth.

"And?"

He rolled his eyes. "Okay, I was a jerk to you in middle school. You didn't deserve it, and I want to make it up to you."

Ding, ding, ding!

Now, we've hit the jackpot. My pride fluttered in the wind. I could let it blow away and accept Sebastian's help, or I could hunker down. The reality was if I could master the technique of a double leg take-down—and I'd have to master it to avoid becoming vulnerable—then

I might be able to out-maneuver my opponents that were slightly stronger than me. But I'd have to spend extra time with Sebastian to do it, and probably be nice to him.

I wasn't sure either of those things held enough appeal to win me over.

"So what do you say?"

"I'll think about it," I said, this time meaning it maybe a little.

He grinned, and those blue-green eyes sparked. "Good enough for me."

CHAPTER 13

AND I DID THINK ABOUT IT.

The next day, and even into the weekend. At Friday night dinner with Mom and Ashley, my sister wouldn't let me think of anything else.

"I hear you and Bash had interesting practices this week," she said.

I pushed a roasted Brussels sprout around my plate. "It's so weird that you call him Bash now."

"Everyone calls him Bash, except for you and his mom."

Even weirder.

"I call him Sebastian," Mom offered.

"Correction–his mom and *our* mom."

Groan.

"You know he's Nick's best friend. It would make life worlds easier if the two of you could get along."

I forked the Brussels sprout into my mouth, unconcerned about my rudeness to eat and speak at the same time. "We get along fine."

"You get along like two inmates from rival gangs."

"Is this true?" my mom asked, pouring me more water. "I know he irritates you, but…"

I glared at Ashley, and she bit her lip. "It's not true, Mom. Sebastian and I are teammates, and we get along like teammates."

"He's not giving you a hard time for being a girl?"

"Not exactly."

"Explain," Mom said.

I dropped my fork against the plate with a clink, realizing we weren't getting out of this conversation without diving into details. "At first, he was freaked out to touch me, which made drilling with him hard. He might be getting a little better at that. Coach had us doing some hand fighting, whizzer kick drills, and other situations. Mostly preseason prep stuff. Every time I had to press my leg between his, he jolted backward and fell."

"So he likes you?" Mom said.

"Not every boy who is freaked out about wrestling a girl likes her. Some are just jerks."

"And you think that's what Bash is?"

So now my mom decided to call him Bash, too?

"No," Ashley said. "I'm pretty sure he likes her."

"Ashley!"

"You're the one who got away."

"What does that mean?" my mother asked.

"Nothing," my sister and I both said.

"Can we please have a nice family dinner without talking about Sebastian?"

"Of course," my mother said.

"Let's talk about Nick," Ashley said.

So we did.

***

THE NEXT MORNING, DOM PICKED ME UP FOR A TOUR-nament way too early. My stomach growled at the sight of my breakfast on my lap, but I couldn't eat until we weighed in. An hour later, we tipped the scales and collapsed onto a blanket in the corner of the gym to devour our food.

"They're not coming," he said, when he caught me searching the room for the Forest Run wrestlers. "They're committed to some other open up north."

"Great," I said. "Good luck to them."

Dom's news didn't prevent me from scanning the room for Mrs. Errico. Ever since my mom had asked me whether I wanted to help the sanctioning movement, the thought twitched at the back of my mind. Never grasping my full attention, but always there.

Dom snapped his fingers in front of my face. "What's your goal today?"

"Work my ankle pick and a single leg takedown. Beat Trevor if he's here. Generally, get ready for the season.

"Specific and right on, as usual. My goal is first place."

Fair goal for him, and after seven matches that landed him unde-feated, it panned out without causing him too much trouble. Obnox-iously, he'd asked me to help him carry his oh-so-heavy first place trophy to the car.

"Can't," I said. "I have my third-place medal to carry." A fair accomplishment in a field of all boys.

He fist-bumped me. "Yeah, you do."

Still, the medal couldn't mask my disappointment. I'd missed the volleyball state championship matchup to make the tournament. Trevor hadn't been there, so I missed the chance to kick his butt again. And, I would have landed in the championship match if I could have worked a double. My opponent had kept wriggling free of my ankle pick, and I hadn't been able to get a single on him either.

I tapped my toes in the passenger seat while Dom drove home, hating that I was seriously considering letting Sebastian help me work the move. I'd have to admit my physical weakness to plot strategies to make the double work despite that.

Letting Sebastian help me? Showing vulnerability and weakness around him? It was another question in a long series of outstanding dilemmas in my life.

"Are you all right?" Dom asked at a red light.

"Great."

"Then can you stop trying to tap a hole in my floor?"

I crossed my legs at the ankles. "Sorry."

"Is this about Bash?"

I shifted in my seat, turning toward him. "Do you ever feel like you don't know what to do?"

"Sure. I guess. So you like him?"

"No! It's not about him. It's about me. I can't decide anything. Do I submit these fall paintings for the art show? I don't know. Do I help this sanctioning movement or spend my time focusing on wrestling? I don't know. If I do help, what would I do? I don't know. Do I ask Sebastian to help me with my doubles?"

"Let me guess," Dom interrupted. "You don't know."

"Exactly."

"I'm sorry, Lise. If it makes you feel any better, from the outside, you seem totally fine."

"I guess. Maybe. Perception is a powerful thing, right?"

"Sure, it is."

Maybe I could hide behind that perception while I figured out the answers to all of life's questions. Dom dropped me off to find Sebastian in the garage with Ashley. I couldn't believe she was already back from the state championship. I ran to her, and she lifted me into a hug.

"How did it go today?" I asked.

"We played great, but you'll have to watch the broadcast online for the finer points."

I swatted her for her lack of detail and vowed to watch the matches as soon as they were posted to catch every play myself. And then I realized I hadn't addressed the fact we weren't alone.

Thankfully, I'd cleaned up my studio in the corner the night before and stored my paintings since my mom had mentioned something about spraying the winter salt off the cement floor. That meant Sebastian wouldn't see my work before I was ready to share with the world, especially him. But still, what was he doing there?

I eyed my sister suspiciously.

She smiled. Maybe a little too encouragingly. "Bash is helping me with something."

A two-by-four rested on the floor between them. Ashley held a massive, black marker above pieces of white poster board. Lined up next to each other, the pieces resembled a tall ruler.

I tossed my wrestling bag in the armoire that served as my garage locker. "What exactly?"

"I'm asking Nick to winter formal."

Wow. That was fast. Guess I shouldn't have been surprised after her marathon love fest at dinner the night before. "Congratulations," I managed. "Is this the grand proposal?"

"Yep. Nick's height is always the talk of wrestling circles, like he can't be a good wrestler because he's tall, and you know how I won't date a guy shorter than me. No offense, Sebastian."

"None taken."

"I have my own insecurities, too, as a tall girl. So I thought we could celebrate that and do this little video of me standing next to the ruler with a sign that says you have to be this tall to take me to the dance."

"Clever," I said.

"And Bash has been a great sport. He's going to stand under the ruler mark and be rejected in the video since he's not tall enough."

My eyes nearly popped out of my face.

"It's cool," Sebastian said. "I'm secure with my manhood."

A voice inside me whispered, *Why wouldn't he be?*

I told the voice to shut up.

It didn't.

You've felt how strong his arms are. And imagine those legs wrapped around–

Okay, brain! Enough.

"How was your tournament?" I asked Sebastian, if nothing else to chase away the evil thoughts haunting my sanity and bring my breathing back to a normal pace.

"Not good. Eliminated early."

"Sorry," I said and surprisingly meant it.

"It's cool. I see you did well."

I lifted the third-place medal hanging around my neck. "Yeah. It was a good day. I have some things to work on." I caught his eye and swore he knew exactly what thing I meant. "But the season is young."

"That it is."

Okay. Awkward silence, and let's wrap this up. "Thanks for helping out my baby sis, Sebastian."

"Any time."

Ashley looked back and forth between the two of us and smiled that wicked, knowing grin of hers. Insistent on changing the subject, I asked how long she would be, so I could use the garage to paint.

"Probably a while. I'm sorry."

"No problem," I said. "I'll get a shower and do some sketching in my room."

"You can help us if you want," she said.

I glanced at Sebastian. He was diligently attaching the paper to the wood.

"I'm good. Thanks though, and good luck." I left them in the garage to work but didn't get far.

Ashley chased me down in the kitchen. "I was hoping you would film the video for us."

"Ashley…"

"I know. You don't want to spend more time with Bash, but he's been nice to me, and he's Nick's best friend. If he's on board, then Nick can't say no."

"What makes you think Nick would say no anyway?"

"He could." Darkness passed across her face. "I don't want to be humiliated. I really like Nick. Please."

I sighed. It was impossible to refuse my big little sister. "Fine. But I have to get some sketches done." And I'm not hanging with you two all day, I thought, but luckily did not say. "Come and find me when it's time to film."

Ashley kissed me on the cheek in the most obnoxious way a sister can. "Thank you!"

I locked my bedroom door and retrieved the clothes I needed for after my shower. Couldn't have Sebastian wandering in. Ugh. Could you imagine? I shivered away the embarrassment and reminded myself it was only a fear, not a reality. I turned the shower water on and checked my phone while it warmed. Hmm. I had a message. Not sure how I'd missed it, I tapped on it to play and realized it was from Coach Law.

"Hey, Annalise. Sorry to bother you at home. I heard from Mrs. Errico. Do you remember her from duals a couple weeks ago? Anyways, she wanted to know if I could give her your phone number. I wanted to check with you and your mom first. I'll text you her information in case you'd prefer to contact her directly. See you at the club soon."

Yet another loose end. With my wrestling goals and the art show application hanging over me, I didn't think I could take anything else on, but if I could, it would be to help Mrs. Errico because that meant helping other girls like me.

I messaged Coach Law back that I'd get in touch with her.

When I was ready.

CHAPTER 14

SHOWERED AND DRESSED, I LAID MY SKETCHES FROM
the last year out on the floor, looking for anything I might have missed
for the art show submission. I hated myself for questioning my fall
painting series. I'd worked so hard on the pieces. Months earlier, I'd
been certain they'd score me a spot in the show.

I jumped up to my go-to thinking spot–the pull-up bar hanging
from my closet doorway.

In the middle of my reps, Ashley knocked at my door that I'd
unlocked after showering. "Come in."

As the door opened, the thought struck me that Ashley never
knocked. I stopped after fifteen and looked over my shoulder.

Sebastian.

"Don't stop on my account," he said. "I have quite the view."

I let go of the bar and glared at him. "Why do you say stuff like
that?"

"What?"

"Commenting on the view. You go from hitting on me at a party
to being a decent person to my sister and then making inappropriate
comments again. And you wonder why I can't trust anything you
say."

He stepped closer. Too close. "Maybe I don't know how to act
around you."

"That makes no sense."

"Sure it does. You're practically my ex-girlfriend."

I literally laughed in his face. "I was *never* your girlfriend. You made that perfectly clear."

"Okay, fine. But there was something there. And you've clearly hated me ever since," he continued. "But now we're teammates and even in the same crew with my best friend dating your sister. So I don't know what you are to me."

Or what you want me to be? I shook my head, urging the question to hide far away from my mouth.

"I'm nothing to you, Sebastian." My words pushed him harder than my toughest collar tie ever could.

He lowered his head and turned toward the door. "Your sister's ready for you. She asked if I could tell you that."

He disappeared down the hallway, leaving my insides burning the way my muscles should have been from the pull-ups. No. I pushed the guilt away like I would an aggressive shot on the mat. It wasn't fair for me to take on that blame. Sebastian had humiliated me.

That humiliation had stayed with me. For years. Every time a boy showed any interest in me—which was rare considering I could kick the asses of most of the boys in my school—I'd questioned his motives.

The thing was, as a wrestler, I'd learned to trust people's actions. Opponents might fake a move or pretend not to care they were wrestling a girl, but their actions told me everything. I watched their hips. I anticipated their moves.

But I couldn't see clarity through all the mixed messages Sebastian sent me. He'd hit on me. Clearly. Several times, but I couldn't decide if anything was real. He masked his actions too well. History had taught me that, and you know what they say about people who ignore history.

I had no interest in repeating my mistakes with Sebastian.

***

I FILMED CLIPS OF ASHLEY AND SEBASTIAN LIKE SHE asked. Different angles. Different speeds. Sebastian had shaken off whatever happened between us in my bedroom and committed to the humor of the video. First, he nodded at Ashley suggestively, but she shook her head. Next, he flexed his bicep. I bit my lip behind the camera, but my sister crossed her arms, unimpressed. When Sebastian pulled his shirt over his head revealing a perfectly sculpted torso, my mouth went Arizona-desert dry. Ashley pretended to consider it, but ultimately, she pointed to the sign she'd made that read, "You have to be this tall to date me."

Sebastian's rejected look of horror made me laugh so hard, we had to retake the shot.

He'd have to take his short off again. How unfortunate.

"I love it!" Ashley said when she watched the clips and pulled Sebastian and me into a three-way hug. His shoulder pressed against mine, but his hand stayed far away from any part of my body. "Thank you both so much."

I separated from them the first opportunity I had. "What's the next step?"

"I drive to his house, send him the video, and then when he comes outside, I measure him against the ruler. If he measures up, he's mine."

I actually said, "Aw." Really. I did. "That is the cutest thing."

Ashley clapped her hands. "I know. You'll come with us, right?"

Sebastian filled my peripheral vision, but I refused to look at him. "You have to."

"Okay," I said. "Anything for you. You know that."

"Good because I have a favor to ask you later."

"Only one per day."

She smirked. "I'll wait until tomorrow."

Dread settled around me at what she wanted and whether it had anything to do with Sebastian.

***

A PERMAGRIN DONNED NICK'S FACE WHEN HE emerged from his front door in sweats, his shoulder-length hair messier than usual. Ashley didn't mind. She measured him, and after he agreed to go to the dance with her, she buried her fingers in his hair and kissed him like they were getting married.

"Wow," Sebastian muttered. "That's some passion."

"Yep. Good thing his parents aren't home."

"They're watching from the window."

"Ouch," I said and laughed.

"You need a ride home? It looks like they could be at this for a while."

He wasn't lying. Ashley and Nick headed for his house, snuggled arm in arm. But riding home with Sebastian?

"I promise to take you right home and only say nice, appropriate things."

I thought of my paintings in the garage, waiting for my attention. "Okay. Thanks."

He opened the passenger door for me. I widened my eyes at him, and he nodded before walking around the car and letting me close my door myself.

After a few minutes of silence, letting him settle into driving, words pushed at my throat, fighting to fill the emptiness.

"They really are the cutest," I said.

"They are," Sebastian agreed. "I'm glad he found her to be honest. It's been kind of sad thinking about leaving him after graduation. And with the school merger…"

I studied his face as his voice trailed off. Was he being for real? He did seem to care about his friend. A lot. And he'd spent his afternoon helping Ashley. But this was a sensitive Sebastian that I hadn't seen—deep breath—since our conversations under the stairwells and in the back hallways of schools when we were thirteen years old.

"Why are you looking at me like that?" he said.

"Waiting for you to finish," I lied.

"I was worried his senior year would suck. He doesn't deserve that. Now, with Ashley, he has a chance to make it awesome, actually. They both do."

"What makes you think they'll still be together in a year?"

"What makes you think they won't?"

I pressed my fingertips against my temples.

"I'm sorry," Sebastian said immediately. "I don't want to fight with you. Actually I want to make you a promise."

I totally didn't mean to, but the smallest snort might have escaped me.

"I get it. You don't trust me. And you're right. I haven't given you much reason to. But I love Nick, and he's clearly falling for your sister. And you love your sister. And we're teammates. I want to get along, so I'm promising you that everything you see from here out will be the real Sebastian Love. No more games. No more quippy comments."

"You know you're asking me to trust that I can trust you?"

He nodded. "I do. But I'm also going to prove you can. Every day. Starting this week. At practice, I'll help you with your doubles."

"Doubles are not my go to move. They're yours." But as soon as I spoke the words, I thought of the match I'd lost that morning, and how maybe a double would have brought me a win.

"But they could be. Your ankle pick is so strong. If you had the double as a backup, nobody would be able to get away from you."

Not nobody, but it would definitely make it more difficult. I glanced sideways at Sebastian again as he slowed to turn into our driveway. The tension in my shoulders that had me sitting straight in the chair disappeared, letting me relax into the curve of the leather. But a second later, my whole body stiffened.

My guard. I'd let it go for a second.

I shook my head.

"You okay?" Sebastian asked.

Okay? My heart pumped so viciously I thought my throat might close right up. Years. Years! That's how long I had despised Sebastian. Years of hoping I wouldn't see him at tournaments, in my bracket, in my life. And now, without any control or warning, I was supposed to welcome him into my space, and let him teach me? Part of me knew it would make me better, which is all I'd wanted.

Part of me knew it was a risk I couldn't turn back from.

"I'm fine," I lied.

He stopped the car and put it in park. "Let me help you."

A simple sentence. As if that's all this was.

Simple.

I made the mistake of looking into those blue-green eyes that had enraptured me since the first moment I'd seen them. He gave me a slight nod, and despite the reality that was our life for the past four years, I felt myself disarming.

He'd worked his way through my defenses, but that didn't mean we'd become anything more than friends—if we became friends at all. Nick had grown up. Even Grant had. Maybe I could, too.

"Fine," I said. "For Ashley and Nick."

He shook his head. "No. You do this for you."

Letting Sebastian into my life–the right thing for me? Those two realities didn't belong in the same sentence.

But it also didn't feel like the universe was giving me much of a choice.

"Okay," I whispered, looking out the windshield at our garage, a view much safer than gazing into Sebastian's eyes. "For me."

"Then it's a deal. See you Monday."

I was not looking forward to it.

CHAPTER 15

I URGED THE HANDS ON THE CLOCKS IN EVERY CLASS-
room to slow Monday, but they didn't. They plowed along in their
tick tock glory teasing that I'd see Sebastian soon, and he'd help me
with my doubles. I doodled on my notebooks in every class, mulling
over my options. Sebastian's kindness seemed genuine, but that was
the problem. I'd thought it was genuine when we were in middle
school, too. I'd let him in, and he'd humiliated me completely.

I understood beauty to be many things, but I wasn't the first
choice. I wasn't the homecoming queen or even on the homecoming
court. I'd never win a beauty contest, and I didn't practice perfect
makeup or hair or poses for my online profiles.

I accepted my identity with a certain reality. The reality of being
a strong girl who dominated a boys' world like wrestling meant that
guys wanted to laugh at me or beat me more than they'd wanted to
date me.

With Sebastian in middle school, I'd forgotten that reality. I didn't
want to forget it again.

That afternoon at practice, he caught up with me on our warm-up
jog. "Hey, Annalise. How you doing today?"

"Good. Thanks."

He nodded.

Feeling rude, I asked, "How are you?"

He didn't seem to notice how stiff the words sounded.

"Good. Ready to work."

We passed the swimmers again, but this time, he didn't even glance their way.

"So about the doubles, the key is to get elbow deep when you reach behind the knees. You have long arms, which is why the ankle pick works well for you. You can definitely get elbow deep if you lower your level and explode into it."

My brain warred with itself over my response. Mostly because I didn't know how to be nice to Sebastian. "Thanks," I managed. Original, I know.

"We can practice that today in our warmups if you want. It's always good to work that motion slower before we go live."

"Yep."

"You okay?"

I sighed. He was trying.

Or lying, a voice whispered. *My* voice.

"Adjusting," I said.

He grinned, and I nearly tripped over the smooth floor. I looked away.

"Being nice to me isn't exactly your norm."

I wouldn't look at him again, not if he was grinning like that. "Like I said, adjusting."

"Fair enough."

As we warmed up and stretched, he lectured me on the strategy behind the double, all the tricks he'd learned perfecting the move over the years, and even how I could manipulate my leverage to overcome any "strength variations" between me and my opponent. Something told me he'd chosen those words carefully.

"You mean if someone's stronger than me?" I blurted, and he blushed.

"I…I…"

I laughed, and he rolled his eyes.

"Are you messing with me?" he asked.

"How long did it take you to select those two words—strength variations?"

He tilted his head back, so only the ceiling could see his expression. "About an hour last night."

Ouch. An hour of sleep lost for a wrestler was exponential. "And then I went and ruined your efforts."

"Pretty much," he said.

"My apologies."

He smiled at me again, more relaxed than I think I'd ever seen him. "You're teasing me. This is progress."

Or dangerous. Guess it came down to perspective.

We moved into shadow wrestling. Side-by-side, we drilled the double. When coach called for partners to go live, Sebastian naturally stepped in front of me.

"Remember your head position," he said, and gestured for me to come at him.

I took a deep breath. "You're going to counter me, right?"

"I'm going to fight you with all my strength."

I nodded. "Okay."

Like we'd practiced, I pushed the back of Sebastian's neck with a collar tie. When he pulled his head up, I was already lower than him. Before he could react, I dropped my knee to the ground and wrapped my hands around the back of his legs.

His thighs.

He broke free, and I shot upright to avoid him gaining a dominant position over me.

"The knees. You have to hit behind the knees, especially with a strong opponent."

Behind the knees.

"Go ahead."

This time, I almost caught him with an ankle pick, but he pulled his head up and stretched out my arm that had the collar tie. I adjusted to try and get a double. Pulling behind his knees, I pressed the side of my head into him. He sprawled and pushed my head away, but I didn't relent. I maintained my grip on his legs, but the weight of his chest was heavy on me. I tried to knee slide up.

Still, he managed to hold strong.

Coach blew the whistle and called for us to switch partners.

"It's okay. You're doing great. We have a full week to work on it."

"No," I said, determined to get him down on the mat. "Kurt and Cory, give us one more go."

They looked at each other and shrugged before going back to wrestling.

Speed. That's what I needed. I'd catch Sebastian off guard. We shook hands, and the second he released mine, I took a shot. No collar tie this time. Before he could recover his stance, I pulled at his knees and pressed my head into his side. It wasn't pretty, but he lost his balance and hit the mat. Normally, we'd keep wrestling, but I'd achieved the takedown. It was time to switch partners. So we both stopped.

Um, which consisted of me on top of him staring into his eyes and both of us breathing heavily.

Ashley's voice whispered in my mind, "I'm pretty sure he likes her."

Did he?

The blue and green in his eyes gripped me, but then his gaze dipped lower. To my lips. *This was not happening. Sebastian Love was not looking at my lips. With those eyes. Move!*

Now!

I shot up, kneeing him in the crotch on the way. "Oh my gosh. I'm so sorry."

He groaned and rolled onto his side. "No. You did great. You got it."

"Thanks. Are you…okay?"

He grunted a sound that was supposed to be affirmative. I think.

"Maybe we should switch partners now," I suggested.

"Yeah," he managed, but he still hadn't gotten up from the mat.

"Can I help you up?"

"I'm good. Kurt!"

Kurt and Cory watched from a few feet away, both covering their grins. I glared at them and mentally promised to make them pay for their ill humor. Cory was my first victim. I practiced the double on him and hit the move again.

"You gonna knee me in the balls, too?" he asked from underneath me.

"Don't tempt me," I said, and he snort-laughed.

I couldn't look Sebastian in the eyes the rest of practice.

***

THAT NIGHT, I STEWED ABOUT MY LIFE OVER MY MOTHer's beef vegetable stew. Sebastian had promised to show me himself. No games. Total honesty. But that look in his eyes. If that was real, then that meant Ashley might have been right. That kind of hot smolder didn't happen between two people that felt nothing for each other.

I groaned at the thought of what that might mean about my feelings.

Or, Sebastian lied. His smoldering looks were meant to confuse me. Maybe he planned to cut weight and wrestle me for my weight class, and he wanted to soften me up to beat me. What was that saying about fool me once and fool me twice?

"You okay?" Ashley asked, buttering a beautiful piece of butterscotch banana bread next to me. I eyed it longingly. "Sorry." She tucked it behind her bowl where I couldn't see it. Like I'd forget the sugary goodness was there.

"Fine."

"I know when you're not fine."

"What made you want to invite Nick to formal?"

"I like him."

"Just like that?"

"It's that easy. If you let it be."

"Maybe for you."

"True, but I don't have the trust issues you have."

I scowled at her.

She rested her hand on my forearm. "I mean that in the best possible way. No use hiding from the truth."

"You trust Nick? You haven't known him long."

"I trust myself and how I feel when he's around. He's hot. Obviously. Funny. The boy doesn't have an ounce of body fat, and I thought it might be good for him to get to know everyone since he'll be going to Iron Valley next year."

"That's altruistic. You almost convinced me you invited him out of the goodness of your heart," I teased.

She bit into that tempting bread. "No. I think you should invite Sebastian out of the goodness of yours."

I dropped my spoon. "You. Are. Not. Serious."

"C'mon, Lise. Chandra is taking Grant, and Sebastian has no one."

How did we become the Forest Run wrestlers' groupies?

"What about Elizabeth?"

"The girl he brought to that party?" Ashley scrunched her face into a thoughtful expression. "I think she lost her appeal when she didn't serve the purpose of making you jealous?"

Not touching that one. "Is this why you begged us to spend time together this weekend?"

"No. I needed your help."

"And you need it again now?"

She shrugged.

"What about Melanie?" I suggested.

"She's taking her own boyfriend, obviously."

"Find one of your other volleyball friends to take him or something. I cannot go to a dance with Sebastian."

"Then come with us as a group."

"A group of couples with me and Sebastian?"

"Lise, I want to spend time with you."

"Go with your friends. I'll meet you there and we can dance together. Okay?"

"But we're getting a party bus and taking pictures at the park and—"

Her mouth kept moving, but all I could think of was the look in Sebastian's eyes when I'd succeeded in taking him down on the double.

"Ashley, I can't."

She sighed. "I knew it was a long shot, but I had to ask."

"Sorry."

"I get it. I thought since you've been getting along as teammates—"

"We're tolerating each other, Ash. That's a far cry from going to a dance together." Or facing anything else that might be going on. *If* I let it go on.

"What about you, though?" Ashley persisted. "Don't you want to go to your last winter formal? With a date?"

Once upon a time, I'd wanted a boyfriend. A boyfriend with blue-green eyes who wrestled and made me laugh. Then I learned he'd been playing me the entire time, and I wasn't girlfriend material. I was a fascination. Fodder for a good story. A joke about whether a guy could get further with me on the mat or off. Winter formal always fell during wrestling season, at the height of the intrigue of the girl wrestler. Which obviously exacerbated the whole issue.

Letting Sebastian help me learn the double-leg takedown was as far as my trust could stretch. Anything beyond that was not happening.

I had no intention of changing my point of view.

CHAPTER 16

WITH EARLY MORNING LIFTING, GOING LIVE WITH SE-
bastian every day after school, and three evening training sessions
at the club that week, I collapsed onto the couch Wednesday night
and vowed to stay there the entire Thanksgiving weekend until duals
on Sunday.

Friday morning while the rest of the country rushed through the
busiest shopping day of the year, I pulled the gallery's winter art
show application up on my phone and reviewed it again, something
I did every week. I hadn't advanced beyond typing in my name and
address. I promised at least this time, I'd get to my phone number.

Such a go-getter.

I'd chosen a fall theme because I'd started the paintings in fall,
my favorite season, but as winter gripped our corner of the world,
my inspiration for fall had faded. Now I had to recreate the images
from memory. I could have selected winter as a theme—all white,
blue, and glitter—but that meant entirely reworking my series in less
than two months.

I weighed my other options.

Painting a couple pieces from each season? I could choose my
favorite pieces from the fall series and then add to them with a couple
paintings from each of the other seasons. Oh, I might even have a

summer painting in storage.

Still, though, I didn't think I could manage it with practices and tournaments. I'd need an unparalleled burst of creativity and inspiration.

I'd have to stick to fall.

"Earth to Annalise."

Ashley stood in the doorway to the family room with wide eyes.

"Huh?"

"I've only been calling your name for the last ten minutes."

Seemed exaggerated, but okay. "What's up?"

"Come dress shopping with me."

I groaned.

"Please."

"I'm very busy here."

She rolled her eyes.

"I am! I'm filling out my art show application."

"You gonna write more than your name and address this time?" she quipped.

Sisters.

"I have to finish this."

"Yes, you do," Ashley said, climbing onto the couch next to me. "You need to take

photos of any number of the paintings you have sitting in the garage and finish your application. I completely agree. Can I help you with that?"

I glared at her. I wasn't ready, and she knew it.

"That's what I thought." She shook my shoulders. "So, please. Come with me. You need a dress, too."

"I can wear something in my closet. Or in yours."

"I need your opinion, and dresses are on sale today," she said in a sing-song voice.

I covered my face with a pillow. "Where are Chandra and Melanie this weekend? Don't you want to go with them?"

"Melanie shopped with her mom and her sister, Elle. Chandra's mom insisted on going with her since this is her first big dance."

In a year, I'd be away at college with no option of doing things like this with my sister. I rolled off the couch, my muscles angry to be stripped of their rest. "Let me change real quick."

Ashley pulled me up off the floor and hugged me. "You are the best sister ever."

I wasn't sure she still felt that way an hour later when we were standing in the dress store at the mall.

"You don't like any of them?" she whined.

"Let's keep looking."

"We looked at everything. The only other rack is out of my price range."

"Then I'll have to tap into my piggy bank. My sister needs the perfect dress."

"Lise, I love you for that, but I can't let you spend college money on my dress."

"Consider it an investment. Resell the dress at a consignment shop after the dance and pay me back."

She scrunched her mouth to the side in that adorable pensive look of hers that went back about fourteen years, and I knew I had her.

"I guess it won't hurt to look."

I looped my arm in hers and led her to the most expensive rack in the store. We gaped at each other with wide eyes.

"Expensive dresses have more sparkles," Ashley said.

"Better shapes."

"More style."

The metal hangers clacked against the circular rack as we slid the dresses this way and that, studying them. Within minutes, Ashley had four dresses to try on, and I had two of my own.

"I thought you weren't getting a dress," she said.

"So did I, but do you see these sequins?"

Ashley sighed. "I do. If we're going to do this, better do it right."

"Shoes," we said in unison.

We swiped heels of every color from the shelves and laughed our way to the fitting rooms.

"I wanna see every one of them on you," I called over the divider that separated us.

"Same!"

I looked at the dresses hanging on side-by-side hooks against a backdrop of off-white plainness. My favorite, an ombré pattern, had black sequins on the bottom that transitioned to a blend of black and silver around the waist and then silver around the plunging neckline. My mom would kill me. Better try that one on second, and only if the other wasn't love at first fit. I shifted my attention to the royal blue mini skirt, also sequined to the max.

"Sequins must be everything this year," I said.

"Yep," Ashley answered. "You almost ready?"

I slid the dress over my shoulders and positioned it tightly against my stomach and hips. It showed every curve of my body, which for someone who worked out like I did was a blessing since I didn't have an abundance of curves.

I went with the silver, three-inch heels and threw my hair up in a messy ponytail.

"Ready," I called to my sister.

She squealed. "Me too."

We stepped into the hallway at the same moment, and it was my turn to squeal. "You are not my little sister."

"You are wicked hot."

I stood tall, as tall as someone my height could, and looked over my shoulder in the mirror. She wasn't lying. My shoulder, back, and arm muscles were on full display, and my quads and calves showed off their edges.

"I feel like we're all grown up," I said. "You know mom is going to cry."

"Try sob."

"Is that your favorite?"

She shook her head. "You?"

"No."

We laughed and ran back into our changing rooms. If the blue dress was wicked hot, I couldn't even guess what word my sister would utter when she saw the black and silver one. It came with a subtle built-in push up bra that served its purpose, allowing my chest, shoulder, and arm muscles to stand out even more somehow.

A little school color nostalgia, I chose three-inch purple heels from the line up and studied myself in the mirror of the small changing room. "I found my favorite, Ash."

"Me too," she said.

"On three?" I asked.

"One."

"Two."

"Three."

We popped out into the hallway and gasped at each other. Ashley's dress was red to the max with black heels. Her short brown hair and thick eyeliner gave her an edgy look. She'd accessorize it perfectly– fierce and glam. Nick was going to drop when he saw her.

"It's definitely the one," I said.

"And you, look...wow. I've never seen you wear anything so sexy."

Over her shoulder I glanced in the mirror and spun. "And you will be the only one to see me in it."

Ashley pouted. "Fine. Then at least we need a few pics."

"No posting them."

"Promise. But we have to go out there." She pointed to the store, out of the dressing room. "Store rules."

"Whatever. Two minutes though."

"Two minutes," she repeated and pulled a few strands of hair out of my ponytail, so they hung around my face. "You look seriously hot."

"As do you."

She grabbed my hand and pulled me into the store. Laughing and giggling, we posed for selfies across the spectrum of funny to fierce. Until a familiar voice interrupted the fun and said, "Dang, Ashley."

Arm-in-arm, we spun to face Nick and, of course, Sebastian. So much for only Ashley seeing me in the dress. Sebastian's eyes worked their way down my body, his mouth opening wider the further they got. He swallowed hard at the sight of the shoes. A voice reminded me that purple was his favorite color.

Ashley pressed herself into Nick's arms. "What are you doing here?"

Yeah. What was he doing here? At the same time we were? I glared at Ashley.

"Picking up my suit for the dance. You told me I had to today because they were on sale."

"Right," Ashley said, avoiding my gaze. "I forgot about that."

I bet she had.

"I was going to text you about the tie color. Please tell me it's red."

She stepped back and struck a pose. "That depends. Do you like it?"

His mouth moved, but no words came out until he managed, "Yes. Yes, please. I like it very much."

Even I laughed. Until I side-eyed Sebastian, and he was still staring at me.

"You look incredible," he said, his mouth still hanging open.

Ashley reached for his lip. "You have a little bit of drool there." Sebastian's face reddened.

"I'm not buying this dress," I said. "Just having some fun with my little sis."

Sebastian nodded.

"Actually, I'm gonna change. Be right back, Ash." I turned away before she could protest. As I walked back to the fitting room, my heart pummeled my chest, and I knew Sebastian was watching me. At the doorway, I couldn't help myself. I glanced back. Those blue-green eyes were locked on me. I wasn't sure I could label the emotions simmering inside me at that moment, but anger at my sister for setting us up was definitely not one of them.

CHAPTER 17

SUNDAY MORNING, I PEELED MYSELF OUT OF BED LAT-
er than usual, a whopping six a.m. With my bag already packed for
duals, I brushed my teeth and braided my hair before starting my car
and watching from the dining room window until the frost worked its
way off the windshield. I could scrape it myself, but that's the kind
of thing nobody should have to do on a weekend.

When my front seat blared heat onto my butt and the car was
warm enough, I tossed my bag onto the passenger seat and started
the twenty-minute drive to the tournament. My sister and mom would
come later, but since it was so close, there was no reason for them
to rush out of bed.

A memory of Sebastian's expression when he'd seen me in the
dress Friday night brought a smug smile to my face. How could it
not? His eyes tortured me on the daily. No shame in a dress torturing
him a little. Except we were supposed to be friends. Or on the verge
of friendship. If I enjoyed torturing him, we weren't friends. And if
knowing he found me attractive made me feel anything at all...no, I
wasn't entertaining that thought.

We were friends.

Like I had to practice my technique with wrestling, I had to practice being his friend. That was all.

Part of me hoped I wouldn't see him that day at duals. I was wrestling the girls' bracket only. I wanted to focus on my freestyle and get to know some of the girls better. It could help if I decided to work with Mrs. Errico to lobby the sanctioning of girls' wrestling as a statewide sport, something still dancing around in my already crowded mind.

And sometimes, a girl needed a break from boys.

Funny that the first person I saw then when I finished weigh-ins was Nick. He wore a state championship singlet, showing off his dominance. I couldn't judge. I wore mine, too.

"Okay, state champ," I teased.

He pointed to me. "I only have one title. I defer to your brilliance."

I smirked at him. Nick had gone from zero to hero in the last few weeks, and if that could happen, maybe Sebastian and I could be friends. If I practiced.

And reminded myself of that often.

"Come with me." He headed for the girls' mats where a younger girl wrestled, working moves with a coach. I pegged her to be about twelve or thirteen, way too young for Nick, who happened to be dating my sister. My confusion dissipated when I saw the look of pride on Nick's face.

"Is that your little sister?"

"Yep. Fallon."

She took a quick shot. He rolled with the move to give her practice, but she'd definitely have landed that in a real match.

"She's tough," I said.

"She loves wrestling. She's much better at the sport overall than I am."

"I don't know about that, Nick. You're pretty good. It takes a lot for me to say that about an opponent-slash-teammate."

"Thanks, but I mean the stuff off the mat, too. She's up every morning before school, working out, doing pull ups, lifting. She barely eats any sugar. She's so disciplined. Evenings, she works out with her team and at the club."

"Sounds like the kind of dedication she needs to win," I said, especially if she has to keep competing against boys.

He nodded. "She was upset when our club closed, but I think it's for the best."

"I didn't realize your club closed." Was anything surviving in Forest Run?

"Last week. It sucks, but they didn't do much freestyle, and that's what she needs now.

"They do good freestyle training at my club."

"That's what we heard. She starts there this week, actually. She's gonna need freestyle training. She's entering a lot of the girls' brackets. Today, she's wrestling on your club team."

"Wait. She's in my club now?" And although I had all but invited her to the club to learn freestyle, I heard the real question in my voice. Were the other Forest Run wrestlers following Fallon to the Keystone Club?

"We all are," Nick said.

We? As in…?

"Sebastian, Grant, and me."

Practice being a friend. Practice being a friend. Practice being a friend.

"That's...great!"

"Nice try."

"At least you can tell I'm trying."

"It's a start. So what do you think?"

"Are you asking me to look out for your little sister, Nick?"

"Maybe…"

I glanced back at Fallon on the mat, learning the basics of freestyle. I remembered my first experiences with the new style and my frustration that only the girls had to compete in two different styles. It only took a few weeks for me to learn to love freestyle more than folkstyle, though. Then it felt more like an opportunity and less like a burden. Maybe I could help Fallon see that, too.

"I'd be glad to," I said.

"Good because I have another selfish request," Nick said and took a deep breath.

Uh oh.

"She wants to meet you."

I laughed.

"I'm serious. You are her idol."

"I don't want to be anyone's idol, but I'd be glad to meet her. She's part of our club now. We're teammates."

"You have the same love for your new Forest Run teammates?"

I sighed. "Working on it."

"Even Sebastian?" Nick asked.

"Working on that a little harder."

"Good. Ashley wants to see you get along. If it's something Ashley wants, I'm ready to move mountains to give it to her." He rested his hand over his heart and tilted his head to the sky, oh so dramatic.

"The mushy look doesn't suit you, Nick."

"This year hasn't gone anywhere near how I expected. I thought we would wrestle our last season at Forest Run and compete at our club. Everything came crashing down on us. It was a lot, and I guess one of the blessings in all that was meeting Ashley and getting a chance to apologize to you. Seeing Sebastian on the verge of happiness."

"You keep bringing up Sebastian's name. You do realize that, right?"

"Do I?"

"Nick."

He waggled his eyebrows at me. "He liked your dress the other night."

My stomach flipped, and a breathy laugh escaped my lips. "Liking a dress and liking a girl are two different things."

"Not always."

I reached out to the universe for patience.

"Nick, you and Ashley have this love at first sight thing going on. And it's great. I'm happy for you, but Sebastian and me—we don't."

"But—"

"We don't, Nick."

"Fine," he said. "I won't push anymore."

"Thank you. Now that we have that settled, I want to meet Fallon."

Nick called her over during a water break. When she found us on the side of the mat, she smiled at her brother, but then her eyes practically popped out of her adorable little baby face at the sight of me.

And I knew love at first sight, too.

"Hey, Fallon," I said. "So good to meet you. Your brother's been telling me all about you."

Fallon glanced at Nick and then back at me. "He told me he knew you, but I thought he was lying."

"He doesn't know me. He begged me in the hallway. I've never seen him before."

Nick nudged me with this hip.

"Okay, he stalks me at home. It's kind of creepy."

Fallon giggled.

"How's your freestyle training going?"

Her face squeezed in fear so tight, you'd thought I was about to suplex her myself. "Today's my first match. I'm gonna get creamed."

"Nobody wins them all."

"But I feel like I *have* to learn freestyle if I want to wrestle in college even though that's like forever away. It kind of sucks. I was just getting good at folkstyle."

I knew that dilemma well. "Can I tell you the truth?"

"Sure."

"Once I learned freestyle, I liked it better than folkstyle."

"You did?"

"Yep. And it's fun to spin someone over and over on a mat."

She laughed again.

I glanced at my watch. "I have at least an hour before my first match. Do you want to go over some moves together?"

"Oh my gosh. Yes, please!"

So we did. In the corner of the gym, I showed her how to transition her current takedowns to freestyle turns. If she could take someone down and roll them even once before her opponent stopped her, she had a chance.

Before I knew it, my watched buzzed. Good thing I'd set the timer.

"We have to go. Our first match is about to start. Are you ready?"

"I'm ready to try."

I smiled at her attitude, and I could see why Nick adored her. I found him and Sebastian waiting at the girls' mat. Fallon excitedly told Nick everything we'd worked on. I watched her to avoid making eye contact with Sebastian.

Until a voice in my mind whispered, *Practice.*

Stupid voices.

"Hey," I said.

"Hey," he answered. "Good luck today."

"You too."

There I'd done it. I thought—until I glanced at Nick, and he rolled his eyes at me. Whatever. I didn't say anything mean. Progress was progress.

The structure of the event was to start with the lower weight classes first and then work your way up to the heavier weights. That meant Fallon would be going first. Part of me wished I could wrestle first to show her some of the moves I taught her in a live situation. Instead, I gave her a pep talk.

"Fallon, you got this. You have the strength and skill from folk-style. You can use the same takedowns. Think of this as a practice. Work on the turns we talked about. Okay?"

"Okay. Thanks, Lise."

"Any time."

Nervous, I kneeled on the mat, ready to cheer Fallon on. Nick and Sebastian kneeled on either side of me. Sebastian watched me with a weird expression.

"What?"

"Do you let everyone on the planet call you Lise except me?"

I could not work out the pretzel that was that mess right now. "Fallon's up," is all I could manage.

The match started. After some circling, Fallon got taken down, but she pressed her arms wide into the mat and refused to be turned. The ref called them back to the upright position.

"Good job, Fallon. You got this!"

She nodded to me with a sudden ferocity in her eyes. I knew that look. At the whistle, she attacked and earned herself a takedown. In perfect position, she used the leg lace I had taught her and rolled her opponent twice before the other girl could stop her momentum. I screamed and squeezed Sebastian's arm. Oops. I'd meant for it to be Nick's, but whatever.

"Did you see that? Let's go, Fallon."

She'd thought she'd be destroyed, but she was winning by four points. Again off the whistle, she shot hard, but her opponent sprawled, and they both circled up to their feet. After two more attempts, neither of the girls could get a takedown, and the period ended.

"She's doing great," Nick said, looping his arm in mine. "I'm so proud of her."

"You should be."

As the match progressed, Fallon's opponent tired, but she didn't. Chalk it up to those early morning workouts and the lack of sugar. In the second period, she took her opponent down again, and with two more turns, she was the winner.

When she came off the mat, the first person she hugged was her brother, but I was next.

"I'm so proud of you."

"Thank you for all your help."

"Yes, Lise," Nick said. "Thank you."

Fallon slipped sweats over her singlet and grabbed a granola bar from her bag. "Anyone else want one?"

"Thanks," Nick said, "but we have to run."

I looked back and forth between him and Sebastian. They'd miss my match. The pang of disappointment that tore open my chest surprised me.

"I'll cheer for her loud enough for all three of us," Fallon said.

"Good luck, guys," I managed.

"Thanks," they said.

CHAPTER 18

I FINISHED THE DUALS UNDEFEATED. FALLON WON more matches than she lost and couldn't stop smiling about it. We'd spent the day between competitions working on moves and chatting. I could see why Nick adored her. We were fast friends, unlike my friendship with her brother.

The guys competed in a separate room, so we missed watching each other the rest of the day. Probably for the best, especially since I couldn't shake Sebastian's voice from my mind. I drove home wondering if he wanted to call me Lise. I'd told him my friends called me Lise. I'd told him I was trying to be his friend. Didn't that mean I should let him call me Lise, too?

Except hearing Sebastian's voice say that name might transport me to a time that erased any good will built between us.

Back home, I showered and broke out my massage gun. The vibrations against my traps, quads, hamstrings, and even glutes had me pain-groaning. An alert popped up on my phone. Rebecca Watterson's show would close the next day, a reminder that made me groan for real. I'd forgotten. And wanted to go nowhere, but the printed version of the art show application taunted me from my desk.

This is what it means to be an athlete and an artist, I told myself. I messaged Dom to drop everything and meet me at the gallery and gave in to the vibrations for five more minutes, sacrificing that time I could have been styling my hair. Instead, I dried it quickly, threw it up into a loose bun, grabbed a winter dress and leggings from the closet, and brushed minimal makeup on my face.

Longingly, I said farewell to the massage gun and left.

***

REBECCA WATTERSON'S EXHIBIT HAD BEEN A HIT AT the gallery. Locally born, she now spent most of her time in New York City. Despite the exhibit having been on display for weeks, people packed the space for the last viewing.

I shook my head. A well-respected artist on display in my hometown, and with wrestling practices and my own workout schedule, I'd almost missed it. The colors of her pieces greeted me first. I'd spent weeks painting yellows, reds, and oranges, but Rebecca created with the brightest greens, purples, and blues. Her centerpiece featured geometric shapes in the three colors with white puppy paw prints and white cat paw prints moving in all directions across it.

The little paws told a story. So did the photos mounted on the walls around the work. They chronicled the real-life pets pawing their way across the canvases. Rebecca had positioned both abstract paintings of shapes and realistic landscapes around the floor of her studio with dipping stations around the edges. With the help of a few friends, who caught the pets when they exited the path of paintings, re-dipped their paws, and set them loose again on the canvases, she was able to systematize the process. Still, the photos told a story of silliness and laughter throughout the whole experience. Under one of the photos was a quote from Rebecca that read, "Our pets walk all over us in the best possible way. As an artist, I wanted to show that."

Brilliant.

I guess that was the thing about art. It connected with people in different ways. I got lost in the painting again, a deep yearning rising from inside me that my fall series would be accepted. I wanted someone to see it. I wanted someone to stand in front of it like I was standing in front of Rebecca's paintings, admiring them, *feeling* something.

"Annalise?"

Pulled from the depth of the moment, I spun to face Sebastian. "What are you doing here?"

"I wanted to catch the show one last time."

"You've seen it before?" I asked, confused. "And you're back?" Sebastian liked art?

"Yeah. My aunt's the artist."

Oh universe, you saucy thing. Of course she was.

"I helped her with this one, actually," he said with a laugh. "It was so cool."

I studied the photos of her helpers again. Sebastian pointed to one where he dipped the puppy's paws into the white paint. I hadn't looked closely enough at the helpers' faces to notice him before.

"We laughed so hard." He snickered then from the memory of it. "She had to throw away a few canvases. They were too destroyed."

I couldn't help my curiosity. Sebastian had the inside knowledge of a true artist's process, and I wanted it. "What do you mean destroyed?"

"One time, the cat rolled around in the paint and then all over the painting. It became a big blob of yellow."

"Oh no!"

"Exactly. Aunt Bex knew the risks, though."

I nodded, taking the extra few seconds to digest his words. Rebecca Watterson was Aunt Bex to Sebastian. The boy walked in sunshine.

"Wanna meet her?" he asked.

"What?"

"Meet her? Aunt Bex?"

I stuttered.

"Annalise Fiori," Sebastian said, shaking his head.

"What?"

"You're cute. Come with me."

He took my hand. My hand. My skin on his. To meet his aunt, the artist. Too many emotions collided inside me. I couldn't sort them, and I definitely couldn't assign one specific emotion to the feeling of his hand in mine.

My mouth moved, but no actual words came out. Maybe a few embarrassing sounds, but let's ignore that. In the back room of the gallery, I spotted Rebecca Watterson immediately. I'd seen her picture online, but she also stood out with a special elegance among everyone in the room. Her clothing was sleek, a black jumper, fitted at her thin waist with a chic, silver belt. The pants flared at the bottoms over red, heeled boots. A collection of silver necklaces contrasted against the black of her clothes. She tossed her head back in the easiest laughter, and I sighed at my realization that I'd love to be like that someday.

"Aunt Bex!"

"Bash, darling! You came!" She hugged him and kissed his cheek. Seeing his aunt adore Sebastian so completely was nearly contagious.

Nearly.

"I want you to meet someone," he said. "This is Annalise Fiori. She's on my wrestling team."

Rebecca's eyes widened. "Annalise! Of course. I love watching you wrestle."

"You do? I mean, thank you."

She smiled. "You're welcome. I remember when you beat this one." She wrapped her arm around Sebastian's shoulder. "He was heartbroken for weeks."

Heat rushed over my cheeks at the mention of the dreadful tournament when Sebastian and I'd faced off. And the kiss he'd stolen from me earlier that day. "You were there?"

"Our whole family was, expecting Sebastian to take away the first-place trophy as usual, but you stepped in and shocked us all."

Sebastian blushed but managed to keep eye contact with me. Thinking back, I remembered how he'd reacted after the match. Clearly disappointed, but still respectful. How could the same kid who'd embarrassed me over a kiss behave so maturely after I'd beaten him at the sport he loved? In front of his whole family? With the kind of father who pressured him at every opportunity.

"Thank you," I managed. "Your art is brilliant. I love the paw prints."

She held her shoulders back and smiled. "Thank you. It's not for everyone."

"No art is," I said.

"You like art?" She smiled in a genuine way that invited me to spill my life secrets.

"I paint. I'm working on a fall series to submit to the art show here. Mostly reds, oranges, and yellows with some mixed media."

Rebecca crossed her arms and a little line formed between her eyes. "What kind of media?"

"Leaves, acorns, and seeds mostly. I'm considering adding candy to my Halloween painting."

"Interesting," she said. "How's it coming along?"

Terrible.

"Good. I think. When I can manage between wrestling practices."

"It's hard to find time," Rebecca said, "but you will."

I hoped so. Across the room, Dom looked around the crowd trying to find me. I waved to get his attention, and he hustled our way, his eyebrows raising at the sight of me with Sebastian.

"Rebecca, this is my best friend, Dom."

"Nice to meet you. The gallery is closing soon, but we're having an after party to celebrate the show. You should join us as Sebastian's guests."

I glanced sideways at Sebastian who was pointedly not making eye contact with me. My tongue stuck to the roof of my mouth.

A guy in a suit leaned toward Rebecca to whisper something in her ear. "I have to go close a sale. See you in a bit."

"I have to go, too," Sebastian said. "Say hello to a few people. I guess, I'll um, see you at the after party."

When he was gone, I grabbed Dom by the wrist. "We have to leave."

"I just got here. And the artist invited you to the afterparty. Isn't that like the Holy Grail?"

"She's Sebastian's aunt."

"That boy is clouding your judgment, Lise. It's not about him. This is your opportunity to chat with artists and the owner of the gallery. The one you're applying to show at in weeks. You want to bail on that because a guy was a jerk four years ago?"

I crossed my arms and slumped against the wall. "You're kind of making sense."

"Good. Now walk your best friend through this place and tell me everything you know about the art. That way you'll be ready to rub elbows with the important people, and I won't be totally clueless."

I looped my arm in his. "You're kind of smart."

"That's what I've been telling you."

CHAPTER 19

I'D TAUGHT DOM TOO WELL. AFTER MY LESSONS, HE introduced himself to a group of girls and reiterated my lecture to impress them.

It worked.

So I wandered off on my own, casually envisioning my own paintings hanging on the walls. Which would only happen if I could finish them. And the application. And if the committee liked it instead of immediately rejecting it like the years before.

I bounced on my toes.

"You okay?" Sebastian offered me a bottle of water. "You look a little…"

"Stressed?" I took the bottle. "Thanks."

"Wanna talk about it?"

I applauded myself for not laughing in his face. Progress!

"I want to show you something," Sebastian said, when I didn't answer him.

The last few seconds felt dangerously like an experience that could occur between two friends. Friends. Friends with Sebastian? All this practicing was getting me somewhere.

"Lead the way," I said.

For the first time in four years, I saw Sebastian smile. The way he had when we'd hid in the corners of the lobby, under the stairwells, and behind the bleachers to talk and laugh as kids. When I'd thought things were real.

Before I could think about the words escaping my lips, I said, "You know what? I think this is a bad idea."

"Annalise, let me show you where it is, and if you want to be left alone, then I'll go."

I sighed.

"I promise," he insisted.

"Fine."

He nodded. "Fine." Behind another curtain, he pushed a heavy door, and a cool wind gusted into the room. I followed him up a flight of cement stairs to an expanse of rooftop lit with candles and twinkle lights.

I raised my eyebrows at him.

"Okay, so it's kind of romantic, but that's not why I brought you here. Look at the ground."

An oval with three lines running through it, flirted with the edges of the space. "A track?"

"No idea why it's here. Wanna take a lap?"

Desperately. Sebastian followed. I didn't feel right sending him away. He'd gone out of his way to be nice. He'd introduced me to his aunt. Maybe thinking of him with kindness would prove a fool me twice, shame on me situation.

Maybe not.

"You're always so quiet around me," he accused.

"I'm quiet around everyone."

"Not around Dom or even most of the guys on the team."

"They're my friends," I said before I actually heard the words and calculated their implication.

"Ouch," he said.

"Sorry. I didn't mean to…" What? Be honest?

"It's because of what happened in middle school, isn't it?"

My mouth went dry. I definitely wasn't ready to be that honest. "What happened in middle school?"

He laughed. "Okay. I get it. Let's talk art then. You like art, right?"

"Obviously."

"Who's your favorite modernist?"

"You know about modernism?" I asked, skeptical.

"I guess you'll have to find out. Answer the question."

I thought about the books I'd read about art and the summer camps I'd spent at the Carnegie Museum of Art in Pittsburgh. I never fully "got" some of the modernists. Only two stood out to me, but one was a clear favorite. "Jackson Pollock."

His wide eyes showed his surprise. "The guy was a jerk."

"Were you asking about the person or the art?"

"Fair enough. I'm surprised, I guess. You seem so moral."

"There's beauty in the chaos of a Pollock painting," I argued. Standing in front of his work always made me feel like he'd reached into my mind and pulled out the image of my world with all its strands pulling me in different directions—art, wrestling, school, family, friends—never enough time for any of it. A tangled mess of colors that I loved too much to let any of them go. "I try not to look beyond that."

"Makes sense."

"What about you?"

"Have to go with the local guy," he said, sweeping his arm toward the lights of Pittsburgh in the distance.

"Warhol?"

"Silver clouds, Campbell's soup, Marilyn Monroe."

"Have you been to his museum?"

"Only a million times. My aunt convinced my parents to host my fifth birthday party there."

I imagined all of Sebastian's five-year-old friends trying to understand the work of Andy Warhol instead of bowling or playing laser tag and laughed.

"And my tenth birthday, actually."

I laughed harder. "That's great."

"Next question."

Was that what this was? Some sort of interview to get to know each other like coach had made us do the first day of practice? Or a way to avoid talking about anything that mattered like what had happened in middle school? I glanced at the sky as if the stars knew the answer. "Do you like impressionism?"

"I prefer post-impressionism."

"That's specific."

"I personally don't see a huge difference between the impressionists and post-impressionists, but if I wasn't specific, Aunt Bex would be disappointed in my training. Seriously, she's taken me everywhere in the United States to look at art."

"I'm surprised she hasn't swept you away to Europe." I planned to go the first chance I got with study abroad in college. I couldn't wait to stand in the great museums of Paris, London, Florence, and Amsterdam.

"She's working on my parents now. She wants to take me for a graduation gift."

"I'm jealous."

"Aunt Bex is the best," he said. "Back to my post-impressionist. Seurat. A Sunday Afternoon on the Grand Jatte."

I knew it vaguely, but every time I considered post-impressionism, I got lost in my absolute favorite—Vincent Van Gogh.

Sebastian's eyes lit up. "Pointillism…I can't explain it. Putting together a picture with only dots. Doing that digitally now is one thing, but he painted those dots by hand almost one hundred and fifty years ago."

I groaned.

"What?"

"I kind of agree is all."

"Wow. We agree on something."

"Don't say it too loud," I whispered. "But seriously, sometimes I look at the world and see all the dots that make up the image."

"It's cool, right!" Sebastian grinned.

My chest did a flopping squeezed thing I wasn't sure I liked. "I never knew you were this passionate about art."

"That's not true. We talked about it once."

Once. Right. When we were in the hallway of a high school for a wrestling tournament. Images of Warhol reprints danced around my memories, not standing still long enough for a clear picture, but definitely a memory, just the same. Sebastian had praised them and the artist.

"I thought you were joking."

"You thought wrong."

I swallowed hard, afraid to let that comment fully absorb. I couldn't let myself believe I'd thought wrong about Sebastian. That would be too dangerous. "Favorite classicist?"

"Gentileschi," he said.

"Over Caravaggio?"

"Of course. Caravaggio only got the attention he did because he was a male. Gentileschi out painted him on her worst day."

Sebastian had never struck me as a feminist. "If you love and respect female artists so much, who is your favorite?" I mentally guessed what he might respond before he had a chance to answer me. He'd pick one of the most prominent female artists no doubt. Mary Cassat or Frida Kahlo.

"Besides my aunt?" he asked with a smile.

I rolled my eyes at his attempt to be obviously adorable. "Yes. Besides your aunt."

"Sofonisba Anguissola."

I didn't know her. As if reading my thoughts, he said, "Look her up."

I nodded, making the mistake of looking directly at him. The moonlight highlighted his face, reminding me Sebastian was as cute as a senior in high school than he had been when we were younger. His face was more defined on the edges, and his bright eyes sliced through those edges in a way that threatened my insides.

He watched me with patience, giving me the space I needed to turn these thoughts over in my head, to realize that the current Sebastian Love was as alluring as he'd always been, but something about him was more refined, more sure of himself.

More open with me.

Our gazes locked together like two hands in a wrestling match, bound for penalty points.

With Sebastian, everything led to penalty points.

"I should go," I said.

I turned, but he stepped in front of me. "Don't, Annalise. Please."

"I have to."

"I get it. I was a jerk four years ago. We're teammates now. Can't we try to move past that?"

"Move past what exactly?"

He exhaled so heavily you would have thought he'd been holding his breath since we were kids. "You're gonna make me say it?"

I took a deep breath, too, prepared to be fully present when he gave me the apology I'd been waiting years for without realizing it. "Whenever you're ready."

He lowered his head and closed his eyes, leaving me to wonder how the apology might go. *I'm sorry I pretended to like you when all I wanted was to beat you in the championship. I'm sorry I stole your first kiss on a lie and didn't actually care about you at all.*

Something like that.

He took another breath and raised his eyes to mine. In the moonlight, candlelight, and twinkle lights, they sparkled bright blue. Good thing I wasn't eating. I'd have choked.

"Annalise, I'm sorry that when I was in middle school I didn't have the guts to tell my friends how much I liked you."

My body froze. My brain froze. My eyes froze and lost focus.

How much he'd liked me?

He'd *liked* me?

That wasn't possible. I shook the numbness away. Sebastian was lying. He wanted on my good side. He'd never liked me.

I turned back to the track and walked. And walked. And walked.

"Annalise, wait!"

"Sebastian, I can't." I rushed for the stairs but met a horde of people climbing them to admire the lights.

Dom was in the crowd and caught my eye. His forehead creased. "What's wrong?" he mouthed.

Without any other choice, I moved out of the oncomers' way and right into Sebastian.

He stepped backward. "I'm sorry," he whispered to avoid drawing attention. "Can you please tell me what's going on? I apologized to you, and somehow made you more angry."

What was going on? I'd spent the last four years of my life believing Sebastian never liked me, that he'd played me. That boys were liars.

If I believed Sebastian now, then that meant he hadn't played me. That, as a person—as a girl—I was likable. My heart wanted me to believe him. Who didn't want to be likable? But if I believed him, that meant what had happened between us in middle school had been real.

That was too far from the reality that'd consumed me ever since. I couldn't let the foundation of my world shake. I couldn't let the questions that might follow roll in.

I couldn't trust Sebastian's words to do that to myself all over again.

"Lise, you good?" Dom asked.

"I want to go."

"We just—"

"I want to go!"

He scowled at Sebastian. "Okay. Let's go."

CHAPTER 20

AFTER THE ART SHOW, I PLOWED INTO ASHLEY'S ROOM with my pillow and stuffed bunny.

Lying on her bed under the covers, she looked up from her phone and raised her eyebrows. "Sister sleepover?"

I climbed under the blanket with her, a clear response in the affirmative.

"What happened?"

I angry sighed. "Every time I think I can forgive Sebastian and be his friend, the universe proves me obnoxiously incorrect."

"Okay…"

Another angry sigh.

"And what proved you obnoxiously incorrect this time?"

I pressed my face into the pillow. "He rom ee he rara whyd ee a mama ool."

Ashley pulled the pillow away. "One more time?"

"He told me he'd liked me in middle school."

She waited. "And…?"

"And what? That's the thing—the whole thing!"

"Oh, Lise. Of course he liked you. We all knew that."

"We all didn't. We thought he played me to soften me up, so he could beat me on the mat."

"No." She pointed to me. "*You* thought that because he embarrassed you, and you needed a coping mechanism to get through it."

I pathetic sighed. "If that was my coping mechanism, and it's gone now, how do I, you know, cope?"

She snuggled next to me. "Sister sleepovers?"

I closed my eyes. Yeah. That could help. Until I had to go to practice and drill with Sebastian. Until I looked into his confusingly colored eyes. Until I started questioning how I could forgive Nick for being a stupid middle school boy but not forgive Sebastian for the same offense.

I *hadn't fallen for Nick*, my own voice answered. I'd given Sebastian a piece of myself, and he'd wrecked it.

***

TO MY SHOCK, THE SEASON ROLLED ON WITH SOME sense of normalcy. Sebastian focused. I focused. Coach had us drill our best moves. And on it went for two weeks of practice. We worked repetitions of our main throws and turns, so we'd feel ready to use them at our first meet. Coach also had us drill our weaknesses, giving us pointers on how to overcome them on the mat. Then we had our first wrestle-offs. None for me. I was the only wrestler in my weight class.

Nick and Dom were set for a bout though, until they agreed to rotate their weight class. They'd take turns at 160—their actual weight—and 172, the next weight class up that we didn't have a wrestler for. That way, the team would not have to forfeit a weight, and they'd continue challenging themselves.

Our first match of the year was at Riverport in mid-December. I climbed on the bus with my eighteen male teammates to travel a whole fifteen minutes to their school. We stretched and warmed up in their gym while fans from both schools trickled in. Tournaments and school matches differed in a lot of ways, but what stood out to me was how intimate school matches felt. Only two people wrestled at a time. At tournaments, rows of mats wrestled.

I focused on the steps of my takedowns. I envisioned myself walking off their mat with a victory. A pin even. When the bleachers filled to standing room only and the ref confirmed everything with the head table, the teams lined up on the mat for the national anthem and our introductions. Mine was followed by a warning to my Riverport opponent from one of his teammates, "You better not lose to a girl."

The wrestler said it loud enough for me to hear when I ran by, but not loud enough to get into trouble. Somehow, though, Nick had heard it, too.

"Screw that," Nick said. "You're gonna crush that kid."

My teammates agreed, patting my back and complimenting me one after the other.

"Guys, I'm good," I said in response to all of the attention. "I got this."

I hoped.

Our team dominated from the first match.

Ethan White pinned his opponent in the 106-pound weight class. Vinny Romano and Cory both won their matches, leaving me to continue the streak at 126 pounds.

"Remember what we practiced," Sebastian said, squeezing my hands, any awkwardness lost between us in the moment of competition. I bounced on my toes, and my teammates pounded on the padded gym wall behind our bench as the announcer called my name.

"You got this, Annalise!"

I ran to the head table to check in for the match and then out to the center of the mat. I drilled the moves of the double-leg takedown in my mind. I'd never wrestled my opponent before—a junior named Landon—a rarity given all the wrestling I'd done. Maybe he was new.

Didn't matter. I was ready.

The ref blew the whistle. We circled each other. I watched his legs for a chance to lower my level and take a shot, but he protected himself. We tied up with some hand fighting, but broke free of that, too. I thought the period might end before either of us got a shot off. Seeing an opening, I grabbed him in a collar tie and pressed his head down hard. Lowering my level, I shot forward for a double, my right knee pad sliding across the mat. He tried to sprawl and get his hips back, but I lifted against him, wrapping my arms elbow deep around his knees and used my head to push into the side of his body like Sebastian had drilled with me. Every muscle worked for this same goal—taking down my opponent.

As I pressured into him and held his legs, there was nothing Landon could do to stop from landing on the mat. As soon as his hands and legs hit with me behind him, the ref called a takedown. I'd scored the first two points.

My teammates screamed so loud I couldn't hear Coach Joseph. My next logical step was trying to get back points, a challenge since my opponent was staying strong in his base on his hands and knees. I struggled to break him down to his stomach. When he pushed back into me and brought his legs out from under him to sit out, I took the opportunity to slide my left arm under his armpit. In a quick motion, I hooked my right hand around his chin as I scooted my body out of the way and sucked him backwards. I pushed his back towards the mat, and the ref followed, getting into position to count back points and look for a pin.

"Dammit," Landon muttered.

With his elbow on the mat and his bridging, I couldn't see scoring the fall, but the back points I'd take. He struggled harder and was able to shift his hips and body to a sideways position. I started losing my grip. *Hold onto it. Hold him!* But I couldn't. He bellied out, and the ref raised two fingers for my back points.

I followed Landon's body with my hips and stayed behind him. Both exhausted, we lost steam. He didn't try to escape, and I stayed in position to ride out the period with me leading 4-0.

I was *so* winning this match.

"Good work, Annalise," Coach Joseph said from the sidelines and pressed his open palms downward in his signature nonverbal cue to slow down the match and take only the best shots I could. It was time to be conservative.

I nodded to make it clear I'd gotten the message.

"You got this," Coach said.

The ref flipped his coin that had green on one side and red on another. The coin landed on red, and the ref pointed to Landon—he'd have the first choice of position to start the second period since he wore the red ankle band.

He deferred the choice to me. I chose down. As I moved to get into position, Landon made eye contact with me and revealed his entire strategy with a ferocious look in his eyes. He was coming fast. This was gonna be fun. With my elbows tucked close to my body, I sat on my feet, pulling them under me as much as possible to avoid Landon grabbing an ankle. He'd probably try to muscle me from the whistle, so I'd have to stay in a strong base. Sometimes bottom was the toughest position for me when I wrestled boys. Their strength could sometimes come into play too much. I had to use clean technique and not make any mistakes.

The ref blew the whistle. Landon pressured my left, but I planted my right foot to stand and grabbed the arm he extended around my waist. Once I had wrist control, I pushed backward against him as I stood, tucking his hand into my back pocket. From there, I spun to face him, earning an escape point and pissing him off even more.

As expected, he shot hard and fast, but he didn't set up his shot and made an attempt from too far away. I used good head and hands defense and stuffed his shot. I could tell that his frustration was growing. Frustration led to mistakes. I hoped for a chance to use one of the throws I knew, like a lateral drop. The move would be risky, but Landon would never see it coming. Hopefully. Instead of tying up, he closed the gap between us and faked a shot before shooting a single leg. He tried to bring my leg up in the air and trip me, but my leg ended up between his own legs. I immediately remembered the whizzer drill. I curled the leg he held around his leg and shifted my weight to his side. We hopped until I yanked on the whizzer, pulling him to the ground. He quickly tried to stand, and we went out of bounds. The ref brought us back to center. The period ended with me still leading, and my opponent even more frustrated.

That frustration exploded in the third period when he selected the neutral position—I have no idea why—and he pushed hard into me, becoming careless. Using his momentum, I kept my upper body tie and hit a beautiful lateral drop. The crowd actually gasped at the sight. Lateral drops always looked more impressive than they were. He'd pushed against me and had practically flipped himself over. I, on the other hand, managed to adjust well once we hit the mat and got the pin.

The ref lifted my arm, and my teammates wore pride on their faces. They pounded on the wall pads for Sebastian to take the mat in the 132-pound weight class while I sipped Gatorade and caught my breath.

Sebastian's first period started slowly. He and his opponent were hand fighting hard, but neither wanted to commit to a shot.

"Let's go, Bash," Nick yelled.

I cheered for him, too, but more quietly. Like in my head.

Finally, Sebastian set up a smooth ankle pick, a nod to me for taking on his signature move. It landed him two points from the takedown. He threw legs in on top and cranked a power half, earning back points. When he readjusted, his hips slid off the side, and his opponent almost reversed him.

"No!" I yelled before I could catch myself, but my teammates were as wrapped up in the match as I was.

Sebastian bailed out and allowed his opponent to escape rather than get behind him, giving up one point. Better one point than a pin.

Sebastian tipped his head back and stood strong as the first period ended. In the second, the ref pointed to him for choice. He took bottom. Immediately off the whistle, he exploded up to his feet. Before the ref could even award a point for escaping, Sebastian shot on his opponent, took him down with a double, and transitioned to a tilt for two back points. Rolling back to their knees, Sebastian let him up.

A memory struck me in the way they sometimes do—as if floating through time out of nowhere and connecting with your consciousness. When we'd chat for hours at tournaments as middle schoolers, he mentioned that sometimes, he'd let his opponent back up to his feet, so he could take them down and earn back points again. Then the opponent escaped, and he'd take them down and earn more back points. It was almost a game he played that his opponent had no idea they'd become collateral damage in.

In the third period, Sebastian started on top and after a tough ride, he got the pin.

And smiled at me as the ref lifted his arm in victory. That smile was like a thunderstorm, raining all of the awkward back down on me until I was soaked through.

After the match, I tried to be anywhere except next to Sebastian. We chatted with the friends who'd come to see us wrestle. Ashley and my mom hugged me and congratulated me with a grilled chicken sandwich. As soon as I took my first massive bite, someone tapped my shoulder. I turned, covering my mouth, to see Sebastian's Aunt Rebecca.

"Hello!" she said, and I nodded and pointed to my mouth. "Oh, I'm sorry. Please, eat. You were incredible out there. Congratulations!"

"Thank you," I managed after swallowing.

She looked around and then leaned close to whisper, "I think that boy you wrestled might need some support. Do they always get so distraught when they lose to you?"

"Almost always. Although you'd think some of them would be used to it by now."

Rebecca laughed. "You'd think! I know my brother was ruthless on Sebastian when you beat him as kids, but Bash took it in stride. He said you were good, and that was that."

Why did she have to keep mentioning middle school? It endangered my health.

"How's the painting coming?"

I groaned.

"That bad, huh?"

"I thought I knew what I wanted to submit, but now I'm second-guessing everything."

"Been there," Rebecca said. "If it would be helpful to you, I could look at your paintings. Give you some feedback. Only if you want it though. I don't want to appropriate your work or anything."

My work? I was a real painter with work!

"No," I said in the calmest voice I could manage. "That would be everything."

"Okay. I'm leaving town in a few days, but I could stop by before then. Why don't I get your number from Bash, and then we can set something up?"

"Or I could give it to you now," I suggested, not wanting to interact with Sebastian to coordinate.

She waved the suggestion away. "Nonsense. You eat. He won't mind."

Across the gym, he laughed with Nick and Dom. As if he could feel my gaze on him, he turned and caught my eye. Air whooshed from my lungs. He'd liked me. He'd really liked me.

He didn't look away. Neither did I.

"Great match, again," Rebecca said. "You're so impressive out there."

"Thank you."

She patted my shoulder. "I'll be in touch."

Rebecca had offered to help me figure out my art show application, but it was another puzzle flirting with my consciousness that held my attention. When we'd met at the gallery, she'd told me Sebastian had been heartbroken the day he'd lost to me.

Not disappointed. Not embarrassed. Not defeated.

Heartbroken.

Ashley knew it all along, and maybe deep down I had, too. All these years I'd been wrong. I couldn't sort through the implications of that standing in the middle of the gym with a chicken sandwich in my hand, gazing at Sebastian across the mat.

What I did know is that it meant something monumental.

CHAPTER 21

EVERY DAY, MY WORLD FELT MORE AND MORE LIKE THE
chaos of Pollock's paintings, and while I had no idea how to make
sense of the splashes of color that represented Sebastian, finalizing
my gallery application felt like low-hanging fruit.

I'd pick it off the branches, and then the chaos would not be so
chaotic.

Hopefully.

Sebastian texted me later that night with Rebecca's number and
another congratulations on hitting my first double-leg takedown of
the season. "Here's to many more," he'd written.

My fingers hovered over my phone screen, swirling through the
air until I managed a decision on my reply.

"Thanks."

Epic.

I messaged Rebecca. She agreed to stop by the following evening after practice. That felt so soon, yet so far away, but it came
soon enough. I showered quickly and repositioned my paintings in
the garage roughly three-hundred-thousand times until I still wasn't
convinced they were right. The doorbell rang, though, signaling I
had no more time.

Rebecca waited on our front porch looking grand and glorious in checkered dress pants, black heels, and a gorgeous red winter coat. "Annalise! Your house is so hidden back here. I love it!"

"Thank you," I said and led her through the kitchen to the garage. "Can I get you anything to drink before we look at the paintings?"

"No. Thank you. You're sweet to offer. I have dinner later with an investor. It's a whole thing. So!" She rubbed her hands together. "Where are your pieces? I'm so excited!"

I led her across the garage to the table I'd set up along the wall. My best two pieces perched on the easels. The others leaned against the wall or laid flat on the table.

"I love the use of the leaves as a painting sponge. There's a beautiful chaos in that, like the paw prints."

My lungs filled with magical, sparkling air. "Thank you."

"The colors are gorgeous. Cohesive, yet contrasting. I love your use of chunks of paint, too."

Impossible. Rebecca Watterson was not saying such amazing things about me. My paintings! Rebecca Watterson!

"But…"

But? Oh no.

"While the creativity shows you have real talent, I don't feel the emotion in the pieces as much as I'd like."

They were leaves. They didn't have emotions.

"What are the feelings of fall?" she went on. "How can you evoke them in your audience?"

"Um…"

"Don't get me wrong, Annalise. Your paintings are beautiful, but I want to challenge you to dig a little deeper. Does that make sense?"

It did, but I wasn't sure how to dig. Maybe that was stupid, but it was true.

"When I first started painting, I painted what I wanted. That's what everyone told me to do. If you don't want to paint it, it won't become your masterpiece."

"I want to paint fall," I said.

"Exactly, but the thing is that after a few years, I realized that advice was terrible. I shouldn't be painting what I want. I should paint my passion. The strong emotions I have about my passion will carry into the painting, and then I'll have something special. After I learned that, I scored my first gallery show."

It made sense, but there was one little problem. "Painting is my passion. How can I paint painting?"

Rebecca smiled at me. "You sure that's your only passion?"

Wrestling.

"My nephew seems to think you're full of passion for your sport. I think it's one of the reasons he likes you so much."

I choked on her words and wondered how she hadn't, too. Had Sebastian told his aunt he *liked* me? Or did she mean as friends?

"What is it about wrestling that brings out your passion?" Rebecca asked, bringing my focus back to where it should have been. "Find a way to put that on canvas, even for an experiment. See what you think."

The fall canvases lined up in my garage evoked the most beautiful moments of the season. That had been my goal, but maybe Rebecca was right. If I wanted to get into a good art program and gallery shows, I'd have to show something relevant, something only I could present. I'd read it on so many websites and articles. Bring your voice to your art. Paint something only you could paint. I'd thought the fall display worked because I loved the season, and I watched it closely from the windows of our home on the edge of the forest, but other painters lived similar experiences.

Was my painting voice meant for wrestling? I scanned the fall canvases around me. Would I have to repaint them all?

I'd never finish in time to apply to the art show.

"I'll think about it," I said. "Thank you, Rebecca."

"You're welcome. I'd love to see it when you finish."

I nodded, but I couldn't make eye contact with her. My eyes wouldn't leave the fall paintings I'd clearly failed.

"Thank you for sharing your work with me, Annalise. It's an honor." Her soft voice aimed to encourage me, but nothing could.

The Pollock painting that was my life was even more chaotic than ever.

"It's an honor to have you review it," I whispered and meant it.

Rebecca hugged me, then held me gently by the shoulders. "Don't break my nephew's heart. It's a fragile little thing."

My mouth went dry. Did Rebecca think Sebastian and I were

dating? He adored his Aunt Bex. Did he tell her something that I didn't know?

Or maybe that I did know but refused to admit I knew?

Rebecca sauntered back through the kitchen to the front door. "Goodbye, Annalise! Have fun with your painting."

She left me with a pile of blank canvases waiting to be beautified with my passion and a head full of the kind of confusion that had become second nature in my life.

***

LIFE ROLLED ON WITH A SCHEDULE THAT DIDN'T QUIT. Wrestling and school demanded most of my time, but I snuck into the garage at every opportunity, dabbling with colors and canvases. No real sense of direction. The day after Christmas, which was less than three weeks before the application was due, I finally had an idea.

With the garage doors closed and the industrial heaters on blast, I got to work. I printed pictures my mom had taken of me wrestling. I circled the details that stood out to me. Wrist control. Cross faces. Looking intense as I tried to find an opening to shoot. Cradles and arm bars. Grimacing on bottom as I tried to hold my base. All the technique that had to be flawless for me to beat some of the boys who were stronger than me.

And I stopped there.

Glancing from the printouts to the canvases, I had no idea how to create something real with emotion. I could copy the images for sure, but what would copying them do?

"Hey," Ashley said from the kitchen doorway. "You wanna watch a movie with us?"

I assumed "us" would be Chandra and Melanie. Or maybe Nick. "No, thanks. I'm trying to figure out the primal artist's question."

"Okay. If you change your mind, we're in the basement."

"Thanks."

Ideas. I needed ideas. I could paint the zoomed-in sections of the pictures, the moves that I circled. But what would that show? Instructions for correct wrestling moves. That felt colder than the warm and fuzzy emotion that Rebecca had suggested.

But she hadn't said the paintings had to be warm emotions. Could cold emotions work, too? Were emotions cold? Itching to move a brush across the canvases, I started with the background. I'd rolled over a million wrestling mats. Painting one came easily. The faded lines. The creases. I played with the perspective until the shape came together perfectly. I stood back to admire the canvas, and I could swear I was looking at a photo of a wrestling mat.

"Impressive."

At the sound of Sebastian's voice, I dropped my paintbrush on my foot. I hadn't seen him for a few days. Before Christmas, he and Nick had traveled out of state for a tournament and with the holiday that meant four long days without Sebastian. Longer than we'd been apart in months.

Not that there was any takeaway from that observation. He was gone. That was all.

But now, clearly, he was back. And coming to see me.

I took a deep breath and bent to wipe away the excess paint from my shoe.

"Sorry. Didn't mean to startle you."

"I didn't realize you were here."

"The whole crew is," he said. "Chandra and Grant. Ashley and Nick. Melanie and Harris. And me."

"That explains why you wanted to get away," I said as politely as I could. And why Ashley had invited me. She needed to stop with this Sebastian-Annalise match making. Rebecca's voice flooded my memory like a can of paint being poured over my face—impossible to ignore. "*Don't break my nephew's heart. It's a fragile little thing.*"

I allowed myself to look at Sebastian, and I could feel my own heart cracking. Nothing about him appeared fragile, and everything about the way looking at him sent my insides into a tragic combo of earth's natural disasters—tornadoes, volcanoes, hurricanes, floods— all at once every time our eyes locked made me feel more fragile than ever.

"Can I help you?" he asked.

"I don't think so."

"Oh." He tucked his hands in the pockets of his jeans and lowered his head.

"It's not you. I don't know what I want to do yet, and until I figure that out, I'm kind of stuck."

He pointed back to the kitchen. "You wanna take a break and watch the movie then?"

"Um…"

"Look, Annalise. I know there have been some awkward moments between us, but we could be friends. I think."

I scoffed. "You don't sound convinced?"

"I'm not, but I'd like to try. I'm trying to try."

"I see that," I whispered. "I do. But…"

But what? You wrecked my heart for years. Literally years. And it might be too wrecked to make space in it for friendship? Or if I was honest with myself, what I may have wanted, which was more than friendship?

Suddenly the dark basement where nobody could talk to me or see my face sounded like the best idea of the year.

"Let's watch that movie," I said.

His eyes widened in surprise. "Yeah?"

"Yep." I sealed up my paints, pulled off my splattered smock and shoes, and headed inside. "You want some popcorn?"

Sebastian squinted at me, as if I were a complicated wrestling maneuver he was trying to mimic. "Sure. I love popcorn."

"Me too! It's a whole grain. And lightly buttered. Unless you don't want butter."

"I'll live on the edge. I have a couple days until our next tournament."

I washed my hands and moved around the kitchen like I didn't feel his eyes on me. Popcorn out of the pantry. Opened and in the microwave. Bowls from the cupboard. Pop. Pop. Pop.

"Need anything to drink?"

He laughed.

"What?"

"This is oddly normal for us."

"Friends can be normal."

"Yeah. I guess they can."

Normal. Right. Nick and Ashley curled up on the love seat. Chandra ran her fingers through Grant's hair on the couch, and Melanie and Harris cuddled on the recliner. That left the massive bean bag on the floor.

For me. And Sebastian.

"You can take it," he whispered, not wanting to interrupt the movie.

"You're the guest. You should have it."

"Where are you going to sit?"

There was sort of room on the couch next to Grant and Chandra's entanglement. Sebastian and I looked at each other, both grimacing at the thought of sharing with those two.

"I'm down for the bean bag if you are," he suggested, not meeting my eyes.

Snuggling next to Sebastian on a beanbag chair in the dark with three other couples in the same room?

So. Not. Normal.

CHAPTER 22

"YOU DID WHAT LAST NIGHT?" DOM SHOUTED INTO THE phone.

"Can you please keep it down? I think my mom heard you through the wall."

"No. I can't, given the situation. Sebastian? *The* Sebastian Love?"

"I know. I know. It was the only seat—"

"Who do you think you're talking to?" he interrupted. "The floor is a seat. Subconsciously, or consciously, you wanted to sit next to him."

Flashes of Sebastian's arm brushing against mine while we ate our popcorn, and the closeness of his breathing, and when he adjusted his weight and had to brace himself on the table behind us almost like his arm was around me.

I closed my eyes and fought back the sob of recognition threatening to escape my throat.

"I like him, don't I?" I whispered.

"Yep," Dom said. "Damn."

Yeah. Damn.

We sat in silence, observing the death of my hatred for Sebastian, grieving the ease of the past when walls of anger protected the softer emotions from the pain undoubtedly coming my way.

"What are you going to do?"

"Nothing," I said.

"Nothing?"

Ashley knocked at my door as she passed through it and jumped on my bed. "I can hear you debating your love affair with Sebastian through the wall."

I scowled at her.

"Who is that?" she asked. "Dom?"

"Hi, Ashley," Dom said into the phone.

"Do you two want to talk?"

Ashley crossed her legs and got comfortable. "Sure. Put him on speaker."

"I wasn't being serious," I muttered but put my best friend on speaker just the same. "As I was saying, he's my teammate. It's already complicated."

"He's also gorgeous," Ashley said. "I'm rapturously in love with Nick, and I see that."

"Everyone with eyes sees that," Dom agreed.

"Yeah, but did you hear me say complicated?"

"I did. Did you hear me say gorgeous?" Ashley batted her eyelashes.

"That can't be everything."

"How about this then," my best friend said, bulking up his voice like he was about to dual in a debate competition. "You have been into him forever. He is the only boy to catch your attention in five years. He is the only boy that had enough of your heart to hurt you."

"But he did hurt me," I reminded them.

"Four years ago," Ashley countered. "He's apologized. You think you're punishing him, but did you ever think you're punishing yourself?"

"I don't want to risk it." My voice was a gasp of air fluttering and floating until it dissipated into nothing. Maybe my feelings for Sebastian would do the same. "Besides, I can't know what he wants with me. Yeah, there's something there, but I'd need him to be, like, totally honest about what he wants. Boys don't do that."

"Nobody does that," Dom said.

"And how would it affect the team?"

"Would it make you happy?" Ashley offered.

Her question stopped my mental spiral.

"Lise?"

"I don't know," I admitted.

"I hate to agree with Ashley on anything," Dom said.

"Thanks," she threw back.

"But I think it's time you figure it out."

A huge part of me wanted them to be wrong. But without question, I knew they were right.

"There's a party tonight," Ashley said. "Sounds like the perfect opportunity."

***

TO BE CLEAR, I WAS NOT GOING TO THE PARTY TO FIG-
ure things out with Sebastian. I was going to spend time with my friends. Or more specifically, my sister's friends. Chandra pulled up to the Forest Run house party and parked behind an SUV that resembled Sebastian's. With a wrestling decal on the back. So yeah. Sebastian's SUV.

"You okay, Lise?" Ashley whispered when the girls adjusted their clothes and purses. "I want you and Sebastian to get together because it would be so awesome for the four of us, but you don't look so good."

"You told me this outfit was hot!"

"Not the outfit. You look terrified."

In other words, I was being transparent.

"Maybe I was wrong," Ashley said with concern. "Maybe everything that happened in middle school is too much. I know how you feel about being vulnerable."

Not like I was alone in that. Who liked to be vulnerable?

Ashley did.

The girls' boots clacked against the cold, snow-shoveled pavement, an ominous march. I held onto Ashley's arm. She squeezed my hand, worry creasing her face.

"I'm fine," I said.

Chandra led us into the party. Within seconds, Grant and Nick found us, greeting everyone before planting kisses on Chandra and Ashley, respectively. Sebastian wasn't with them. We moved through the packed living room and kitchen, loud music sparking huddled conversations and obnoxious dancing. Any moment, I told myself, I'd see Sebastian with his arm around some girl. I repeated the expectation in my mind. I'd be ready.

We settled in the basement around a ping pong table. Nick challenged Chandra, and the competition began with the kind of intensity you'd expect from two varsity athletes. The tick-tock sound of the ball hitting the table, paddle, table, and then paddle again became the background noise for our conversations. After a few minutes, Chandra crushed the ball to the corner. Nick dove for it and launched himself into the wall, setting off a chorus of laughing and teasing.

I leaned back against the stool of a high-top table in the corner, and a warm arm wrapped around my waist.

"Hey, Annalise," Sebastian whispered in my ear.

I swung my body away, spinning to find him sitting in the stool I'd leaned against. When had that happened? I'd practically sat in his lap without realizing it.

He grinned, his arm still resting on my hip, and his hand flirting with the curve of my back. An inch lower, and it could be said he was grabbing my ass.

I had been so wrong. I was not ready for Sebastian to have his arm around some girl, not when that girl was me.

"I didn't know you were sitting there," I said. "I'm sorry."

"Don't be," he whispered, his eyes never leaving mine, and I knew without a doubt I could take one step forward and press my chest to his. I could drape my arms around his neck. I could kiss him even, and he'd let me.

More than that, he wanted me to.

I wanted to. Oh, gosh. I really wanted to.

I stepped back instead. "I'm going to grab a drink. Do you need anything?"

He bit his lip and shook his head, disappointment on his face.

I nodded and backtracked through the basement and up the stairs to the kitchen. I grabbed a water bottle from a cooler without ice on the back porch. When the temperatures were this low, the porch itself was the refrigerator.

I closed my eyes and remembered Sebastian's fingers like fire against my skin. He'd wanted to touch me as much as I wanted him to. What if I let him? What would it be like to feel his fingertips along my arms, my back, my stomach, my cheek?

Stop!

I shook the thoughts away with a shiver. Back inside, I leaned against the counter in the kitchen and drank half of the bottle. Down the basement stairs, my friends played an innocent game of ping pong. Sebastian sat on a stool in a corner.

Waiting for me? Maybe.

Or maybe I should go. I could call Mom and ask her to pick me up. Before I could sort through my options, a guy I didn't know draped his arm over my shoulders. I pushed him away, moving out of the kitchen and into the open living room.

"Chill," he said. "You're that hot wrestling chick from Iron Valley, right?"

"And you are?"

"I don't mean hot in the physical sense," he said, making a jab and sending his drunk friends into fits of laughter. "I mean hot as in everyone's talking about you."

His insult awakened my snark. "If you're the judge of what's hot, then I guess we're in serious trouble."

His grin faded. "I could take you."

Oh, here we go. Macho stupidity at its finest.

"You're scared," he taunted. That's how it usually went. Teasing. Taunting. Then all out harassment and bullying until they got what they wanted—a shot at the girl wrestler.

"You're an idiot," I said.

A few guffaws came from the growing crowd. I needed to work my way out of this, like now.

"Afraid what it would be like to touch a real man, not one of those wrestling boys."

"Oh, a real man?" I said. "I thought you were offering yourself, but if there's a real man here, maybe I could take him on."

He moved so close to me, he spit in my face when he said, "Fight me, bitch!"

Before I could push him out of my space, someone else did.

"Back off," Sebastian said.

"The big, bad wrestler lets her boyfriend fight for her," the idiot continued.

Sebastian didn't even flinch at the suggestion he was my boyfriend, but it made my throat go dryer than if I'd been running in the summer heat.

"She doesn't need my protection," Sebastian said. "You do. Trust me when I tell you she'll leave you broken and embarrassed."

"Bullshit."

"Oh enough of this," I said. Moving quickly, I locked my arms around the guy and flipped him over my shoulder, suplexing him into the carpet face-first. The room exploded with cheers and laughter, and before my nemesis could get off the ground and realize which way was up, Sebastian wrapped his arm around my waist and pulled me out of the house.

CHAPTER 23

WITH SEBASTIAN'S HAND IN MINE, WE RAN TO HIS CAR
and jumped in, laughing. He started the engine and turned up the heat
to fight the chill threatening us from outside.

"I can't believe you did that," he managed before pounding his
hands against the steering wheel and laughing again. "Did you see
his face?"

"I shouldn't have," I said, lowering my head into my hands.
"Coach will be furious if he finds out."

"What's a little wrestling skill if you can't defend yourself?"

"Was that self-defense?"

"I'd testify for you."

The memory of the obnoxious stranger's face when I dropped him
made me laugh all over again.

"You smell like beer," he said, making a face. "I think he dropped
his cup on your shirt when you suplexed him."

My mom wouldn't like me coming home smelling like alcohol.
Explaining why would not gain me any points either. Even if she secretly respected it, which she probably would, she'd feel all maternal
and try to teach me a lesson about self-control.

"I have a hoodie in my backseat," Sebastian said, reaching for it.
"If you want it."

He handed me his shirt, and my breath caught. The cotton smelled like the clean version of Sebastian, not his rugged scent when we were on the mats. I wasn't sure I could wear it and not crumble into a pile of regret and desire.

"You okay?" he asked.

"Fine. Thanks." I pulled my shirt over my head. Sebastian flinched and turned away.

"It's fine," I said. "I'm wearing a cami." I sniffed my undershirt. The beer scent was faint on the waistline, but it would do. Within seconds, Sebastian's hoodie, and his scent, surrounded me.

Sebastian's eyes found mine. They darkened, and his lips parted. And my insides exploded.

"Thanks again," I said, stumbling over the words. "I'll get it back to you tomorrow. Or Monday, I mean. Not that we're going to see each other tomorrow. Unless you're going to duals. I never asked. But, right. Thanks."

Shut up, Annalise. I grabbed the door handle, but Sebastian reached across the car and covered my hands with his. I ignored the tingles popping in every spot our skin touched.

"You're not going back in there."

I slipped my hand away. "I'm not going to hide."

"Annalise, he's stupid and drunk. And you embarrassed him. Bad combination."

"My sister's inside."

"Nick won't let anything happen to your sister. Your victim probably doesn't even know you're related," he said with a smile.

"My victim? Whose side are you on?" I teased.

His lips curled into the hint of a smile. "Yours. Always."

I tried to swallow but couldn't. I tried to breathe, but that body function didn't work either. As a thirteen-year-old girl, I'd been awed by Sebastian, but four years had passed since then. We'd both grown up, and with that growing came other emotions and desires. Everything I'd felt for Sebastian in middle school had expanded exponentially.

I couldn't look away from those bright eyes, more green than blue in the moonlight. After a few seconds, I realized he struggled to breathe as much as I did. My fear and vulnerability were reflected on his face.

He lifted his arm and brushed his fingertips against my cheek. I gasped. His face inched closer.

And closer.

I shouldn't do this.

Not with Sebastian.

When he was close enough to kiss me, he leaned his forehead against mine and whispered, "I've thought about being alone with you like this a million times."

Me too but couldn't bring myself to speak.

His lips pressed against my ear when he whispered, "Come to the winter formal with me."

"What?" I'd expected him to kiss me, not invite me to a dance.

"Please, Annalise. I want to dance with you, touch you, flirt with you. And maybe…"

I gulped.

"Kiss you," he finished.

There it was. I swallowed. Twice. I shifted in the seat, and his scent from the hoodie wafted around me again. Oh gosh.

"Why do you want to go to the dance with me?" I asked, urging my mind back to something sensical.

"Because you're the most incredible girl I've ever met. I knew it four years ago, and I know it now. I'm trying to be brave enough to do something about it."

My voice was the next function to fail me.

A thumping sound on my window made me jump closer to Sebastian.

"Open the door," my drunk nemesis shouted. Another victim of the suplex, he held a red tissue to his bleeding nose.

One of his friends grabbed him and pulled him back from the car. "Dude, chill!"

"Go, Sebastian!" I yelled.

He tore out of the parking space and down the street until the sound of the party was too distant to reach us anymore. At the first red light we came to, we looked sideways at each other and laughed.

I pulled my phone out of my bag. "I better text Ashley."

"She won't believe you're letting me take you home."

"Any more than she'll believe I suplexed someone in the living room?"

We both laughed again.

"Besides, you took me home once before."

"Yeah," he said. "I guess you're right."

We drove in silence for a few minutes, and I wondered if he mentally replayed the conversation we'd had before my window was attacked.

I was, but no matter how much I wanted to believe Sebastian, we had unfinished business.

"You hurt me," I said. "When we were younger."

"I know," he said quietly.

"Do you know how much I hate to even admit that? I don't let anyone get enough of me to hurt me. Not since then."

"I know that, too. Ashley told me."

"So much for being a loyal sister."

"I think she's secretly rooting for us."

"Or not so secretly," I said.

"Or that," he agreed.

"The thing is, I don't know if I can let you in. I can already tell it's different. Or it *could* be different."

"It could be more," he said.

"Yes."

"I want it to be more, Annalise. I wanted it then, and I want it now. The difference is back then I was too much of a little kid to say it. I'm not going to make that mistake again."

I didn't want to make the same mistake either, and a voice in my head shouted that I was on the verge of doing exactly that.

Sebastian drove down our street and into the driveway. He put the car in park and turned to me with so much hope in his eyes that I had no choice but to look away.

"Give me a chance. Please."

At my core, I knew looking him in the eye and giving in to what he wanted—to what I wanted, too—would feel like falling off the edge of a beautiful cliff, with wind in our hair and sun shining against our skin. Each moment would be breath-taking and magical and perfect.

But then we'd land.

As much as he wanted to, he couldn't promise me a soft surface. "I can't, Sebastian."

He rested his forehead against the steering wheel.

"I'm sorry," I whispered. "Thanks for the ride."

I passed my paintings in the garage, leaving them untouched. I brushed my teeth, washed my face, and slipped into pajamas.

Before I climbed under the covers, though, Sebastian's hoodie hanging over the back of my desk chair caught my eye. The softness fell over my head and wrapped me in the kind of warmth I knew Sebastian would gladly offer with his own arms.

If I'd let him.

CHAPTER 24

SEBASTIAN FLOODED MY DREAMS. THE FEEL OF HIS arm brushing mine on the bean bag. The steam rising inside me when he looked into my eyes. His forehead against mine in the car, but in the dream, he hadn't asked me to the dance. Instead, he'd tipped his head low and pressed his lips against mine. If I thought there had been explosions between us before, I'd been wrong. The explosions when he kissed me in the dream even came with beeping. Loud beeping.

Of my alarm.

I tapped the snooze button and caught my breath. Wrapped in my blankets, I'd never felt so warm or comfortable in my bed. I closed my eyes and replayed the fragments of dreams I could remember.

And smiled.

I *smiled*.

Sebastian made me happy. More than happy. What was I doing? I'd said that I wanted Sebastian to tell me exactly what he wanted and how he felt. He'd done that the night before, but I'd walked away.

He'd apologized. He'd grown up. He'd been my friend. He'd helped me with wrestling. What more could he do?

It'd be different if I didn't want him, too, but I did.

The alarm beeped again. I tossed the warm covers off, and the coolness of the morning bit at my bare legs. And that was it. My safety and comfort were like being under that warm blanket. If I trusted Sebastian and gave us a chance, it would be like peeling back those covers and taking a risk with the elements.

Leaving a warm blanket behind in the winter was a hard thing to do.

Twenty minutes later, my mom, Ashley, and I piled into the car and headed for a duals event in Ohio. Ashley curled up in the backseat and slept. I watched the snow-covered hills pass outside the windows and wondered if Sebastian would be there.

My phone buzzed.

"Who's messaging you this early?" Mom asked. "Dom?"

"I don't know." I glanced at my phone and saw my sister's name. Over my shoulder, she tapped at her phone screen. Her message read, "So Sebastian asked you to the dance last night, huh?"

News traveled fast.

I turned my phone off and shoved it into my bag. Ashley sat up and leaned forward between the two front seats. "Okay. If you're going to ignore my stealth messages, we'll do this in real time."

"Ashley," I warned.

"Sebastian asked Annalise to the dance," my sister announced.

"Ooh," Mom said. "And?"

"I told him no."

My mom actually gasped.

"Mom!"

"Sorry. I thought that, 'he irritates me' stuff was for show. He's kind of adorable, sweetie."

I groaned.

"I'm not going to say anything," Ashley said, which I found hard to believe. "But, he's crazy about you, Lise. And I know you like him, too. Please get over your pride and be happy."

The memory of his lips on mine in my dream was like pin pricks on my heart. "I don't want to talk about it."

It had been a dream. Not reality.

Ashley shook her head and curled back up in the backseat. Mom glanced sideways at me but didn't say anything. She didn't have to. My mind turned the situation over and over, studying it from every angle. No need for anyone else to weigh in.

A few minutes later, she dropped me at the main entrance and parked the car. I checked in and made my way to the cafeteria where I'd agreed to meet them. I stared at my phone screen, not wanting to look around at the growing crowd. What would I say if I saw Sebastian?

Since I had no idea, best to avoid him.

I watched clips from my recent matches, studying the moves of my opponents and theorizing how I could work harder. A few minutes in, Mom sat next to me.

"Hi, darling."

"Hey, Mom."

"Wanna put that down?"

Oh boy. I tossed my phone in my bag and turned to her, ready for a Mom talk.

"I know you're struggling," she said. "I've seen it for a while, but I wanted to give you the space to work it out for yourself. I'm not sure that's going well, though."

"It's not," I admitted.

"I want you to go into today's competition as clear-headed as possible, so why don't we hash it out?"

I sighed. "Everybody thinks that Sebastian and I should be together."

"What do you think?" my mom asked.

"I think it's a bad idea."

"Honey, you've had a crush on him forever. What makes it such a bad idea?"

"Mom, in middle school it was more than a crush. We were... talking. And…"

"And?"

"This is so embarrassing. And he kissed me at a wrestling tournament."

"Oh." She sat upright and nodded a few times, digesting the news. "Was that your first kiss?"

"Yep. Then his friends saw us together, they teased him about it, and he blew me off and said it was his way of getting to know the competition."

"Ouch."

"Exactly."

My mom smiled in that knowing way she did. "Is that the tournament you beat him in the championship, refused his congratulations, and kept the trophy next to your bed ever since?"

"That would be the one."

"That makes a little more sense now. Look, when I was in middle school, I did a lot of stupid things. When I was in high school, I did other stupid things. And in college, guess what?"

"More stupid things?"

"You got it. You grow over time, and hopefully you do fewer stupid things, and they have fewer consequences, but there's no wrong answer here. If you decide you want to give Sebastian another chance, then give him another chance. And if you decide that you can't trust him with your heart, then don't trust him with your heart. Whatever you decide is okay. You don't have to be with Sebastian because your sister is with his best friend, and you don't have to give him another chance because people want you to. You have to do whatever's true to yourself, and honestly that's the best lesson you can learn. Probably you'll do fewer stupid things if you do."

"That all makes sense, Mom, but what if I don't know what I want? What if I don't know what being true to myself looks like? You're right. I've had a crush on Sebastian forever, and he's the only boy that has ever made me question things about myself, has ever made me want to give in to my feelings. What if I regret not giving him a chance? It was a lot easier when he wasn't on my team and didn't go to my club and didn't show up to my house for movie nights."

"Maybe a lot easier to ignore, but it doesn't mean it's the best for you. You could wonder in college, or when you're a grown woman what things would have been like if you would have dated Sebastian."

"And what if he hurts me again?"

"I'm your mother. If I could protect you from getting hurt, I would. A million times over. But the reality is getting hurt is a part of life. Hurting other people is too and learning from those experiences is what it's all about. Most relationships end. If you give Sebastian a chance, it could end. There's no way of telling if or how, but it could also be worth it."

Key phrase in that sentence being "no telling." I leaned against my mom, settling in to the vulnerability of the conversation. My sister had said I didn't like being vulnerable. She was right. Growing up on a mat will do that to you. My wrestling strategy had always been to protect my weaknesses and avoid being vulnerable. It started with a strong stance—a solid base with a low center of gravity and always being squared up to my opponent. Then, I'd worked on my head and hands defense to counter my opponents' shots. I'd mastered moves one at a time, only working them in a match when I had the utmost confidence.

Year after year, I mastered more moves to avoid becoming vulnerable. In this cafeteria, being vulnerable with my mom was one thing. Allowing myself to be vulnerable with Sebastian—that felt like throwing off my center and letting my strong stance crumble.

CHAPTER 25

MY PHONE BUZZED, INTERRUPTING OUR HEART-TO-
heart. "Ashley messaged. Our team is about to be up. I'm going to
chat with Fallon. Make sure she's ready."

My mom nodded. "I'm proud of you for looking out for her. I
know you've never wanted to be the face of girls' wrestling, but
maybe this is how you advance the sport. Helping the younger girls."

Maybe. I still hadn't called Mrs. Errico, mostly because I didn't
have a plan for how to help or time to. I hoped that would change
eventually, but all I could think of right now was helping Fallon
through her match and then preparing for my own. We hustled
through the crowd and the field of chairs, pop up playpens for the
littles, and older kids playing catch or practicing wrestling moves on
our way to the girls' mat.

Next to Coach Law, Fallon bounced on her toes in her headgear,
ready to go.

"How are you feeling?"

"Nervous. What if she suplexes me?"

I grinned. "What if you suplex her?"

She laughed and hugged me. "Thank you, Lise."

I hugged her back. "You got this, Fallon. I promise. I've seen you
training. Remember, go hard on your takedowns and get some lift.
Nothing soft. Get those extra points, okay?"

She nodded.

"No matter what takedown you hit, lead it right into one of your turns."

"And if she takes me down, hold my arms out to the side, engage my core, and refuse to let her roll me."

"Exactly."

"I can do this."

"Yeah, you can," Nick said from behind us. He picked up Fallon and squeezed her. "You got this."

"Thanks." His sister grinned shyly. "Hi, Bash."

I spun to find him standing there, too.

"Good luck," he said, and then glanced at me. My breath stopped like it did too often when Sebastian looked at me. Fallon's red cheeks revealed the whopping crush she had on her big brother's best friend. I couldn't blame her.

"Hey," I managed.

"Hey," he answered.

"Those are the two most weighted 'heys' I've ever heard," Nick said, and Ashley swatted his arm.

Before anyone could say anything else, the tournament director announced over the loudspeaker for everyone to rise for the national anthem—a welcomed interruption. When it ended, I dodged Sebastian's gaze and kept my eyes on Fallon, walking onto the mat with intense eye contact pointed at her opponent. Oh, the intimidation tactic. I hid my smile, not wanting to give Fallon's strategy away, especially because the wide eyes of her opponent, Gina, told me it might be working.

I kneeled on the mat next to our coaches. "You got this, Fallon!"

Nick knelt next to me. "I'm freaking out."

"Me too," I said.

We looked at each other and laughed.

"She can do this," I said, and he nodded.

"Do you know her opponent?"

"Yeah. Gina has more experience than Fallon, but Fallon's stronger."

Nick nodded. The ref signaled the girls to shake hands, and the match started. After twenty seconds of both girls moving in their stance, Gina shot a single leg takedown and took Fallon to the ground.

The ref raised his arm to signal two points for her. "That's good," I said. "A four-point takedown would have hurt her more."

Like she had been taught, Fallon reached her arms out to the side and pressed them to the mat. Gina wasn't able to turn her with the gut wrench she was attempting, and the ref stopped the match to restart them in the neutral position.

"That's it, Fallon!" I yelled. "You got this."

The girls circled again, Gina faking shots and reaching noncommittally for Fallon's legs. Eventually though, Gina committed, hit the same single, and took Fallon down again. Two more points.

Gina couldn't outmaneuver Fallon on the mat, and they were back to neutral.

"Let's go, Fallon," Nick shouted.

They circled for only a few seconds before the ref signaled the end of the period. I helped fan Fallon while the coaches talked to her. She nodded, taking in every piece of strategy and technique they offered.

When they finished, Fallon turned to me. I kept fanning her, and said, "Take her down hard. You can do this. Get lift and the full four points. Then turn her."

She nodded.

"Go hard."

She nodded again, this time with a smile.

The ref called her back onto the mat, fire in her eyes. "She has this," I said.

Nick rubbed his hands together. "I hope so."

Fallon and Gina tied up, both fighting for inside control, but this time, Fallon perfectly timed a head outside single and lifted Gina into the air before taking her to the mat. The ref held up his arm. Four points for Fallon. I grabbed Nick's arm and squeezed.

"Turn her," our Coach yelled. "Turn her, Fallon! Go!"

Fallon locked around Gina's waist and rolled Gina once in a gut wrench.

Six points.

She rolled her again.

Eight points.

It was the crucial moment. At that age, once someone started turning, it was hard to stop. Either Gina would fight long enough for the official to put them back on their feet, or Fallon would take her over again. Gina reached for the mat, pulling with her arms, but Fallon rocked back on her toes and drove forward. Her strength was too much for Gina, and she turned her again. From there, she couldn't be stopped.

After two more rolls, the ref crossed his arms to signal the match had ended. Nick and I high fived each other and clapped, huge smiles on both our faces. After chatting with the coach, Fallon jumped into her brother's arms.

"Aren't they the cutest?" Ashley said, and I couldn't lie. Seeing Nick with his baby sister definitely revealed his softer side.

While everyone congratulated Fallon, I stepped back from the mat, far enough that I could immerse myself in my music and warm up my muscles but still watch the matches and keep up with the progress of my team.

"Good luck," Sebastian said.

"Thanks. Are you staying?"

He rolled his eyes at me. "Of course, I'm staying."

I nodded and took a deep breath, hoping my music could pull me away from this moment and into a headspace reserved for wrestling and competition. I closed my eyes and let the beat take me away, checking every few minutes to see how the matches were going.

When my weight class and name flashed on the sign, I tucked everything into my bag and checked in for the match. Nick, Fallon, Ashley, and Sebastian sat together. I wouldn't zoom in on them. I wouldn't let the fact that Sebastian was there to watch affect me. He'd seen me wrestle before.

He'd wrestled me himself.

My only focus was my opponent. It would be a good match. I had a few good matches lined up for the day, which is why I went with the girls' bracket only. I doubted I'd be able to throw her for five points, but I'd try.

I slipped my mouthpiece in. In the center of the mat, the ref signaled us to approach and then blew his whistle. I took my own advice and pushed hard, like Fallon had. My opponent hadn't expected it. Instead, with all my forward pressure and being heavy on her head, I easily hit my ankle pick.

"Two," the ref called.

Off my ankle pick, I worked to secure a leg lace, but she knew enough to push her hips back into me. I engaged my core, planting my feet, and managed to roll her once before I lost my grip on the lace. The ref stopped us, and we went back to the neutral position.

I glanced at the score. I was winning 4-0.

Circling again, I reached one hand towards her legs, but she was more focused now and immediately pulled her leg back. Neither of us could get much offense going for the rest of the period, and the ref stopped us before I could take her down. Fallon and my teammates fanned me with towels while Coach Law pumped me up.

"Be patient, Annalise. You'll outlast her. Don't give up any points being sloppy and forcing something."

"Yes, Coach."

The ref called us back onto the mat, and I could hear my mom and sister shouting. I didn't hear Sebastian. Probably for the best.

I'm not sure what her coach said to her during the break, but she started the period with a collar tie that almost made my ears ring. As I tugged my head back up, she lowered her level and shot on me. I responded fast and stuffed her shot. As she came back to her feet, I hit a reshot and got a great lift on a high crotch.

"Four!"

"That's it, Annalise," Coach yelled.

She fought my attempts to lock around her waist and immediately thrust her hips back when I tried to drop to her legs for a leg lace. I transitioned again, but realizing it wasn't working and knowing the ref would stop us at any second if I didn't secure a turn, I jumped to a new move I'd been working on, a side headlock. I drove hard. She grunted. With her back locked out, she had no choice but to go with the pressure.

I rolled her, and the ref blew the whistle.

I laid against the mat and exhaled.

"Nice match," she said in a groan-whisper.

"Thanks."

The ref lifted my arm. I shook hands with my opponent's coach and then headed for my own. To find Sebastian standing behind him with the proudest grin on his gorgeous face.

My heart crumbled, and I knew in that second—I was a goner.

CHAPTER 26

OUR CLUB TEAM HAD A BYE IN THE NEXT ROUND, SO I slipped away from my friends and family. I found a spot on the floor in the corner and ate, checking the website every few minutes to see when Nick and Sebastian were wrestling on mat fifteen. When they were on deck, I snuck closer to the action, across from them on mat sixteen. Everyone was in their corner. Ashley, Fallon, even my mom. As his time came closer, Sebastian looked around the crowd for someone.

For me.

Was that presumptuous? He'd asked me to the dance. He'd stood right behind my coaches while I wrestled. He'd said he wanted more.

The match in the weight class before Sebastian's started. He paced back and forth and stretched his neck and shoulders. And still looked around. The match on mat sixteen ended. The ref and the coaches cleared, leaving me alone, standing on its edge.

Sebastian looked across the empty mat and saw me. Our gazes locked like they had the first time we'd ever seen each other, also across a mat, only this time he was getting ready for a match, not me.

He smiled. I mouthed the words, "Good luck."

"Thank you," he mouthed back.

I came closer, kneeling on the empty mat to watch his match.

Sebastian's opponent gave him some competition in the first period, but by the middle of the second, Sebastian pinned him, ending it.

When the ref raised his arm, turning him in both directions, I clapped and wondered if I wore the same look of pride he'd worn when I'd won. Not that he'd notice. After the match, Sebastian's father wrapped an arm around his shoulders, pulled him to the side, and coached him quietly for several minutes until Nick's match started.

Nick won, too, pinning his opponent in the first period.

Sebastian shook his hand and patted him on the back before nodding at me. That nod! I folded myself back into the crowd, my heart racing as if I'd just finished my own match. Sebastian wasn't anywhere near me, but I felt him. All this time, had I been punishing myself instead of him? Was my big, little sister right?

Ashley texted to meet her, Fallon, Nick, and Sebastian to celebrate our wins. I closed my eyes, my decision made.

"I'm doing this," I said, and then more confidently, "I'm doing this."

My stomach was a butterfly garden as I crossed the indoor football field to where they all sat in a corner.

"Congrats, guys," I said.

"Thanks for watching," Nick said.

"Yeah," Sebastian nodded. "Thanks."

"Thanks for watching my match," I said.

"You up again soon?" Nick asked.

"About forty-five minutes. You?"

"Same."

The four of them chatted and munched on crackers and fruit snacks. I pretended to watch the action on the mats in the distance. The struggle, which is the definition of the word "wrestling," reflected the feelings in my chest. You can do this. You can do this, I told myself. You want to do this.

"Do you want to sit?" Ashley asked.

I worked to keep my voice even. "Actually, I was going to go for a walk."

"Okay," my sister said.

I took a deep breath. "Sebastian, would you want to come?"

Nick pumped a fist, and we all laughed. I covered my red cheeks, somehow still grateful for Nick's silliness despite my embarrassment. Sebastian jumped up and dusted the turf pieces off his clothes. "See you guys," he said.

"Yeah, yeah," Nick said.

My face flamed redder than it did at the height of a workout. "That wasn't embarrassing or anything."

"I'm not embarrassed."

"Good," I managed.

We walked through the halls and up the stairs to the balcony overlooking the wrestling mats. Neither of us spoke, but halfway up the stairs, Sebastian had reached for my hand and smiled when I'd squeezed his back.

"I'm afraid to ask any questions," he said. "About what this is. What you're thinking."

"I'm afraid to say what I'm thinking."

"After last night? I put myself out there."

"Yeah," I said. "And I kind of shut you down."

"Brutally."

"I'm sorry."

He shook his head. "It's fair. I hurt you."

I nodded and tried to find the words to explain what had changed. "You did, but seeing you there, after my match—I wanted you to be there. More than that, it felt natural having you there."

Like a warm blanket in winter.

"Same."

"I thought that things between us couldn't change. That there was too much resentment and hurt, but without my even realizing it, it did change. Part of me feels like I have to accept that."

"What does accepting that mean exactly?"

Knowing the outcome, I looked into those eyes that mesmerized me every time. He ran his fingertips along my cheek again, like he had in the front seat of his car, but this time I leaned into him.

"Does this mean you'll go to the dance with me?"

"I don't have a dress," I said.

"I think you do."

A dance with Sebastian. His arms around me with that low cut dress. His hands pressed against my bare back. My head on his shoulder. I took a deep breath and closed my eyes. I could do this. My mom had said there were no wrong answers. I should go with what I felt.

A flash of the first moment I'd seen Sebastian four years earlier struck me. I'd joked with Nick that not everyone could be love at first sight like him and my sister, but Sebastian and I had been. We'd each known it when he'd given me that first nod from across the mat in eighth grade.

It was time to do something about it.

"Yes," I said, finally.

A slow smile crept across his face. "Really?"

I laughed. "Really."

His hands slid along my waist to my hips, pulling me to him. We smelled like a mix of sweat and wrestling mat, but that was us. His eyes at that close distance were a kaleidoscope of blue and green.

They closed, and our lips touched. It had been four long years since I'd kissed Sebastian Love. Our first kiss had been tentative and sweet, but this was different. We'd grown up since then. Our kisses had, too. His hand pressed at my lower back. Not willing to relinquish all the power, I wrapped my arms around his neck and ran my fingers through his black hair. He moved his lips against mine with passion and nudged me into the railing. His body all around me triggered magic, fireworks, everything the beauty of the world had to offer. When I thought the kiss was ending, he brushed the tip of his nose against mine and kissed me again until I was utterly breathless and wanting so much more.

He leaned his forehead against mine and whispered, "Annalise."

"Wow," I managed, and he laughed.

"Yeah. Wow."

Both of our phones beeped in unison.

"What is that?" I said, pulling my phone from the pocket of my hoodie. A group chat from Nick, Fallon, and Ashley exchanged rapid fire messages that were mostly firework-exploding emojis.

"I'm guessing it's not a coincidence those messages came in the exact moment we kissed," Sebastian said.

In the corner of the turf room below, the trio in question waved from the spot where we'd left them. They weren't sitting and snacking anymore. They were jumping up and down. Dancing. Pumping their fists in the air.

"They saw us," I said.

Like his friends had seen us in middle school. When Sebastian had pretended he didn't care about me to avoid embarrassment. This time, though, he put his arm around me and waved back before leading me down the hallway into a doorway that gave us a little more privacy.

And we kissed until I thought my legs might crumble beneath me.

CHAPTER 27

"WE HAVE TO GET BACK," SEBASTIAN SAID AFTER THE most magical however many minutes of my life.

I nodded.

"I'm afraid when we leave this hallway, something's going to change. Or more accurately, your mind is going to change."

"I said I'd go to the dance with you. I don't back out of my commitments."

Sebastian pulled me in for a hug. "Thank you."

"For what?"

"For trusting me enough to give me another chance. I won't mess it up. I promise."

"Deal."

Hand in hand, we made our way back down the stairs and toward the mats. The boys' team for the Keystone Club was set to compete on mat eighteen next. The girls were all the way at the other end. We'd have to watch each other from a distance.

Sebastian brushed a kiss on my cheek. "Good luck."

"Same."

He smiled, shook his head, and ripped his hoodie off as he walked away, leaving me with a beautiful view.

"Did I see what I think I saw?"

I jumped. "Mom! You scared me."

"So, I guess you made your decision."

"Guess so."

"You okay?"

"So far," I said.

Sebastian had faded into the crowd of parents, coaches, and wrestlers. He'd promised me he wouldn't mess it up. The only choice I had was to have faith.

"That's the thing about dating, honey," Mom said. "You have to take a risk."

I only hoped my risk didn't crush my heart.

Again.

***

LATER THAT NIGHT, I STOOD IN OUR KITCHEN AND stared at my phone, quiet and alone on the island.

Ashley came into the room dressed in adorable jeans and a tight long-sleeved tee. Her hair and makeup were flawless. Nick was clearly on his way over.

"What are you doing?" she asked.

"Waiting for my phone to do tricks."

Her eyes widened knowingly. "Is one of those tricks ringing with Bash on the other end."

"Maybe."

"You should call him."

"What if he doesn't want me to?"

"He made out with you in public today. I'm pretty sure he'd be good with you calling him."

The thought of his lips on mine knocked me into a parallel universe where the only emotion was utter euphoria.

"Damn, Lise. You have it bad."

And the euphoria was gone. "Shut up."

"Stop overthinking. Stop looking for the exact right thing to do and stop pushing him away. Sebastian knows you. He gets you, and he likes you."

All difficult points to fully believe.

"Okay?"

"Okay," I said, not entirely sure, but committed to trying.

"Do you want to invite him over to watch a movie? Nick's on his way."

Despite my sister's big speech, I didn't feel ready to sit calmly next to Sebastian and watch a movie. My insides were circling the mat, so to speak, not ready to engage yet, but also not able to sit still.

"No. Thanks. I'm gonna paint."

She scowled at me.

"I promise I'm good. I have a deadline is all."

The doorbell rang.

"That will be Nick," she said.

"I'll be in the garage."

***

I LINED UP MY SERIES OF WRESTLING MAT PAINTINGS and stared at them while Ashley's words played in my head. That old saying about the thin line between love and hate rang true. All these years, I'd thought I hated Sebastian, but my heart sat on the edge of loving him the whole time.

Risking stepping off that edge terrified me.

Part of me knew, though, I didn't have a choice anymore. It was a matter of coming to terms with my reality, not fighting it.

I refocused on the paintings. None of them stood out to me. Maybe the purple mat since the color differed from the norm. Rebecca had suggested I paint my passion. That meant wrestling, but I hadn't gotten further than the background.

Maybe the background was wrong.

Or maybe everything happening between Sebastian and me muddled my passion. If he'd become my passion, did that mean I should paint him?

Authentic art was hard.

Someone knocked at the door to the kitchen.

"Come in," I called.

Before the door opened, I knew who it would be. Nobody in my family knocked.

"Hey," Sebastian said.

"Hey."

"Your sister told me you were out here. I hope it's okay. I don't want to interrupt your creative process or anything."

"It's fine."

He nodded and closed the door behind him. He wore a pair of faded, worn jeans and a Forest Run wrestling shirt, torn at the collar. He definitely hadn't dressed up, and that soothed me in a way. He wasn't trying to put on some facade of perfection. He was flawed and torn. We both were. But he was there. In front of me.

He stood with his hands in his pockets like all the walls we'd knocked down that day at duals had somehow found their way back into position. If we let them.

Being even ten feet away from him, though, tormented me. I dropped my paint brush into the water can and closed the distance between us. His arms wrapped around me without hesitation, and he exhaled a deep breath when he pressed his face into my neck.

"Hey," I whispered again.

"Hey," he answered with a chuckle. "I was scared there for a second."

"Me too."

He squeezed me tighter.

"I'm sorry if I'm making this too hard," I said.

"My favorite activity in life is competing in one of the toughest sports in the world. I think I can handle hard."

I kissed his cheek and led him to my painting corner.

"What are you working on?"

"My passion."

"Wrestling mats?"

"That's the problem," I said. "Your aunt said my fall paintings showed talent, but they weren't packed with emotion. I'm supposed to find my own voice and tell the story only I can tell, but through paintings."

"Wrestling is definitely your passion, so that makes sense."

"It does, but what's my angle? What do I have to say about wrestling?"

He shrugged.

"Obviously it makes sense to paint wrestlers on the mats, but anyone could do that. I don't see how painting wrestlers because I like wrestling is showing my passion and my unique voice." I slumped onto my stool and absentmindedly swirled the brush through random paint colors until I had a mess.

"Aunt Bex always says you can't force creativity. If the painting isn't working right now, do something else that might inspire you."

"Such as?"

He moved behind me and ran his fingertips along my arms. I shivered. He pressed his lips against my neck and whispered, "Is there anywhere you want to go? Anything you want to do?"

A moan escaped my lips. I leaned back against him. He wrapped his arms around my neck and snickered.

"What's so funny?"

"This. Me being here. With you."

"Okay…?"

"The day you came to my aunt's gallery exhibit—" He paused and took a breath. "I saw you about fifteen minutes before I had the guts to talk to you."

"Why?"

"You looked so gorgeous. I mean, when we were kids, you were cute, but since then, you've become this…" He breathed again.

"Are you okay?"

"Kinda terrified, actually," he said with a laugh.

I spun on the stool to face him.

"That might be worse."

"You know I agreed to go out with you, right?"

"I do, which is the only reason I can even attempt to tell you this kind of stuff."

I suppressed a grin. Seeing Sebastian so nervous redefined cute. "By all means, continue your attempt."

He smirked at me, and damn. Phew. He had no idea what he'd become in the last four years, too.

"You were gorgeous, and the way you looked at the paintings. Like, straight on. With this pensive look on your face. It was like a whole world of thoughts and ideas were locked up inside your head, and I wanted to know every one of them."

Now it was my turn to breathe.

"If I would have known we both liked art, I would have tried to use it a long time ago to get your attention."

"Right. Like you've been missing me for four years."

"Are you kidding? I've been watching you wrestle from the depths of gyms across the state—across four states even—wishing I had the right to talk to you but knowing how I'd screwed that up."

The thought of Sebastian watching me wrestle while I was doing my best to avoid the sight of him twisted me up in ways I couldn't explain.

"I avoided you at every tournament because looking at you…" I lowered my eyes and whispered, "It destroyed me."

"Annalise, I'm so sorry."

"I know."

"I started this whole conversation because I thought it could be inspiring, but it went dark fast."

His brutal honesty made me laugh, and it gave me an idea of something that could be inspiring. "How cold is it outside?"

"Freezing."

I leaned into him. "Then we better bundle up."

CHAPTER 28

"WHERE ARE WE GOING?" SEBASTIAN ASKED.

I didn't answer. I was already rounding up everything we needed. Flashlight. Coats, hats, and gloves. Even a couple hand warmers from our camping stash.

"Are we going on an adventure?"

"You could say that."

"Do we need sleeping bags and a tent?" he asked, a little too excited about the idea.

I rolled my eyes at him. "Freezing to death? Not romantic."

"Fair point."

Once we were bundled, I slipped my gloved fingers into his and opened the garage doors. The cold air and a few random snowflakes rushed toward us. Our boots crunched in the snow as we carved our way through the grass toward the woods.

"Is this where you tell me you've been pretending to forgive me all this time, and you're really going to kill me?" he asked.

"You're on to me," I teased and knocked him into the snow.

"Hey!" He pulled me down, too, and within seconds, our lips found each other's and warmed themselves in a deep kiss. "Was this your plan?"

"I could have kissed you in the warmth of the garage," I said.

"But this is more romantic."

"If you think this is romantic, buckle up." I dusted myself off. "Seriously. You're going to love this."

"I already do."

Aw. The sweet, cheesy comments. We were becoming those people.

And I liked it.

Starlight sparkled on the white crystals of snow all around us. The landscape was a painting that should have been in a museum, but it didn't hang on some wall, untouched by humans. It enveloped us in romance, intrigue, and the kind of cold that made you want to hold onto someone and never let go. We reached the edge of the yard, and Sebastian stopped.

"Are we going into the woods?"

"Yep."

"At night? In the dark?"

"Yep." I tried to take a step, but he wouldn't budge. "Are you scared?"

"No. Okay. Maybe a little. Aren't there bears back here?"

"You're not willing to wrestle a bear for me, Sebastian?"

He raised an eyebrow.

"No, seriously. We can't be together then."

"Bears are a little out of my weight class," he said.

"I'm so offended."

Sebastian didn't laugh at my teasing.

"Sebastian, I don't expect you to wrestle a bear. Besides, they're hibernating. I think."

"It's not that. Sorry. I thought of something that kind of took me out of the moment."

"Anything you want to talk about?"

He took a deep breath. "No. Thanks. My dad and expectations and stuff."

"Your dad expects you to wrestle a bear?"

He laughed. "Close."

"I get it," I said. I'd seen everything on the mat. Parents yelling at their children about why they would lower their head or reach back when they were on bottom or roll toward their backs. Even the occasional declaration from parent to child, "You suck." Which would then usually result in the wrestler throwing his fill-in-the-blank and threatening to quit the sport altogether. "There are no parents like wrestling parents."

"Yeah, but your mom doesn't seem like that."

"My mom and I made a pact when I started. I promised to listen to my coaches and try not to make mistakes, and she promised to let me learn from my mistakes without getting in my face."

"My dad and I don't have that kind of arrangement."

"I'm sorry."

"Thanks."

"Do you mind if we walk while we talk? Otherwise, our feet may freeze to the ground."

With the tip of his nose turning pink, Sebastian shivered. "That might actually be possible. It's colder than I thought out here."

"You want to go back?"

"No," he said. "We're on an adventure, remember?"

I pulled him forward onto Home Path. The night was as quiet as it was cold. All of the animals hid from the chill, missing out on the moonlit beauty.

"Ever since I was a kid, one of my most favorite things in the world to see was snow piling on top of branches. That contrast of white and brown is so artistic. You know?"

"Secretly, I look forward to it from the second the leaves are off the trees."

"Me too!" I said.

We were deep in the woods by then, to the spot where the paths split. Ahead of us were the path signs Ashley and I'd made as kids. One pointed to the left and read Sunset Path. I'd painted a sunset on the sign. The sign to the right read Deer Path with a terrible painting of a deer.

"You have paths?" Sebastian said. "Paths with names?"

"Yep. Ashley and I made them when we were kids." I pointed behind us. "That's Home Path."

"Aptly named. Is there a village back here, too?"

"Not a well-populated one. Unless you count the deer and squir-rels."

I pulled him left onto Sunset Path. We side-stepped down the slope to avoid sliding like a sled-ride gone wrong, and after a few minutes, we made it to the clearing where my family went to watch sunsets.

"Wow," Sebastian said.

No matter how many times I walked the paths, I felt the same way. The clearing was high above the river, overlooking the cliffside. In the summer, trees on the hill and in the woods behind us blocked some of the view, but in the winter, you could look left and see all the way down the river toward the city of Pittsburgh. To the right, the water extended into Riverport. Across was our rival, Pacific, with all the lights from the houses built along the hillside climbing from the river's edge sparkling off the water.

"I never knew you could see this from here."

"Everyone says that," I said. "You should see it on the Fourth of July. The fireworks go off right over the water."

"Is that an invitation?"

Warmth spread across my cheeks, fighting the cold of the night. "Maybe."

He squeezed my hand. "That's not a no. How often do you come here?"

"A lot," I said. "It's a great place to think. I've painted it a few times, but no brush can do this view justice."

"This is definitely the kind of inspiration I was talking about."

"It's better with you here," I said, shocked at my boldness. He wrapped his arms around my shoulders, and I leaned into his warmth. I closed my eyes, letting the peace of the night wash over me until a memory struck me with more force than the cold.

And I groaned.

"What?"

I shook my head.

"Tell me."

I took a breath, puffing a cloud of steam into the cool air. "See that stump over there?" I pointed to the edge of the clearing where a tree stump dangled over the cliff.

Sebastian nodded.

"That's where I sat after *the* tournament…"

"What tournament?"

I gave him a knowing look.

He closed his eyes. "When I hurt you."

"I think that was the only time I won a tournament and still cried."

Sebastian hugged me so tightly I thought I wouldn't be able to breathe. "I hate myself for being so stupid."

The pain of that day had shaped me. No denying it, but Sebastian was right. He'd been a scared kid, embarrassed and confused. He'd apologized and changed, and it wasn't fair for me to hold it over him anymore.

"I'm letting it go," I said.

"What?"

"Right here. Right where I cried over it. With you standing beside me, I'm letting go."

"Thank you, Annalise."

I kissed his cheek and whispered in his ear, "Don't you think it's about time you call me Lise?"

He chuckled and then whispered, "Lise," before kissing me on the cliffside with a whole town of people across the river as our audience.

CHAPTER 29

"DO YOU WANT TO GO BACK?" I ASKED HIM AT THE IN-
tersection of Home, Sunset, and Deer paths.

"There's more?"

"As long as you're not going to lose a toe."

"I think I can hang on a little longer."

"Good."

The path narrowed, so I walked in front of him with the flashlight. When our destination was about to come into view, I stopped, and he bumped into me.

"Close your eyes," I said.

"This is where you kill me?"

I punched his stomach. "Stop. Seriously. Close them."

He did, and I fumbled through the snow to our family's gazebo. We'd decorated it with solar twinkle lights over the summer. Surprisingly, they worked better in the winter with all the leaves down and the sun, even limited, able to poke through. The lights clicked on, and the woods sparkled even more.

"Okay. Open."

Sebastian obeyed, and he raised his hand to block some of the light. "What is this?"

"Amazing, right? C'mon."

He stepped up into the gazebo and joined me on the bench inside.

"You have a gazebo?"

"Yep."

"And a river view?"

"Yes."

"This is like the scene of some cutesy holiday movie." His eyes widened when he heard what he'd said. "Not that I watch those."

"Clearly."

"My mom has them on from Thanksgiving to Christmas. All day every day."

"Likely story."

"Okay, so I've caught the occasional cheesy detail."

"Maybe I could call them up. Offer the property for a setting or something."

"You should."

Or, I thought, looking into those eyes that had confounded me for years, I could use the setting for my own love story. I couldn't decide if that's what I wanted or if I even had a choice anymore.

"Thank you for showing this to me. And for showing me your painting and talking to me about things that are important to you."

"Thank you for listening."

He spun me in the gazebo and then held one finger up while he grabbed his phone. After a few seconds, soft music played.

"Will you dance with me?" he said.

His words pinned my heart in my chest, and I could barely breathe let alone talk. I nodded, and he lifted my hands around his neck. Just like that, the movie got better.

"You should pinch me," he said.

"It's real," I said, but a voice inside of me whispered: *for now.*

No. I wouldn't think about this ending. I'd live in the moment. In the middle of these quiet woods, with snow falling around us in this gazebo with twinkle lights, looking out over the cliff at the lights of Pacific's small riverside town.

I wouldn't ruin the perfect moment with thoughts of the future.

***

"DO YOU WANT TO COME IN?"

"It's getting late. I have to get home for my morning workout, or my dad won't let me out ever again."

I nodded. "Probably smart to get some rest."

"You think I'm going to be able to sleep?"

I fought a grin. Same, Sebastian. Same.

"I want to take you on a date," he said. "A real date."

"Aren't we going to the dance together?"

"Definitely. You're not bailing on me, but the dance is more than two weeks away. I want to see you before then."

"You mean besides at practice and the club and our matches?"

"Yes. Besides all that. Because at those places, I can't do this." He leaned close, inch by painful, longing inch, until our lips connected again.

"I have one request," I said when the kiss ended.

"Okay."

"No wrestling or workout related dates."

He smiled. "Sure, but why?"

"I can't think of you on the mat. This part of us and wrestling have to stay separate." Or I'd never be able to concentrate in another match again.

"Agreed. I'm glad we don't have to wrestle each other ever again."

"Me too. That, and I'm the reigning champion of that matchup so…"

He laughed and nodded. "Okay."

We stood outside the garage, in the frosty moonlight, staring at each other, knowing the night had to end but not wanting it to.

He kissed me again.

"I love that I have your permission to do that," he said.

"I love that you do it so well," I said, surprising myself.

He grinned. "Glad to hear it, but I should go."

"That's what you said," I teased.

"I don't want to. Today has been unexpected."

"For me, too. In a good way."

"Definitely in a good way," he agreed.

I kissed him because I could.

"Morning workouts," I whispered.

He sighed. "I'll see you tomorrow at practice."

"Okay."

He backpedaled toward his SUV. "Go paint."

"Okay," I said again.

He jogged forward and kissed me one last time.

"Good night," he whispered.

After that day, the night had no other choice but to be good.

***

BEFORE BED, I BRUSHED MY TEETH AND WASHED MY
face like normal. I picked up the few things I'd left around my
room as usual. I set my diffuser with cinnamon, my overnight scent,
stretched, and did my pushups and sit ups.

All part of my routine.

But before I slipped under the covers, I did one thing that wasn't
part of my routine at all.

I picked up the first-place trophy from my nightstand and turned
it over in my hands one last time. I'd earned it by beating Sebastian.
I'd kept it there to remind myself of the pain he'd caused me, of how
I couldn't trust boys.

How I couldn't let myself be vulnerable around them.

I'd believed the only thing I could trust was my training and my
dedication to the sport.

"Some things do change," I said to myself.

I opened my trophy case, and positioned the memory in the back,
putting the moment behind me once and for all. Then I slipped into
Sebastian's hoodie that I still hadn't returned and fell into the deepest
sleep I'd had in a long time.

CHAPTER 30

I WOKE UP AT 6 A.M. TO A TEXT MESSAGE FROM SE-
bastian that read, "Have a good workout."

I texted back, "Same to you."

We both had plans to lift at our respective gyms before the Iron Valley team met for practice later that afternoon.

The snow falling outside didn't dull my spirits. Neither did the cold. It only reminded me of the night I'd had with Sebastian. I started the car with a smile on my face. It didn't go away through my whole workout.

"You're happy today," my trainer said.

Not that I hadn't ever been happy before, but I was a special kind of happy. Dom had plans to bring me a veggie omelet that morning and then paint with me. He was expanding his horizons, his joke about the fact all he did was paint horizons.

We ate our breakfasts in the garage with him giving me a squinty side-eye between bites.

"What already?"

"You sure about this?"

By "this," I expected he meant Sebastian. "No."

"At least that means you're still rational."

I scowled at him.

"You've avoided him for years. And yeah, I think he's an okay dude, but you're one of my best friends, and I know guys. I am a guy."

"Meaning? He wants to sleep with me and then dump me?"

"Hey! I don't do that."

I stabbed another bite of spinach and tomato. "What's your point then?"

"I love you, and I'm looking out for you."

"I get that giving Sebastian another chance is a risk, but isn't every relationship a risk? There are breakups in high school, like, every day. Ugly ones. And that could happen to me and Sebastian. I hope it doesn't, but it could."

Dom didn't respond. I refused to wonder if that meant he was debating how ugly mine and Sebastian's breakup would be.

"I'm taking a chance, and I'm happy. Be happy for me."

"If you're happy, I'm happy."

"Thank you."

"Do I still get to watch you kick his ass at practice?"

I groaned at the thought of practice. Sebastian and I would be rolling around on a mat together. After rolling around with him in the snow and dancing with him in the gazebo and the electric shock that scored through my body when our skinned touched—phew—I might be in trouble.

***

OUR REGULAR ROUTINE, SEBASTIAN RAN WARM-UP laps next to me before practice. He didn't check out the swimmers, but he didn't give me the side-eye either. In fact, he acted like he did every other practice.

Like nothing had happened the day before.

Like he hadn't kissed my neck and wrapped his arms around me in my garage. Like we hadn't walked in the woods and danced under the twinkle lights of the gazebo. Like his lips hadn't known the curve of my mouth and explored the softness of my tongue more than once.

In the middle of stretches, he collapsed on the mat and whispered, "I can't do this anymore."

Wow. That breakup came faster than I thought.

"I'm over here, trying to be normal, when all I want is to sneak away into that back hallway and kiss you."

Tension escaped my body in a laugh.

"What?" he said.

"You were pretty convincing that nothing had changed between us."

"I thought that's what you'd want, things to be normal at practice, and I'm up for trying, but I can't pretend that what happened didn't happen when it's basically all I can think about."

"Me too," I whispered.

"Okay. Why don't you drill with Kurt today, and I'll work with Cory, until we can figure out how to make all this work?"

Relief washed over me. "That sounds good."

"Good. We have a match to get ready for, and I don't think I'm ready to touch you in a, um, well, yeah, this is a good plan." His face flamed red, and we both laughed.

Definitely a good plan. Kurt challenged me, and I held my focus in the more difficult moves when we were live. Our work kept my attention, and I barely looked at Sebastian at all.

Barely.

After practice, he waited outside my bathroom. "Hey."

"Hey," I said, surprised.

"Can I give you a ride home?"

I couldn't stop the grin spreading across my face. "Okay."

He grinned then, too, and we both laughed, our cheeks turning pink.

"This is going to take some getting used to," he said.

"Yeah."

He held out his hand, and I took it. He pulled me close and kissed the top of my head. We walked to his car hand-in-hand, waving to our teammates along the way. If anyone hadn't known before, they'd know now. Sebastian Love and Annalise Fiori were together.

I'd never ever dated one of my teammates before, but Sebastian was Sebastian.

Sometimes you had to break your own rules.

He held the passenger door for me, and then came around the driver side and tossed his bags into the backseat. Once we were moving, he reached across the seat and held my hand again.

"What are you doing tonight?" he asked.

"Eating a healthy dinner and getting an appropriate amount of rest."

"You're so dedicated," he said.

"Like you aren't."

"True. I have a workout at the club, though."

"I'm off tonight."

"Painting?"

"I hope. Still searching for that inspiration."

He pressed his hand against his chest. "I'm hurt! You mean our romantic interlude in the woods didn't do it for you?"

Oh, it had done things for me, but inspiring my painting wasn't one of them.

"Actually," Sebastian said slowly. "I have some news."

"What kind of news?"

"My dad got Nick and me into another tournament. In Ohio. We leave first thing in the morning, and I'll be visiting family through New Year's."

"Oh." Disappointment settled over me at the thought of not seeing him for days. "When will you be back?"

"January 3."

That was almost a week away. A week. Without Sebastian. "I'll miss you." My voice sounded small and pathetic, but Sebastian smiled.

"I'll miss you, too."

We rode the last couple of minutes to my house in silence, letting the news of our separation settle. When he parked in the driveway, he turned his body to me and kissed the back of my hand. "I'm sorry about this. If I didn't know any better, I'd think my dad did it on purpose."

"Why?"

"To keep me focused."

"Are you unfocused?"

He licked his lips and did his best to avoid grinning. "I've had someone on my mind a lot lately."

Me. His dad was sending him to an out-of-state tournament to get him away from me. "Does he do this every time you like a girl?"

Sebastian looked away.

"He does? Wow. That's rough."

"No," he said, turning those stunning eyes on me. "I've never *really* liked a girl. Not like this. I think he sees that, and it scares him."

My tongue stuck to the roof of my mouth. It scared me, too.

"I'll show him I'm focused, and he'll back off. Promise."

Deciding to be with Sebastian had been way complex, but now, with his dad and figuring out practice partners and wondering how our teammates might react—complex had only begun.

"We'll go on a date when I get back."

"Okay," I nodded. "I'll paint while you're gone."

"Don't suplex anyone at a New Year's party."

"Wouldn't dream of it, especially because our family tradition is a party of three—me, Ashley, and our mom. We celebrate our female trio in the last year and do all sorts of rituals to ensure our success in the new year."

"I love that." His lips parted, and he leaned toward me. I sank into his kiss, knowing it would be too long before I could feel the magic of it again. "I will miss you, Lise."

I laughed at him calling me Lise. How had I ever wanted him to call me something else.

"Me too."

CHAPTER 31

I'D BEEN RIGHT. I MISSED SEBASTIAN. A LOT. KNOWING his father would be hovering over him the whole time, I did my best not to message incessantly. Instead, I painted. And hung out with Ashley who was missing Nick as much but messaging every chance she got.

"Can you put your phone down, please?" I snapped at her in the garage when she was supposed to be helping me.

The smile that had been painted across her face faded, and she set the phone down. "Sorry."

"No." I sloshed my brush in the water can. "It's me. Sebastian's dad is not thrilled about him being so into a girl, so I'm messaging him once for every, like, twenty times I want to."

She blew me a kiss. "That's rough. But he does have to wrestle, and you do have to paint. So, how's it coming?"

We stood side by side, studying the lineup. Of incomplete paintings.

"Still haven't gotten past the background, huh?"

"Nope," I said, shaking my head. "But when I do figure out what I want in the foreground, I'm going to have lots of mat canvases ready for it."

"That's positivity."

Something like that.

"How are you doing on your weight?" Ashley asked.

"Good. Down three pounds."

"With five days until your next match? Let's make cookies."

"Ash…"

"Cookies!"

So we made cookies. I ate one. We watched the kinds of holiday movies that could have been filmed in our forest gazebo. Played board games. Worked out. Had sister sleepovers. Watched the New Year's ball drop. Sorted through our closets to prep for back-to-school.

Watched the clock through every period on the first day back after break and rushed to the mat room the second the bell rang. Sebastian must have dismissed from Forest Run early because he waited outside the auxiliary gym doors and dropped his bag the moment he saw me. I ran down the hall, jumped into his arms, and wrapped my legs around his waist. Without a care for who watched, we kissed like we hadn't seen each other forever.

Because we hadn't.

***

PRACTICE WENT WELL. GOOD THING CONSIDERING OUR first school match of the new year would be the next day at Pacific High School. The first person I saw when our team entered Pacific's gym for the match was Mrs. Errico.

She waved. "Annalise! How are you?"

"Good. Thanks. I didn't realize you'd be here."

"Pacific has several female wrestlers interested in their own team. I'm here as moral support."

"What does their athletic director say?"

"They're working on it."

In other words, they were blowing the girls off. Opponent or not, my blood simmered for them.

"Have you given any more thought to helping us out?" Mrs. Errico asked, hopeful.

"I have, but I don't know what I can do."

"I'd be glad to set up a meeting between you and some of our other advocates. They can share what they've done."

For the second time in a few weeks, I stood on the edge of something that could be epic, fearful of falling. I glanced at Sebastian. He grinned back at me.

"Sure. Let's talk more."

She clapped her hands. "That's wonderful, Annalise. I know this is the beginning of an excellent partnership." She tapped into the Notes feature of her phone. "What's the best way for me to reach you?"

I shared my number and my mom's since she requested to chat with her and gain her permission given my minor status. I'd almost forgotten about our chat by the time the team took the mat for the start of the match until Sebastian tapped my shoulder with his stunning smile.

"Lise, you're wrestling a girl."

"Excuse me?"

"A girl. You're wrestling a girl."

Across the mat, one of Pacific's wrestlers I'd seen often in the tournament circuit waved back. She'd cut a few pounds, so we weren't regular opponents, but still. I was wrestling a girl. In a high school, folkstyle match.

Imagine that.

When I hit the mat, the referee hung back at the head table, sorting through something I could care less about.

"I'm Zora," the girl said, shaking my hand. "We've been around of course, but never met."

"Annalise," I said. "You're working with Mrs. Errico?"

She nodded. "Yeah. I had to cut weight to get a chance to wrestle on our team. And the boy who usually wrestles this weight class is sick. It's such crap. We have five girls at the high school that want to wrestle, but some of them won't join unless they're competing against girls."

"I get it," I said. "A lot of my friends quit by ninth grade, sick of everything."

"They want a whole roster before they'll list it as a school sport. It's so backward."

I glanced at my team, waiting to cheer me on. I loved the guys, but maybe that had clouded my experience. What if a girl from Iron

Valley wanted to wrestle but hadn't felt accepted by our team? How many of my classmates had missed out on the opportunity to compete in this incredible sport that taught lessons about struggle and toughness and humility better than anything in life could?

The ref left the head table and came our way.

"Mrs. Errico is setting up a call for us to talk more. I want to help."

Zora smiled. "Awesome. Thanks, Annalise. Good luck."

"Same," I said.

I enjoyed the match more than I should have. I had a chance at a pin early in the first period, but part of me didn't want it to end. Going anything less than my hardest went against everything I believed, but wrestling Zora was fun.

We went back and forth for two periods before I pinned her.

"That was fun," she said with a grin.

I laughed. "For me too. See ya."

Coach Joseph didn't laugh. "You two gonna go to the mall after this?"

"I got the pin, Coach."

"Next time, get it earlier."

"Yes, Coach."

He shook his head. "I won't pretend to get what it's like to wrestle the guys all the time and then have the chance to wrestle a girl, but next time—"

"I know, Coach. I get it."

"Good. Sebastian's up."

He gave me his signature nod from the mat and then gave the opponent his signature pin. I couldn't lie. Sebastian had gotten a lot better over the years. If we had to do it over again, I didn't know that the trophy would be at my house instead of his.

We won our matches Tuesday and Thursday. And then came Saturday. The day of my afternoon mystery date with Sebastian. Ashley squealed when I asked her for help getting ready.

"Finally! Nick and I saw this coming miles away."

"Impressive insight," I said sarcastically. Let's be honest. When it came to Sebastian and me, it was going to go drastically one way or the other. We weren't the kind of people who could do the in-between thing or the friend thing. "He said to dress warm."

Together, we picked out a pair of fleece-lined jeans, a cami under a gorgeously fuzzy oversized sweater, warm socks, and knee-high winter boots. After makeup, jewelry, and the cutest hat and gloves, I couldn't deny it. I looked good.

I had no other choice going in public with Sebastian.

"You look great," Ashley said from the couch where she was cuddled up with Nick. "He's not going to be able to take his eyes off you."

"Probably his hands, too," Nick threw in, and Ashley swatted him. "Sorry. Being honest. You look hot, Lise. And I say that with absolute objectivity since I only have eyes for your sister."

"Thanks, Nick."

Sebastian's car turned into the driveway, and my stomach tumbled like someone threw me for five points.

"Trust me when I say this, Lise. Bash is more nervous than you are," Nick said. "Don't tell him I told you that, but if you could read our messages from this afternoon."

"Ooh!" Ashley said, reaching for his phone. "I want to read them."

Nick shoved it under the cushion, and Ashley dug for it. I left them alone to play their game and coached my feet into moving one step after the other toward Sebastian's car.

He met me in the driveway with a hug that rocked us both back and forth. He tipped my face up and kissed me like he'd been waiting to all year.

"Hi," he whispered after pulling away.

"Hello."

He sighed and grinned. "Annalise Fiori is going on a date with me."

His innocence and excitement made me want to kiss him again. So I did.

"If we keep this up, we might miss the date," he said. "Not that I would mind that much, but I kind of promised we'd be there."

I squinted at him. "Where are you taking me?"

He led me to the passenger side and opened the door. "You'll see."

CHAPTER 32

AS WAS BECOMING OUR HABIT, SEBASTIAN HELD MY hand while he drove. Within minutes, he slowed the car and turned into the parking lot for the local ice rink.

"Are we skating?"

"Do you like to?"

"Not really," I said. Mostly because I had this skill of ice skating with my butt and my knees. Never a good look. And especially dangerous during season when I needed my butt and my knees.

"Good," Sebastian said. "We're here to watch my brother's hockey game."

I squeezed his hand. "Are you sure that's smart?"

"Why wouldn't it be?"

"Your dad? Isn't this like a family thing?"

Sebastian waved my concern away. "My parents can't make it. I'm representing."

Oh. I guess that was okay then.

After opening the door for me and holding my hand through the cold, Sebastian studied a television screen at the rink's entrance for a few seconds and said, "This way." He led me through a crowd of people, most of which said hello to him. He nodded at them. Waved. Smiled.

"Mr. Popularity," I teased.

"My brother's been playing hockey for years. Long practices. Lots of weekend tournament travel. You get to know people."

People. That covered it. Parents, grandparents, and girls. Lots of girls. All eyeing Sebastian—who could blame them—and me, especially the fact our hands were linked.

"Would it be weird if I asked how many of the girls staring us down right now you've dated?"

"None," he said.

"Right. And I've never suplexed anyone on their face."

"Okay, maybe a couple, but never anything serious."

Maybe he hadn't meant to, but his words triggered something in me. Were we serious? When you knew someone for years and had a history, dating was like dog years. Two weeks in real time meant a lot longer.

Either that, or the emotions controlling my every waking moment meant I was in a lot of trouble.

Sebastian pointed to the concession stand. "Hot chocolate? It can get cold in there."

"Sugar? You're living on the edge."

He pulled two packets of low-fat hot chocolate powder from his pocket.

"You bring hot chocolate packets from home?"

Sebastian waved to the guy behind the counter.

"Hey, Bash," the guy said with a glance at me. "The usual?"

"Two this time," Sebastian said. "This is Annalise."

"Hey, Annalise. Wolf."

I raised my eyebrows at Sebastian and whispered, "Wolf?"

He grinned.

"Here you go, man," Wolf said, putting two Styrofoam cups of steaming water on the counter.

Sebastian reached into his pocket, but Wolf wouldn't take his money. We thanked him and carried our hot water to an empty table in the lobby to mix our hot chocolate.

"This is low fat. And without the milk and whipped cream, it's manageable in season."

It'd been so long since I'd tasted chocolate, I had no doubt it would be incredible. Three girls in tight jeans and crop top sweaters passed us. "Hey, Bash," one of them called.

He waved but turned back to me.

"Not sure if I should be impressed they couldn't steal your attention or jealous that they want it."

"Is there an option for both?"

I laughed.

"A little bit of jealousy is kinda hot," he whispered.

"Noted," I said and sipped my drink. The water wasn't so hot that it burned my tongue, and the chocolate rushed over my senses as if announcing the party had arrived. "Oh my."

"Good, right?"

"Delicious. Thank you."

"You're welcome," he said and sipped his own drink.

I watched him watch the crowd wondering what this other part of his life was like. What was he like in school? At home? As big as he'd seemed in my life for so long, I only saw a snippet of his world. The fact everyone else called him Bash was a constant reminder of that.

"Is it okay that I call you Sebastian?" I asked.

"Sure," he said. "Why?"

"Everyone here calls you Bash."

"Everyone everywhere does. My friends. My family. You're the only one that calls me Sebastian, actually. Even Ashley's started calling me Bash."

"And your mom?"

He laughed. "Yeah. She calls me Sebastian."

So it was true. I was on par with his mother. "I can try to call you Bash. If you want." Secretly, I prayed he didn't want me to. Bash Love? Eh. That had a whole connotation I wanted to avoid. Not to get cheesy about his name, but he'd bashed my love life once upon a time, and I was hoping he didn't bash it again.

"Nah," he said with a grin. "I like that you call me Sebastian. It's special. Only for you."

I couldn't hide my own smirk.

"You're blushing," he said.

"I have no idea what you're talking about."

We both laughed, our eyes never leaving each other's.

He glanced at his watch and scooped up the blankets he'd brought from the back of his car. "The game's about to start. You ready to go in?"

"Sure."

The temperature dropped drastically when we stepped through the doorway from the lobby to the rink. I sipped my hot chocolate, letting the drink warm me. Sebastian headed for the glass and watched the skaters zipping around. When one skated toward him and tapped his stick on the clear barrier, Sebastian lightly pounded back. The player skated away, giving us a glimpse of the name on his jersey: Love.

"So that's him?"

"Yep. Christopher."

"How long has he played hockey?"

"Since he was four."

"Wow."

"He's pretty good." Sebastian pointed to an open row on the bleachers. I climbed the steps and helped him position a blanket under us. We sat on it, and he scooted close to drape the second blanket over our legs. "Trust me. You will want every bit of warmth after a few minutes of sitting in this ice box."

No explanation necessary. I was practically snuggling Sebastian in public. I hoped my heart could handle that enough to settle and watch the game.

"Where are your parents?"

"On their way back from a trip," Sebastian said. "How much do you know about hockey?"

I finished my hot chocolate, which was barely warm at that point, and wondered how best to explain my hockey knowledge. Bluntness probably. "I know that they play on ice, and they use sticks to do it."

"Okay. Sophisticated knowledge of hockey. Got it."

I nudged him with my shoulder. "Stop teasing me."

"Right. Because you don't like to be teased."

"I don't," I said, and maybe it was different with Sebastian, but I'd faced too much teasing over the years to say I enjoyed it.

He slipped his hands under the blanket and found mine. Then he squeezed. "Is this okay? Me holding your hand?"

I cleared my throat. "Yes. Fine."

"Sometimes it's like you go somewhere, like you get lost in your head. It makes me curious what you're thinking."

Almost always about you, I thought, but before I had to muster an actual response to the little-too-deep question, the players skated out to the middle of the ice, reminding me of a jump ball to start a basketball game. The ref dropped the puck, and the action began. So different from the building intensity of a wrestling match, the hockey game moved nonstop, shifting from the middle of the ice to one end and then back to the other.

"So it looks like I should be able to hang out tomorrow night after all," Sebastian said. "If you're still free."

"Sure," I said, the thought of more time with Sebastian warming my freezing limbs.

The ref blew the whistle, and the play stopped.

"What happened?" I asked.

"We were off sides." Sebastian explained that the first player to cross the blue line had to be the one with the puck.

"So no fast breaks like basketball where you can pass the puck up the ice?"

"Only into the neutral zone, but a player can't move into the offensive zone before the puck."

Interesting.

Sebastian explained the other common calls—icing, interference, tripping. Christopher scored a goal with only seconds left at the end of the first period, and we both jumped up, dropping the blanket to the bleachers. We clapped and cheered for Christopher, and Sebastian kissed me in celebration, too.

"He's going to be so pumped. He didn't score last game."

I opened my mouth to respond, but someone else did first.

"He played sluggish last game."

Sebastian and I turned to see his parents behind us. Had they seen us kiss? Oh my gosh. So embarrassing.

"Mom. Dad." Sebastian hugged his mom and nodded at his father. "Didn't realize you came in."

"You were a little distracted when we arrived," Mr. Love said, sending a pointed glance my way.

Good thing I'd been mastering my mental strength for years. It took all of it to stand with a smile on my face and focus on the moment instead of any number of alternatives, including spiraling about where Sebastian's father would whisk him off to keep him away from me and my "distraction".

"Right," Sebastian said. "You both remember Annalise Fiori?"

"Of course we do," his mom said. "Hi, Annalise. Good to see you."

"Thanks. You, too."

But Mr. Love did little more than grunt at me and turn his attention back to the game, which basically meant yelling at Christopher for every move he did or didn't make on the ice.

When Christopher missed a shot on a breakaway, Mr. Love stood and shouted at him. Sebastian glanced at me sideways and shook his head. If this was a glimpse of what he faced after every wrestling match—wow. I remembered what Rebecca had said about when I'd beaten Sebastian in middle school. For the first time, I actually felt bad for winning that day. I couldn't imagine what Mr. Love said to Sebastian when he'd lost to me.

Sebastian squeezed my knee under the blanket. "You okay?"

"Fine."

He tilted his head and whispered, "No, you're not."

"Lost in my thoughts."

"Still wondering about them."

I smiled. "Someday I'll tell you."

"I'm going to hold you to that."

Christopher scored again, interrupting my being completely lost in his older brother's words and eyes, and we started the whole jumping, clapping, shouting routine over. His team won 5-2. While Sebastian's parents chatted with other hockey parents in the lobby, Sebastian and I huddled in a corner, waiting for Christopher to leave the locker room.

"I'm not trying to hide you," he said. "I don't want you to get the wrong idea. Just trying to avoid my dad. I hate when he's in a mood."

"Christopher won. Why is he in a mood?"

"Winning is only half the battle."

"Sorry."

"Yeah. Sometimes I think I wouldn't be as good without him as my dad, you know? But other times, I want him to back the hell off."

"Makes sense."

He shook his head. "Enough of that. What are we doing tomorrow?"

"What do you want to do?"

"No hockey. I promise. Me, you, and a romantic, blow-your-mind date."

"Wow. Big expectations."

"I'm gonna back it up. I promise."

We did that swoony eye contact thing. Phew. Neither of us spoke but looking at someone like that was like communicating a million things at once. Like eye gazing told more truths than words ever could.

"Bash!" Christopher shouted from the hallway that led to the locker rooms. His hair, a lighter color than Sebastian's, was wet with sweat. His eyes were without question very blue, and I could imagine him torturing middle school girls the same way his brother had tortured me years earlier.

"Chris! Good game, bud. Two goals. Not bad."

"Thanks, bro. Is this…Annalise Fiori?"

I gave Sebastian a sideways glance.

"It is. I'd know you anywhere. You finally got her to go out with you, huh, Bash?"

"Shut up, please."

Giggles erupted from my throat. "Seems like you have a story to tell, Christopher."

"A few, actually. This guy has been—"

Sebastian covered his brother's mouth, trying to mask the gesture with a hug. "We should be going now. See you at home, Chris."

Christopher pushed his older brother away, not an easy task with a trained wrestler.

"Good game," I said.

Sebastian and I headed for the entrance with him pointedly not making eye contact with me.

"Are we not going to talk about that?"

"Nope," he said.

I laughed again. Christopher's teasing had been cute for sure, but more than anything, it confirmed what Sebastian had been telling me for weeks. Like Ashley had said, I was the one who got away, and all signs pointed to the fact that for years, Sebastian had wanted to change that.

I squeezed his hand and pulled him toward me in the parking lot, surprising him with a deep kiss. He had changed the course of our relationship, and I couldn't have been happier he managed it.

CHAPTER 33

SEBASTIAN AND I COMPETED AT TWO DIFFERENT places Sunday morning. At the advice of Mrs. Errico, I'd signed on for an all-girls tournament and recruited Fallon to join me. More than one hundred girls attended the open, not a huge number, but definitely a worthy showing.

Mrs. Errico introduced me and Fallon to some of the other local advocates working to sanction girls' wrestling in the state. They'd hosted fundraisers and petitions. They'd written proposals for their schools and athletic directors. They'd recruited girls to the sport.

"Any way you can help is great," said Zora, the wrestler I'd faced off against earlier that week at Pacific. "It took me some time to figure out what I wanted to do, so no rush."

That felt slightly less daunting. I filed helping the cause in the same folder as my art show pieces. I'd need time to figure them both out.

"It's kind of cool to think about Iron Valley having a girls' wrestling team," Fallon said with stars in her eyes.

I draped my arm around her shoulder and made a mental note to figure out my plans sooner rather than later. "Do you think your parents would be okay with you helping?"

"They'd love it. Nick could help, too. He still has one more year of high school."

Sometimes I forgot that.

We wished my new friends luck and refocused on our competition for the day. Between matches, I finished every ounce of homework I had to free up my schedule for my date that night. And I messaged Sebastian.

So many messages.

We'd been spending time together for less than two weeks. It felt like my whole life.

Fallon placed third, a huge accomplishment given how new she was to freestyle wrestling. Despite the distractions of the day, I took home the championship trophy for my weight class. Back at home, I put it next to my bed to remind me of my new mission—helping wrestlers like Zora and Fallon compete in the sport they loved.

My phone rang when I got out of the shower. Seeing Sebastian's name light up the screen spread a smile across my face.

"Hey," I said.

"Hey." His voice was laced with dread.

"What's wrong?"

"I'm sorry, but I have to reschedule."

Our date. Our only time all week to spend together between school, practices, matches, and weekend tournaments. "There's no other time we can schedule."

"I know," he said. "That's what makes it so much worse. I have to babysit. My little brother."

"Oh," I said, surprised. "The little brother that skates around an ice rink like an adult and scores hockey goals needs a babysitter?"

"I know. Technically, he's old enough to be home alone, but my mom doesn't trust him. I'm sorry."

"It's cool," I said. "It's nice of you to help your parents out."

"He'll probably challenge me to a Nerf battle and bribe me into making popcorn, so we can watch a movie."

"That sounds perfect," I said, sad to be missing out. "You'll have fun."

"Fun?" His voice had a weird humor to it I couldn't make sense of.

"Yeah. I have a collection of Nerf guns from battles with Ashley. You've seen our property. We're talking epic battles. Hiding weapons in the woods. Building forts. Climbing trees and sitting in wait."

"Do any of your guns still work?"

"Some, I'm sure. We have a couple boxes of them in the garage attic. What are you thinking?"

"That you can show up unexpected and destroy my brother."

"You want me to attack your little brother?"

"Don't underestimate him. He's vicious with his Nerf battles."

"Sebastian."

"I'm serious. One time, he dipped the tip of his darts in hot sauce and shot me in the eye."

I suppressed my laughter. "That's kind of hilarious."

"My eye, Lise!"

No suppressing at that point.

"Please? At least we can see each other then."

"Fine," I said. "But I'm wearing goggles."

"Probably smart. We'll be outside. I'll text the address. See you soon."

***

I PARKED A FEW HOUSES AWAY FROM SEBASTIAN'S and suited up—my white camo snow gear, vest of foam bullets, three loaded pistols, and a rapid-strike weapon, with an extra clip. In all, I could probably shoot Sebastian a good two hundred times. No way was I turning my weaponry on his little brother.

I approached the back yard from the neighbor's house and watched. Sebastian darted through the open space, and darts flew his way. I couldn't even tell where they were coming from. *Impressive, Christopher.*

Sebastian disappeared, too, and the yard went quiet.

Careful not to break any downed branches or sticks and reveal my location, I stepped lightly, searching the winterized porch furniture, woodpile, and tree trunks for a hiding Sebastian. Maybe he was up in a tree somewhere.

"Don't move," said a young voice from behind me.

I raised my hands and turned slowly. Christopher hadn't bothered with camouflage. Not that it mattered. He had more ammo than an armory. Vests. Fanny packs. Overflowing cargo pants pockets. By the looks of it, he even had bullets tucked under his oddly shaped hat.

"So my brother sends his girlfriend to do his dirty work."

I didn't know which statement to refute first—me being Sebastian's girlfriend or the fact I was here to help him.

"You're well-armed, Annalise Fiori. I'll give you that."

"Is that enough to earn me a spot on your team?"

He squinted at me, untrusting. "You're gonna shoot Bash for me?"

"With pleasure," I said.

A grin spread across his face, but he turned serious again. "How do I know I can trust you?"

I leaned forward and whispered, "Because I know how to pick the winning side."

"My brother never stood a chance against me."

"Now we can have some real fun," I said.

"Deal."

"What's your plan?"

***

CHRISTOPHER LOVE HAD A DEVIOUS SOUL. I WOULD call Sebastian's cell, and Christopher would attack his location when we heard it ring. Then I'd circle around the back of the yard by way of the neighbors' houses, climb a tree Christopher had pointed out, and wait for him to lead Sebastian my way. We'd crush him from both sides.

"You ready?" I asked, my phone in hand.

"Always. Don't turn on me."

I shook my head. "Loyal to the end."

The grand declaration satisfied Christopher's battling spirit. I dialed. The call rang on my end, but Sebastian must have silenced his phone. Christopher scowled. I held up a finger warning him to be patient.

"Hello?" Sebastian whispered.

"Hey," I said. "I'm here, I think. I don't know if I have the right house. Do you see me?"

Across the yard, Sebastian poked his head out from behind the woodpile.

"Got him," Christopher said.

I hung up and silenced my own phone. It buzzed immediately. I texted, "Sorry. I found it. I see your car. Parking and suiting up now. Be back there in a minute to rescue you."

"You're evil," Christopher whispered and laughed.

"He's in a perfect position," I said. The tree I'd intended to climb was behind him. "I don't even have to climb. I'll circle around, and when you see my signal, attack."

He nodded.

I took cover behind sheds, playsets, and trees until I made my way around the back of Sebastian's house. From behind the tree, I had the perfect view of him peeking around the edge of the woodpile, looking toward the front yard, waiting for me to arrive. I actually felt a little bad for him. Not bad enough to switch sides, though.

I waved to Christopher, and he charged across the yard, yelling and firing at the woodpile.

"Rookie mistake," Sebastian yelled. "I have the best spot in the yard."

"Think again," I said from behind him.

Before he spun around, I'd already hit him twice in the back. The surprise on his face made me giggle and miss my next shot. I recovered, though, dodging his bullets by hiding behind the tree.

Christopher refilled his weapon. "Surrender!"

"You know that's not my style." Sebastian charged, ignoring the hits I unleashed at him. He grabbed me and used me as a shield.

"I can't let you do that, brother," Christopher yelled. "I swore an oath to protect her." He pulled a blue bubble from his bag.

"No!" Sebastian said. "It's thirty degrees out here, Chris!"

But Christopher kept coming and launched the water balloon at Sebastian's head. He tried to dodge it, dropping me in the process. Christopher grabbed my hand and pulled me toward the house. Sebastian chased after us, but Christopher launched more water balloons at him until he was soaked and more than a little angry. We made it through the front door. Christopher slammed it behind us and turned the lock.

"He'll get in with the code through the garage. We only have a couple minutes. Get your snow clothes off."

We peeled off our boots and outerwear, leaving them on a beach towel apparently left in the entryway for a quick escape like ours. Christopher took my hand, and we ran up the stairs. He slammed the first door we passed. "He'll think we're hiding there." Down the hall, we ducked into another room. A boy's bedroom, clean and tidy. Christopher closed the door.

"Is this your brother's room?" I asked.

"Yep. We need a plan."

A whole garden of butterflies fluttered in my gut. I glanced at the bed, with its blue and red plaid bedspread. That's where he was when he messaged me early in the morning. Or late at night. Did he sleep without a shirt on?

Probably shouldn't think about that.

"I'll hide under the bed," Christopher said. "You take the closet."

The garage door chugged open below us, and Christopher held his finger to his lips. We tiptoed to our positions, reloading along the way. As Christopher had predicted, Sebastian didn't find us immediately, which gave me a few minutes to take in the inside of his closet.

His room had looked like a picture on a website, but the closet told a different story. Clothes had missed the hamper or fallen from their hangers. Shelves begged to be reorganized. So did a pile of smashed shoes in the corner.

A picture frame on the floor caught my eye. I cast light over the image with the flashlight on my phone. No way. Not possible. In the picture, Sebastian stood on the second-place step of a podium. From the first-place step, thirteen-year-old me stared into the camera.

The trophy in my hand in the photo was the one I'd kept next to my bed for years.

Sebastian had kept a picture of that day. A *framed* picture.

The closet door opened, and a foam bullet hit me in the side before I could react. When Sebastian saw what was in my hands, he lowered his weapon. Christopher rolled out from under the bed and shuffled out of the room, firing the whole time. Sebastian closed his bedroom door for cover and with the sound of his brother's footsteps fading down the hall, he said, "I can explain."

CHAPTER 34

HE TOOK THE PHOTO FROM MY HANDS.

"Waiting for that explanation," I said, leaving the closet and standing in his bedroom with my arms across my chest. Yes, things were happening between Sebastian and me, but there was something strange about finding out the boy you avoided for years actually kept a picture of you in his room. Without your knowledge.

"I learned a lot of lessons that day. This picture reminds me of them."

"Lessons? Such as?"

"To have the courage to tell people the truth. That sometimes you lose. That sometimes for the person you care about to win, you have to sacrifice."

"Sacrifice? Like you let me win?"

"No," he said immediately. "You kicked my ass fair and square, but I was happy for you, Lise. I was proud of you."

"Oh."

"I still am."

"Thanks," I whispered, letting my suspicion settle and wondering what had made me suspicious to begin with. Old habits? "Why was it on the floor of your closet?"

"It didn't used to be. I kept it on my nightstand actually, but when we started spending time together, my dad got even weirder about it.

I put it in here the other day."

I sat on the edge of his bed, working to digest the fact that while I kept a trophy reminding me of my victory over him next to my bed for four years, he'd looked at a picture of me beating him with pride.

"Why is your dad weird about us spending time together?"

Sebastian sighed. "Can we not talk about my dad, please?"

I competed in one of the toughest sports in the world daily. Giving up on something didn't coincide with my nature, but Sebastian's expression softened my intensity.

A little.

"Are you two ever coming out of there?" Christopher called. "You know what Mom says about having girls in your room."

"Do you have girls in your room a lot?" I teased, trying to lighten the mood.

"Never. That's what my mom says about it."

I raised weapons in both hands, fully loaded and ready to rejoin Christopher's team. Sebastian tried to block the onslaught. And failed. Christopher dove into the room, his fire enhancing mine.

"I surrender!" Sebastian lifted his pillow as a shield. "Stop, Chris, and I'll make you popcorn."

Christopher immediately stopped. "And let me pick the movie?"

"Yes. After I change out of these freezing, wet clothes."

Christopher glanced at me, and I nodded my approval. We lowered our weapons.

"I owned you," Christopher said.

"Sometimes, I wish you wrestled, so I could kick your butt when you get like this."

"What makes you think if I wrestled, you'd be able to kick my butt?" Christopher fired back causing me to snort laugh.

Christopher Love. A boy after my heart.

***

THE SNACK POPPED IN THE MICROWAVE, AND SEBAS-tian filled cups of water for us.

"Can we have butter this time?" Christopher asked.

"You can," Sebastian said.

Christopher retrieved the butter from the fridge and tossed it to Sebastian. "Even your girlfriend is better at Nerf battles than you. You should be embarrassed."

Sebastian raised his eyebrows at me. "Oh, I'm embarrassed."

Christopher looked back and forth between us. "This sounds like some grown up thing that I don't get. Bring my popcorn in when it's done, please. Thanks."

He headed for the living room, leaving Sebastian and me alone in the kitchen.

"Nothing like a little brother to put you in your place."

"At first, I thought it was silly that he called me your girlfriend, but then I discovered a picture of me in your closet and thought maybe him growing up seeing that picture made a little more sense why he thought I was your girlfriend."

"There's something else I didn't tell you about the picture."

I froze.

"Nothing bad. The truth is I kept it because I liked it. Because I liked you. My mom had all these wrestling pictures printed, and that one—it was the only thing I had of you."

"That's actually kind of cute."

"I wasn't lying when I said I liked you back then. I thought you were the coolest girl I'd ever seen, and I hated myself for being so stupid and messing it up. I guess part of me is afraid I'm going to repeat history."

The microwave dinged, and the popcorn stopped popping.

"Is it in poor taste for me to say that I'm disappointed my little brother got you into my bedroom before I did?"

I threw a kitchen towel at him. "Yes. It is."

He smirked and worked his way around the table, never taking his eyes off mine. "Excuse me for being crazy about my girlfriend."

His words pinned me to the floor.

"Yes," he said. "I called you my girlfriend. Is that a problem?"

I didn't know what to say. Was it? "What does it mean to be your girlfriend?"

He fought a smile. "Like what are the perks?"

"You can start there."

"I won't shoot you with Nerf bullets no matter whose team you're on."

"Go on."

"I bring you low fat hot chocolate powder."

I laughed. "Enticing. Next?"

"So demanding. Okay, what else?" He tickled my waist with his fingertips. "You can kiss me anytime you want."

"Getting warmer."

He nodded and grinned. "I hope so." He gently nudged me against the counter and ran his fingers through my windblown hair before pressing his mouth against mine. My body melted into his. I slid my hands to his waist and twisted my fingers into his shirt, pulling him closer.

"Gross," Christopher said. He retrieved the popcorn from the microwave and poured it into a bowl. "Probably gonna throw this right back up after seeing that."

"And now *I'm* embarrassed," I said, burying my head into Sebastian's chest.

He wrapped his arms around me and sighed. "Thanks for coming here to hang out with us."

"I wanted to see you."

"Good. I wanted to see you, too."

"Movie's starting," Christopher called.

Sebastian laced his fingers in mine, and we headed for the living room. Christopher patted the couch next to him. "Sit by me, Annalise."

"No way, buddy," Sebastian said. "Annalise is my date."

"Gross again. She's my teammate, and teammates stick together."

"He's not wrong," I said, dropping Sebastian's hand. "I'd love to sit with you, Christopher."

He stood to let me get comfortable and then settled in, nestling his head on my shoulder and his bowl of popcorn on my lap. We were all out cuddling. Sebastian raised his eyebrows at me, but I shrugged.

"I like how you call me Christopher," he said.

"Is there something else I should call you?"

"Everyone calls me Chris, but everyone calls him Bash, and you call him Sebastian. It's kinda special."

"Are you trying to steal my girl, buddy?" Sebastian teased.

"She already likes me better than you," Christopher said. "You probably shouldn't put ideas in her head."

I laughed a little too hard at that.

"Let's start the movie," Sebastian said.

"He knows I speak the truth," Christopher whispered, making me laugh again.

"You're a cool kid, you know that?"

He tilted his head to the side and glanced at the ceiling. "Yep."

Sebastian started the movie. Christopher tucked me in with a blanket, and after the first ten minutes, I couldn't tell you what happened. Until Mrs. Love tapped my shoulder to wake me up.

"Oh my gosh. I'm so sorry."

"It's okay. Too many early mornings and workouts. Happens to Sebastian all the time." She pointed to the other couch where he was passed out, too.

Some babysitters we were. "Is Christopher okay?"

"He fell asleep in your arms, sweet thing. I tucked him in already. I hate to send you home half asleep."

"I'll be okay."

"How about some cold water and a few minutes under the bright kitchen lights to wake up?"

Her mothering made me smile. "Thanks, Mrs. Love."

"Sure thing. Sebastian, darling?" She nudged him awake, too, and told him the plan to get me perked up before I got behind the wheel. He took my hand in front of his mom, which made my heart turn in my chest more than the best freestyle wrestling opponent could turn me on a mat. "Nice to see you, Annalise. Thanks for helping with Christopher."

"Any time," I said.

She disappeared up the stairs, leaving me to admire her son and his adorably ruffled hair and sleepy eyes. In the kitchen, he opened a drawer and took out a red container. "Cinnamon gum. It will light your mouth on fire and wake you right up."

"Is this why you always smell like cinnamon early in the morning?"

He handed me two white cubes with red dots. "Yep."

I tossed them into my mouth, and an explosion of cinnamon

popped my eyes wide open. "Impressive."

Sebastian chewed for a few seconds and then pulled me to him against the counter. "That and I wanted to kiss you goodbye."

"Goodbye," I whispered.

He gave me a soft, cinnamony kiss. Then another in the privacy of the garage before he slipped his boots on.

"You don't have to go out there. It's freezing."

"I'm walking my girlfriend to her car, thank you."

He kissed me again in the cold, but mid-shiver, I insisted he go inside. When I drove away, he waved to me from his garage, and I couldn't nudge the smile from my face.

***

SEBASTIAN TEXTED TWO MINUTES AFTER I CHANGED into my PJs and brushed my teeth.

Sebastian: You get home okay?

Me: Yep. Thanks for a fun night.

Sebastian: We literally both fell asleep. Not the most exciting date ever.

I sent him laughing emojis and curled up in bed, eager to fall back into the deep sleep I'd experienced on his couch, curled up with his brother.

Me: Surprised you could sleep with all your jealousy.

Sebastian: You mean because you were cuddling my brother? I had to fall asleep to put myself out of my misery.

My giggles attracted the attention of Ashley who was walking down the hallway to the bathroom. "You look happy."

I inhaled and held onto the breath as if it were my happiness. "I am."

"Good," she said. "You deserve it."

Against my better judgment, I was starting to believe it.

CHAPTER 35

"C'MON, SEBASTIAN," I SAID UNDER MY BREATH. THE
week had passed without much excitement. Without any other choice,
I'd submitted my fall series for the art show deadline, which was that
day. I didn't have big expectations. Maybe the next year would be
different.

Sebastian and I had both won our school matches that week. We'd
woken up early to train and saw each other at the club in the evenings.
He'd given me a ride home from a few practices, sneaking kisses
when he dropped me off.

I'd painted and painted over what I had painted.

The week had felt blah, not in a way I could quantify. Maybe
fewer messages and phone calls from my *boyfriend*. No time together
outside of practice. So when Sebastian had asked if I'd come to his
tournament Saturday, I agreed without a second thought.

Boyfriend or not, I would not be one of those people who pounded
on the mat and screamed at someone who was concentrating with
every ounce of their energy on the same things I was yelling at them.

Mr. Love, though, had other plans.

"Head up! Head up! Off your knees! Don't reach back!" And it
went on.

The clock ticked down. Sebastian needed two more points to take the lead. Twenty seconds. C'mon. Fifteen seconds. He was so close to getting back points. So close!

"Yes! That's it!"

So much for not yelling.

But then his opponent reversed control, and the clock flashed zeros with Sebastian losing by four points. He laid on the mat a few extra seconds, deflated. But then he hopped up and showed the kind of sportsmanship I'd expect.

After chatting with his coach, he lowered his eyes and sighed. My heart lurched, seeing him so disappointed. He walked in my direction, but his dad stepped between us.

And it started.

"What were you thinking? You should have never…"

I turned away to give them privacy, but still heard Sebastian's voice.

"Dad, I know."

Mr. Love raised his voice.

"If you knew, you wouldn't have done it. How could you lose to that kid? You've beaten him five times this season."

"I know that too, Dad."

"How do you expect college coaches to react when you're losing matches like this?" He didn't wait for an answer because I was pretty sure he didn't care for one. "You better get focused. I don't want to see another loss today. You got me?"

Sebastian didn't respond. What could he say? His toughest opponent would be next. Someone he'd never beaten. Someone who'd pinned him multiple times. He could be blinded by his father's flawed expectations, or he could be realistic. He tucked his headgear into his bag and walked away from his dad.

"I'm not done talking to you," Mr. Love said.

"Well, I am," Sebastian said. In a few steps, his arm was around my shoulders. "Do you have a few minutes to walk with me?"

"Sure," I said.

"Bash!" his father called behind us. I turned to see Mrs. Love grabbing her husband's arm and speaking into his ear.

"Is he following us?" Sebastian asked.

"Your mom stopped him."

"He's an ass."

I didn't know how to respond to that. Kind of a losing situation. Sebastian could say anything he wanted about his dad, but it wasn't my place to agree. At least not out loud.

"I'm sorry about your match."

"I'm not," he said with a shrug. "I mean I want to win, but that kid got way stronger than the last time I saw him. And he moved better. I wasn't ready for it. I expected less of him. Lesson learned."

How in the world was his reaction to the loss more mature than his father's?

We walked hand-in-hand down the hallway until we were as far from the gym as we could be. With each step, Sebastian's posture slumped more.

I squeezed him into a hug. No words were needed. He pulled at me, too, and took four deep breaths.

"My dad," he muttered. "He wants me to…"

"He wants you to what?"

Sebastian rested his head on my shoulder. "He wants me to do something I don't want to, and I…I can't."

"Do you want to talk about what it is?"

He shook his head.

"I'm sorry."

We held onto each other. Each squeeze communicated the kind of care we both craved.

"Thanks for being here," he said.

"Anytime."

"No. I mean it. Seeing you next to the mat, being able to walk away with you. I dreaded this season, but I was so wrong."

"Why did you dread it?"

"My dad's expectations. He wants me to wrestle at some big school."

"What do you want?"

"Not sure. Maybe not to even wrestle in college."

"Wow."

"Yeah. Not exactly part of Dad's plans. He's adamant me spending time with you is distracting me."

So his dad hadn't backed off. Not that I should have been surprised. "Is he the reason you've been quieter this week? Fewer messages? No invitations to hang out?"

"Maybe a little. I'm sorry. I didn't realize I was doing that. Are you mad?"

"No," I admitted. "Even though in some ways this doesn't feel new, it still kind of is, and I guess it makes me wonder when you message less if I should read into that."

"You should not."

I took a deep breath. "Okay."

"That was easy," he said.

"I trust you."

He swallowed and nodded. "You excited for tonight?"

The winter formal. An entire evening with Sebastian. Excited didn't cover it.

"I've been having dreams about you in that dress."

Sparks lit up my body. "Oh really?"

He froze. "Do you ever wonder if you said something aloud?"

"Oh, you said that aloud."

"Didn't scare you away, though," he whispered.

"It took a lot to get us here. It's going to take a lot to scare me away."

CHAPTER 36

MAYBE I'D BEEN WRONG. STANDING IN THE neck-plunging dress in front of my sister's bedroom mirror was enough to scare me out of going to the dance.

"You look hot, Lise," Ashley said and whistled.

"Thanks." I took a deep breath. The black lace edges of the v-neck dress plunged in the back and the front with spaghetti straps crossing over my upper back. The dress covered my legs until I walked and revealed the slit up to my thigh. The lace edging gave way to sequins that didn't quit.

I'd never worn anything like it in my entire life.

"I can't tell if I like the back or the front better," Ashley said.

Me either.

"I think Bash is gonna have the same problem," my sister teased.

To my mom's credit, she controlled her surprise with a hand over her mouth when she saw the dress. Her eyes were only as wide as volleyballs for ten, maybe twenty seconds. "Is that even allowed?"

I shook the small plastic box in my hand. "I have safety pins for any spots you think are too much."

"Good thinking." She studied the dress more closely and then put the plastic box down. "You look strong and beautiful. You're a young woman now, and if this is the dress you want to wear, I support you."

I hugged her. "Thanks, Mom."

Outside, a cavalcade of cars with our black party bus leading trailed down our long drive. Nick and Sebastian's families were meeting us here, and then we'd hop in the party bus to pick up Melanie, Chandra, and their dates at Melanie's house. Nick stopped and dramatically placed his hand over his heart when he saw my sister. My eyes found Sebastian and locked onto him as if they couldn't work in any other direction. Lucky for me, he did the same.

"Annalise," Christopher called, running across the lawn. "You look sparkly."

"Thanks, buddy."

"Too bad seniors can't come to the middle school dances. I'd take you in a second."

"But then all the middle school girls would be jealous. I don't want to ruin your game like that."

"You're probably right," he said. "Is this your yard? We could have some great Nerf battles here."

"Anytime."

By then, Sebastian stood in front of me with a wrist corsage in a clear, plastic box. "My brother is trying to steal you away from me."

"As if anyone could manage that," I said, and he smiled wider than I'd ever seen.

"You always know the right thing to say."

"In that case, you look gorgeous."

He grinned. "That's what I was going for. You look even better."

"Better than in your dreams?"

I giggled when pink flushed his cheeks.

"I shouldn't have said that aloud."

I shook my head. "Nope."

"But to answer your question, yes. Definitely. Yes."

The photography marathon commenced. Me and Christopher. Me, Christopher, and Sebastian. Us and his family. Even Mr. Love wore a smile.

"Hello, Annalise," he said.

"Hello, Mr. Love," I said just as formally.

"You look beautiful." The way he said it, you'd think the words had been laced with poison.

Sebastian pulled me into a hug and whispered, "My mom made him promise to be nice. Roll with it."

A lot to unpack there but guess it would have to wait. "Thank you, Mr. Love."

"I hope you and my son have a good time tonight."

I forced an equally pained smile. My mother and sister saved me, asking for a picture. And on it went. Good thing we had early spring weather. Otherwise, we would have frozen mid photoshoot.

"Those shoes look treacherous," Sebastian said, studying the purple heels I'd bought to honor his favorite color.

"You have no idea."

"I like the color."

"I thought you might. Are you going to frame one of these pictures and put it next to your bed?"

He scoffed and then regained his composure. "Yes. Yes, I am."

"I might, too."

"You mean to replace the trophy you earned by kicking my ass?"

"How did you know about that?"

"Ashley."

My sister, the Sebastian and Annalise relationship enthusiast. "Of course. Listen, Sebastian."

"I don't judge."

"No. The thing is, I moved that trophy weeks ago. After we came back from the woods."

"You did?"

I slipped my arm in his. "I thought maybe I should put it behind me."

His eyes sparkled with the most gorgeous colors the planet had to offer, and he didn't release my gaze until his mother hugged him to say goodbye.

The party bus burst with loud music and laughter. We started the dancing early under the flashing, multi-colored lights and the music videos playing on the televisions. When everyone was aboard, we stopped at a local park for more pictures. My face hurt from all the smiling but looking around at these friends. These were my people. So much in my life—my training, my diet, and my sport—was so controlled. Letting loose with Sebastian brought me to this moment.

Excitement. Peace. Home.

And the feeling didn't stop the whole night, not even when the DJ called the last dance. A slow one, music crooned from the speakers, luring me into Sebastian's arms. I rested my head on his shoulder, and he tickled my bare back without saying a word.

"You're quiet," I said.

"Trying to figure out what to say."

"About?"

"Us."

I lifted my head to look at him. "Is there something wrong with us?"

"That's the thing," Sebastian said. "There isn't. Us...this...it's amazing."

"Then what's the problem?"

"Okay, don't freak out. I'm torn between trying to play it cool but then wondering if you didn't know how I felt, would you pull away? Or I could tell you how crazy I am about you, scare you, and maybe you pull away anyway."

His mental dilemma made perfect sense to someone like me. I was allergic to vulnerability. Maybe over the years Sebastian had picked up on that aversion. Maybe he was a little vulnerability-averse himself.

"Didn't you kind of just tell me though?" I said, trying to soften the conversation.

"You weren't supposed to notice that."

"Slick."

"Thank you," he said, deadpan.

But I had a question that wouldn't stop playing in my mind. "Is there any scenario that I don't pull away?"

He laughed. "You tell me."

I pressed my cheek against his and whispered in his ear. "All of them." His cheek pressed against mine harder. My answer had made him smile.

"Sometimes I'm surprised at how honest you are," he said with a chuckle.

"I've always been honest. Think back to a few weeks ago. Wasn't I incredibly candid about how I felt about you then?"

"In the most brutal fashion."

True. "Now you get to see my honesty from a sweet side."

"I'm glad."

"You've earned it."

He leaned his forehead against mine, and I closed my eyes, letting my other senses take over. The feel of his hands on my waist, one cheating as low as he could on my back. His chest and his forehead against mine. His cinnamon breath on my cheek. His clean scent, much less rustic than his after-wrestling smell. The sound of his voice when he whispered the words that worked like magical keys, unlocking parts of myself I'd sworn away for years.

The way his soft lips tasted.

Delicious.

Divine.

Telling me everything I needed to know.

But there was another sense, one that people didn't talk about. Like the pull and push on the wrestling mat, an undeniable magnetism drew me to Sebastian, telling me he was near even if my other senses failed me. It pushed me into his arms, my lips onto his lips, my heart into his hands. The vulnerability of caring about me that also gave me strength by being close to him.

Under no circumstances did that pull lead me away from Sebastian.

CHAPTER 37

LEAVE IT TO PENNSYLVANIA WEATHER. EVEN BY MON-
day, temperatures were still in the fifties, but the forecast called for
a huge snowstorm on Wednesday. One that had teachers scrambling
to reschedule tests and reorganize schedules and Coach Joseph an-
ticipating Wednesday's practice would be canceled.

"We'll have to prepare for Thursday's Senior Night today," he said
at the end of practice. "Does everyone have their escorts planned?"

I glanced at Sebastian, and he raised an eyebrow at me. I nodded,
and he grinned. I guess I had mine, and I couldn't stop smiling about
it.

"For anyone who doesn't," Coach continued. "Figure it out by
tomorrow and let them know you'll need them here before the match.
Next, we'll have wrestle-offs tomorrow since I don't expect to have
practice on Wednesday."

At this point in the season—with only one match left—wrestle-offs were a formality. Nothing new there, so I let my mind wander
to Senior Night. Mom had asked if I wanted to have a special dinner
with her and Ashley. She even said I could invite Sebastian, but
maybe he had plans with his own family. Ashley would get balloons
and flowers, no doubt. Should the seniors plan gifts for the coaches?

I stretched my shoulders while Coach read the short list. After

Thursday's match, I'd have to decide how to spend the post-season. Mrs. Errico had encouraged girls involved with the sanctioning movement to participate in girl-only post-season activities. The problem was they weren't officially sanctioned. If I won a state championship at the girls' competition, I wouldn't be an official state champion, but I was already a two-time state champion in the boys' brackets from when I was younger. It might be cool to earn a title in the girls' contest, too.

"Annalise," Coach said, getting my attention.

"Yes, Coach?"

He looked up from his list.

"Wrestle-offs. Tomorrow."

What? That couldn't be right. There wasn't even anyone else on the team in my weight class. Coach looked back at his list and said, "Sebastian."

I shook my head. He must mean Sebastian was wrestling Kurt for their weight class. Not for mine. But Coach never said Kurt's name.

The next day, I'd wrestle against Sebastian for my weight class.

Words flooded my mind. Not ones that formed complete sentences, and definitely not ones I could say out loud.

"Did you know about this?" Dom whispered.

I didn't answer.

"I'll take the look on your face as a no."

Coach called the end of practice. My teammates headed for the locker room. I sat right where I was, unable to process thoughts or emotions.

Sebastian hovered over me. "Annalise?"

Senior Night. *My* weight class. *My* school. I shook my head. How…? Why…?

"Annalise, please talk to me."

"You cut weight? You cut weight to take my spot? You had your own spot."

"I can explain."

"On Senior Night? Right before the post season?" If I lost my spot on the roster at the end of the season, I wouldn't have the option of competing in boys' states. Sebastian would take it instead. "Why would you do that to me?"

"I…"

"The dance? The other times we've gone out? What was that? Your way of distracting me from working out, so you could take my spot?"

"It's not like that."

I pointed to the mat where he'd been sitting. "You sat there and nodded at me like you wanted to escort me on Senior Night."

"I do."

"My head's going to explode. You want to escort me, be my boyfriend, but then you're wrestling me for my spot on this team without even having the decency to tell me about it?"

"Okay, there's a lot there. Let me start at the beginning."

I collected my stuff. "Don't bother."

"Lise, please."

My nickname on his tongue cut through me, emotions overflowing with no hopes of being contained by my careful control.

I glared at him. "Only my friends call me Lise."

I held it together until I got to my bathroom. In the boy-free sanctuary, I pressed my back to the door, slid down until the floor caught me, and let four years of torturous vulnerability pour through my tears.

***

MY RIDE HOME, DOM KNOCKED TEN MINUTES LATER.

"Lise, you ready?"

"Is the coast clear?"

His footsteps faded down the hall and then came back again. "He's showering."

I threw open the door. "Let's get out of here."

In the front seat of Dom's car, I pulled my hoodie over my face. How had I let this happen twice? That fool me once, fool me twice saying came to mind. Four years ago, I'd come out on top, but I wasn't sure I could beat Sebastian the next day. For one, I'd been distracted. By him and his flirtation and his let's go to a dance crap.

And his lips.

I groaned.

"It's gonna be okay," Dom said.

"I feel so stupid."

"For what it's worth, I think he really likes you."

I tore the hoodie off my face. "Do not defend him. Not now."

He lifted his hands in surrender.

I wanted to crawl under the seat. If I couldn't face my best friend, how was I going to get in front of the whole team and wrestle Sebastian for my own spot? My phone buzzed. Sebastian's name lit the screen.

I silenced the call.

"You're not going to talk to him?"

"No," I said. "I'm going to go home and build a strategy to beat him tomorrow."

"In the grand scheme, this last meet won't matter to you."

"So you think I'm going to lose?"

"I didn't say that."

"It's Senior Night. Of my high school team. Mine. Not his. He doesn't even go to Iron Valley. I've spent my entire school years listening to boys talk about how girls shouldn't wrestle, and boys shouldn't have to wrestle girls, and the only reason I beat boys is because they're too afraid to hurt me. For years, Dom. Years!"

"Don't forget who's been next to you the whole time."

"I know you have, and I appreciate it. This is my last opportunity to wrestle as an Iron Valley Viking, and it's at risk. Not to mention the post season."

"You can beat him."

"Maybe, but we're evenly matched. I have stronger technique because as a girl what other choice do I have, but he's stronger. But you know what else I have?"

He didn't answer, so I took his silence as an invitation to answer my own question.

"I have this rage in my body from being played by him yet again, which you think would be a good thing, but it's kind of balanced by my humiliation. If I let that cloud my thoughts, I give him the upper hand. It could go either way."

"Get it in your head that it's going your way."

My phone buzzed again. Ignore.

Get in my head that I'm going to beat Sebastian in a live wrestling match when I've been dating him for weeks and have been too uncomfortable to even drill with him in practice?

Easier said than done.

CHAPTER 38

AFTER PRACTICE, I DROPPED MY BAGS INTO MY GA-
rage locker and changed into hiking boots. The path welcomed me,
the branches waving lightly in the breeze. A family of deer huddled
in the brush and lowered their heads as I passed. I mentally thanked
them for their solidarity, turned down Sunset Path, and didn't stop
walking until I arrived at the clearing and my thinking stump.

I'd shown Sebastian that stump. I'd told him how I'd cried on it in
middle school. He'd *promised* he wouldn't mess things up this time.

I tossed a branch over the hillside and watched it roll, roll, roll to
the bottom where it crashed against the base of a tree. I bet the rolling
had been fun for the branch. Exciting, adventurous, maybe even a
spark or two. The crashing, though, probably not so fun.

My phone buzzed with a message from my sister. "Where are
you? Nick told me what happened. Are you okay?"

The news was spreading.

I forced my mind to imagine Sebastian on the mat, ignoring the
crushing in my chest. He liked to feel out his opponent before shooting. He always went for the doubles. I could study all the moves to
counter that, but I couldn't outlast him on the mat. He was too strong
and well-conditioned. But with my longer arms and technique, I had

a good shot of taking him down with an ankle pick. At practices, I was usually able to hit it at least once during a live go.

Except he knew all my moves. He knew my strategy. He'd be wrestling to win. This wouldn't be practice.

A small tugboat glided over the glass of the river's surface, pushing a barge of coal. It seemed to glide easily, but in reality, that little tugboat fought for every inch of that river. It pushed a huge weight.

I connected with that tugboat on a deep level.

Footsteps crunched the snow on the path.

"Ashley, I told you I'm fine."

They kept coming. I wiped away the tears from my cold cheeks, not willing to let even my sister see me like that, but when I turned to show Ashley how strong I was, my heart was the part of my body that froze.

"Hey," Sebastian said.

"What are you doing here?"

"I needed to talk to you."

"No," I said. "Leave."

"Annalise, please."

After everything that had happened that day, my heart broke a little more at the sound of him using my full name.

"You promised you weren't going to mess things up," I whispered.

"I didn't mean to. It wasn't—"

I put my hands up to stop him. In a way, I did want him to go, but another part of me wanted the truth. On the ride home, a few details had flashed in my memory. Something Sebastian's father wanted him to do, but he'd refused. The way his father had felt about me. His joke that his father basically expected him to wrestle a bear. "How long has this been going on?"

"What exactly?"

"When did the possibility of you dropping to my weight first come up?"

He closed his eyes, and his shoulders deflated. "The beginning of the season."

Wow.

"My dad thought I could be competitive at that weight. Knock off a few pounds, but still maintain my muscle mass. I told him I didn't want to starve myself. He fought me on it, but then he put two and two together about why I didn't want to drop."

"Me."

He nodded.

We watched the tugboat in silence until it disappeared around the curve of the landscape.

"I told him I wouldn't do it a million times," Sebastian said.

"Yet here we are."

"Look, you don't get it, okay. Your mom is perfect. She supports everything you do. My dad went around me when he didn't get what he wanted. I had this college coach looking at me, but he needs someone at 126. His 132 slot is taken. My dad promised him that wouldn't be a problem and talked to Coach Joseph without me knowing. I found out the same time you did."

I swallowed hard. "Then why do it?"

"I have to."

"No, you don't."

"Yes, I do. My parents made it clear if I wanted to choose my college, then I'd better be bringing money to the table. Either academically or athletically, or both. I can't refuse to wrestle because I…"

"Because you what?"

"Nothing." He took a deep breath. "I'm sorry. I can't refuse to wrestle you, but if there's anything else I can do…"

A memory from my first year of high school wrestling struck me. "There is something."

"Name it," he said, hope in his voice.

"Coach used to talk about the importance of the handshake before and after the match. Have you ever heard this?"

"Yeah. At the beginning of the match, it's all about promising your opponent you'll give them your best effort."

"Exactly," I said. "And asking for theirs. At the end, the handshake symbolizes thanks for giving that effort."

"Where are you going with this?"

"When you get on the mat, I want you to promise me your best effort. I'm going to give it everything, and I want to know the outcome is real. It would hurt me even more if you didn't try as hard as you could."

He paused for a couple seconds and then nodded. "I promise."

"Good. Now, go. I have a match to get ready for."

***

I HIKED OUT OF THE WOODS TWENTY MINUTES LATER to find a pile up of cars in our driveway. None were Sebastian's, thankfully. Still, I couldn't face all the questions and conversations. I snuck in the front door, but Ashley intercepted me. She squeezed me into the best sister hug.

"I'm sorry, Lise."

"Thanks."

"C'mon." She pulled me toward the basement stairs.

"No. I don't want to…" Do whatever she and her friends were doing.

Chandra called my name, and I trudged down the steps out of duty. At the bottom though, my mouth dropped. Dom had his computer hooked up to the big screen with a selection of video files from our matches this year—all with Sebastian's name on them. Melanie held a tray of healthy snacks. Ashley patted the couch next to her where she worked on her laptop.

"We're your prep team," she said. "I'm scouting YouTube for all of Sebastian's tournament matches this season, especially the ones he lost."

"I have our school meets ready," Dom said, and pointed to school supplies on the coffee table. "And a notebook and pencil."

"I don't know what to say."

"Say you'll beat his smarmy ass," Chandra said, scrolling through her phone.

"What's your contribution?" I asked.

"Posting pictures of you in that hot dress from winter formal all over social, so he can see them and think about what he's done."

We all laughed, and, oh, it felt good to laugh.

I held out my arms wide. "You all are amazing."

My crew hustled from their spots into a group hug that almost launched us over the back of the couch.

"Thank you," I whispered.

"We got you," Chandra said, breaking up the hug before someone got hurt.

"Here." Melanie handed me a small paper plate. "Get a snack, and let's go."

We ate and watched film for hours. We studied Sebastian's moves and his few weaknesses. We theorized the best ways to earn points on him, expecting that pinning him would be tough, to say the least.

When I finally had a strategy that gave me a shot, I climbed into Ashley's bed for a sister sleepover. She held me and didn't make excuses for Sebastian.

"How are you feeling about tomorrow?"

I snuggled closer to her. "I've been wrestling boys my whole life. This is just another match against a boy."

"Lise."

"No. I mean it. That's how it has to be. It can't be anything else. I'll push myself. I'll try every strategy and technique I know, and when three periods end, we'll see."

"I'm picking you up after practice. I want to be there for you."

"Thanks," I said.

"And if it's okay, I'd like to escort you for Senior Night."

I smiled. "I can't think of anyone better. Love you, my big, little sis."

"I love you, my little, big sis."

I closed my eyes and urged my mind to go quiet. The noise dwindled slowly, finally dying long after Ashley's breath had grown soft and rhythmic.

Wishing away the day and hoping for a better one tomorrow, I finally fell asleep.

CHAPTER 39

FOCUS THAT DAY IN CLASS ELUDED ME. I FLIPPED through the notebook from our strategy session the night before. I would definitely need to maintain good defense and stop his shots to win, so I mentally ran through the movements that would counter his double leg takedown, expecting that to be his shot of choice. He could switch it up on me, but I couldn't get into that guessing game.

After hours of visualizing my plans, I marched into the wrestling room with my head high. Right past the spot I'd jumped in Sebastian's arms and kissed him. Deep breath. My teammates welcomed me.

Owen Malone draped his arm around my shoulders. "I know from experience how much this sucks."

Owen had competed against his own girlfriend for the quarterback position on the football team, so he was actually probably one of the few people who could understand.

"Do your best. Everyone on this team knows you can win."

"Thanks, Owen."

He nodded and hustled into the boys' locker room. What he hadn't said was everyone on the team probably knows it could go either way. I remembered Dom's words, *Get it in your head that it's going your way.*

After that, the moments passed in a blur of images. Coach calling us into his office to ask if we preferred the team be present or not. Sebastian deferring to me.

"I want them there," I'd said.

Warming up. Working through drills at practice. The wrestle-off hovering. Coach calling me and Sebastian to the side mat, away from where everyone else went live.

"You both ready?"

"Yes, Coach."

"We'll run a full match. Both of the assistant coaches are reffing to ensure fairness and that we get the calls right. I want good sportsmanship. Give this everything you have."

"Yes, Coach," we repeated.

Our teammates around the gym cheered for both of us to wrestle smart. To wrestle hard. I had no doubt we would do both. They pretended to go back to their own drills, but the key word there was *pretended.*

Coach called us to the line, and we shook hands. Sebastian held mine longer than normal, and he squeezed—his promise that he would give me everything. I squeezed back. At the top of page one of my strategy notebook from the night before, I'd written *Don't give in to the emotion.*

At the whistle, we stayed low in our stances. The unskilled eye might say we weren't engaging, but anyone who knew wrestling could see we were holding good position and leaving no vulnerability to exploit. Sebastian took a half shot, but I didn't bite. I kept a good, strong stance, and we tied up, both fighting for inside ties, but again, we dropped back into our stances, a gap between us. I watched his hips and knees, wanting to take a shot, but he kept good position, leaving no opening. If I forced it, he'd take advantage of my mistake. I'd be handing him two points.

Dom and I had both agreed the night before Sebastian and I were so evenly matched that points would be difficult to come by, and I couldn't afford to hand him any. In fact, Dom had suggested that coming out of the first period with a 0-0 score could be an advantage for me in the long run, as long as I could capitalize in the third period. Better to keep it close than to force shots, make a mistake, and provide an opportunity for Sebastian.

The first ended with neither of us taking a shot. And a 0-0 score, like Dom had predicted.

We both took a breath and waited for the toss to determine who'd choose their position to start the second. I got the call and chose bottom. One escape point might mean the difference in the match. I knelt, tucking my feet and ankles under me and safely away from Sebastian's strong hands. At the whistle, I applied pressure backward, but not so much that he could suck me back. I got my legs under me and stood, his arms still around my waist. I peeled off his top hand and held it to one side while I quickly turned the other way to unwrap the tight waist he had. He followed and regained his grip, and we went through the process again. I peeled his top hand, held it in mind, and spun to face him.

My heart lurched when I looked in his eyes. I'd steeled myself the whole day. I'd convinced myself I wasn't wrestling my boyfriend. I was wrestling another guy. Nobody that mattered but facing him like that in the middle of the match, looking in his eyes after letting the tips of his fingers slip through mine—emotion hiccupped in my throat, threatening to wreck me.

I shook the feelings away and refocused, shifting my gaze from Sebastian's eyes and to his lower body instead. Seeing an opening, I shot for a double, wanting to claim the poetic justice of scoring on his signature move, the one he'd taught me himself. I gripped the back of his knees and pushed the side of my head into him, driving with all my strength. He tried to sprawl, but it was too late. I had timed my shot perfectly. We landed on the mat with me behind him and claiming control and my two points for the takedown.

Our coaches stopped us, ending the second period with me leading 3-0. Sebastian and I didn't look at each other. Instead, I caught Dom's eye across the gym. He and Nick were pretending to drill, but really watching every move on our mat. Subtly, Dom gave me a thumbs up. Openly cheering for one teammate over another would not be cool, but my bestie was my bestie. I could only guess Nick silently cheered for his best friend, too.

Sebastian chose bottom for the start of the third period. I took as deep of a breath as I could and still hide that I was kind of freaking out. I could actually win this. Or anything could happen if I let it. I had to keep pushing and stay smart. The whistle blew, and Sebastian hit a changeover and forcefully turned to the right. I followed him with my hips and was able to keep my tight waist, squeezing my arm around his stomach. Sebastian tried another changeover, and I followed him again, not letting him escape. All I had to do was hold on, and I'd win this. On my toes, I got as heavy as I could, counting the seconds.

But Sebastian hit a sit out and hip heisted, turning his body in the air. I lost my grip, leaving a gap between us on the mat.

He'd escaped.

It was 3-1.

Back in neutral position, we dropped to our stances. Still leading, I only had to play good defense, and the match was mine. The Senior Night spot was mine.

As it should have been.

Sebastian attempted an inside tie, but I deflected. He pushed at me, and I could feel his attempt to trick me into pushing him back, so he could score a lateral takedown. I didn't give him what he wanted there either.

"Thirty seconds!" Coach Joseph yelled.

I caught Sebastian's eye. I had to know he was giving it everything. He wouldn't circle for the next thirty seconds and let me know. He'd promised.

But he'd promised lots of things.

He lowered his level and moved for another takedown, this time an ankle pick. I tried to counter him but felt my balance wobble. That's all it took for him to bring me down, but worse than that, I didn't land on my stomach.

I came down on the mat on my back. *Not back points!* I fought to my base, refusing to be pinned, my mind rolling through possible moves, but before I could run anything, Coach blew the whistle.

My body deflated, becoming one with the mat. I didn't even have to look at the score.

I knew.

CHAPTER 40

I'D LOST MY SPOT. THE LAST MATCH OF MY SENIOR year.

To my boyfriend.

Correction. *Ex*-boyfriend.

I ran the wrestle-off over in my mind. Again. And again. Every hold, every grab, every move. I wouldn't have done anything differently, which meant one thing. Sebastian was better than me.

After all these years.

He was better.

A knock pulled me back to the moment—sitting on the floor of my school bathroom. Alone. Because I was the only girl on the team. The only one who'd outlasted years of harassing comments from the boys we'd competed against and the discomfort of puberty among a world of testosterone. Refining my technique to perfection while fighting to maintain the kind of strength that made me competitive. Learning two styles of wrestling while my male opponents only learned one.

Watching states around the country sanction girls' wrestling as a high school sport and waiting for my state to do the same.

I'd outlasted all of that to lose my spot to a boy the last match of my high school career.

The knock sounded again.

"Who is it?"

"Nick."

My sister's boyfriend. Sebastian's best friend.

"What do you need?"

"To check on you."

Because everyone expected me to fall apart. I packed my bag and opened the door. Nick had failed to mention he wasn't alone. Sebastian stood next to him, looking like he'd run over a puppy.

Maybe he had.

"I'm fine," I said, forcing a smile. "See you guys later."

"Annalise, wait," Sebastian said. "Please."

"Have to get to club practice. Sorry," I called over my shoulder.

I wasn't sorry, and I didn't stop walking until Coach Joseph insisted. He pulled me aside in the gym and watched me quietly while my adrenaline simmered down. "You wrestled tough today."

Not tough enough. "Thanks, Coach."

"Justin Chan has mono."

"Oh." I didn't see the conversation going in that direction.

"Kurt is wrestling up to cover 138."

And Sebastian, who normally wrestles 132 is wrestling down in my—what *was* my weight class. In other words…

"We need someone to wrestle 132 tomorrow."

"You want me to wrestle up?"

"I do."

I'd never wrestled up. Never.

"I know the kid. You can beat him. And it's Senior Night. This will give you a match."

Since I'd lost my spot. Still, this was my team. The crumbling girl from the bathroom floor threatened to take hold if I let her.

"Sure, Coach," I said, clearing my throat. "Whatever the team needs."

"I appreciate your attitude. Great work again, today, Lise."

After years, literally years, of watching every bite I put in my mouth, training my muscles to the max, and refining my technique to beat boys my own size, now I'd spend my Senior Night wrestling up a weight class.

Because of Sebastian.

As she'd promised, Ashley waited outside to drive me home. Already knowing the result of our wrestle-off from Nick obviously, she hugged me in silence, and we left, getting home before the snow came. By the time I showered, ate dinner, and settled on the bench next to my window under my fuzziest blanket, white speckles dotted the forest landscape.

"It's so pretty, isn't it," Mom said from the doorway.

"It is."

"Mind if I sit with you?"

"Sure."

She curled up onto the bench next to me, and we shared the blanket. "How are you doing?"

I sighed. "Not sure."

I expected some exquisite Mom speech, but she didn't say anything else. We watched the snow fall. After a few minutes, I leaned my head on her shoulder, and before either of us spoke, at least an inch of white outlined the branches.

"Your father and I used to sit like this and watch the snow."

I sat up and stared at her. "You never talk about dad."

"It was hard when he left. I wanted to talk about him, for you girls, but sometimes, it's easier to lock away parts of yourself and leave them there, you know?"

How could I not when I'd locked Sebastian away for years and now wanted nothing more than to do it again?

"But we had moments like this. Watching the snow. Loving each other. Moments of happiness. And no matter what happened after that, those moments still existed."

"Like the moments I had with Sebastian before he wrestled me for my spot?"

Mom squeezed my hand. "I saw you together. You were happy. I don't know what happened. People make mistakes, teenagers more than anyone. But that boy adores you. I have no doubt about that."

What she didn't say was that I adored him, too. But some scars were too deep, even for adoration.

"About that," Ashley said, joining the party. "There's something you should know about Bash."

Mom kissed my head and then Ashley's. "I'll let you sisters chat. I love you both and am so grateful for how you're here for each other."

When Mom was gone, Ashley took her place on the bench. "Some college coach is looking for a wrestler in your weight, so Bash's dad went over his head and called Coach Joseph with the details."

"I know," I said.

"Oh."

"Sebastian told me."

"The whole thing's a mess," Ashley said.

"Yep."

She put her arm around me. "You want to watch a movie or something?"

I barely wanted to get up from the bench and cross the room to my bed. "After the day I had, I think I'm going to sleep."

Ashley hugged me and kissed my cheek. "You're still badass. You know that, right?"

"One wrestle-off can't change that."

"Hell yes!"

"Love you."

"Love you, too." Ashley blew me a kiss from the doorway and turned off the lights.

CHAPTER 41

THE INSPIRATION CAME TO ME IN A BLUR. FITTING GIV-
en my plan. I rolled out of bed at two in the morning and fired up
the heaters in the garage. I popped up every folding table we had
and lined them along the wall. On top, I organized the canvases I'd
painted of the wrestling mats. I poured my pencils onto the table,
ready to sketch the images that had flooded my sleep.

On the first mat, I sketched a boy clearly dominating a blurry
figure.

In the next painting, the girl would be slightly less blurry, but still
nearly unrecognizable. In the background, I'd show the scoreboard.
The girl had scored two points. In the next design, she'd score eight
while her opponent scored ten and pushed her face into the mat because she had the audacity to nearly beat him.

Then a tie. Overtime.

Then a win.

Finally, a pin. In each painting of the progression, the girl wrestler became less blurry, more defined. More present. More difficult
to ignore.

Until, finally, in the last match, she was completely clear, earning
a first-place trophy, with the *boys* blurred in the background.

And the final image—two girls, face-to-face, ready to start a match. Both clear. Both present. Both with teammates of girls in the background.

I dropped the pencil when I finished the sketches. That was it. My voice. My story to tell. My vision for something that mattered more than me and more than a superficial representation of a season. My contribution to the sanction movement.

I mixed paint until all my fingers were smudged with color. My pajamas, too.

I moved from one canvas to another, dabbing paint to bring my vision to life, letting layer after layer dry while I worked my way through the progression of time in the sport I loved. Light trickled in through the garage windows. Then it poured through.

My house awoke with sounds of pans clacking and smells of bacon in the kitchen.

I painted.

A plate of scrambled eggs and fruit appeared on the table next to my brushes, but I was still alone in the garage. I let the canvases dry while I ate the cold breakfast, admiring them from a few feet away, imagining what it might be like if people saw them. Why couldn't inspiration have struck before the art show deadline?

I rinsed my brushes and worked in more colors. More shapes. More movements. I blurred the edges of the girl wrestlers and then tidied them and blurred them again until the clarity matched my vision.

Grey, green, and brown hues dominated the earlier paintings in the progression. Vibrant colors in the final image reflected the reality of the sport and its potential for the future. I brushed and dabbed, swiped and perfected.

"Lise?"

I looked away from the line of canvases and took a few seconds to refocus my eyes on Ashley, standing behind me.

"Are you hungry for lunch?"

I turned back to my work, exhausted. "No. Breakfast was great. Thanks."

"Do you want to tell me about what you're working on?"

"Maybe when I'm done with it." I studied the canvases again, each taking shape, but none fully mature. "Right now, I'm going to shower and sleep."

***

UNLIKE THE NIGHT BEFORE, I SLEPT WITHOUT A SINGLE mental interruption. It was as if I'd purged my deepest thoughts in the paintings, and now I could rest, but only until they dried. As soon as I woke up around dinner time, I slipped into warm clothes and headed for the garage again.

I opened the door and found Sebastian staring at my lineup of canvases. "What are you doing?"

He jumped and stepped back from the table. "I'm sorry."

"What are you doing at my house?"

He rubbed his hands over his face. "My dad and I…we're not good. I had to get out of there, and Nick was here. He suggested I come and pick him up." He pointed to the fridge. "I was grabbing us a couple drinks for the road."

He and his dad were fighting. Still. About me.

"You think he'd be happy you won the wrestle-off," I said.

"My dad doesn't really do happy." Tears pooled in his eyes.

"Sebastian," I whispered, wrapping him in a hug.

"I'm so sorry." He pressed his face into my hair, and his body shook with sobs. I squeezed him, trying to push away his sadness before remembering my own. No matter the circumstances, Sebastian had hurt me. Again. He'd violated my trust. *Again.* I didn't want him to hurt like this, but I also couldn't be the one to put him back together. When his lips brushed mine and the wetness of his tears ran down my cheeks, I gently pulled away.

"Sebastian, I can't." I avoided looking at him by mixing paints and prepping my brushes. "I'm sorry about your dad. I'll steer clear. That should help prevent some fights."

"Annalise…"

"I don't want to hurt you, but I can't do this. And I need to finish these up."

The garage filled with the sounds of us breathing.

"I'm sorry," Sebastian finally whispered.

I didn't answer, but Sebastian didn't move. He watched me with a look on his face I'd never seen before. His lip quivered and his eyes darkened. His breath caught like he wanted to say something, but his tongue couldn't put together the words. He bent his head forward, and I knew: I was breaking Sebastian's heart. The thing was, he'd already broken mine. And I wasn't ready to pick up the pieces and stick myself back together again either. Not even for him.

Maybe, not ever again.

After he left, his absence chilled me as if the garage heaters had finally clunked their last burst of air. I closed my eyes and took calming breaths until warmth rushed over me. The garage was my studio. My space. My sanctuary.

And this was my art.

I finished the progression late that night, turned off the heaters and the lights, and went to bed. If I woke up in the morning and still liked the paintings, I told myself I'd be done, but I didn't last until the morning. After only a few hours of sleep, I slipped into my robe and slippers and hustled back to the garage. I studied each detail from inches away. Then stepped back and studied the whole.

A slow smile crept across my lips, and I shook my head. I was done. Despite the moments I'd felt like quitting, like I'd never get the pieces quite right—I'd done it. I took pictures of each piece and uploaded them to the cloud for safe keeping. The gallery's website listed the rules for submission, and the deadline to submit stared me in the face in bold letters. Maybe Rebecca would have another suggestion for where to submit the series.

I scrolled through my contacts and found her number. She'd offered to look at my work again in the future, and I had followed her advice. But would she be in New York or back here? Sebastian would know, but I couldn't ask him.

I'd have to text and hope for the best.

Her reply came quickly.

"Annalise! Good to hear from you. You caught me at the perfect time. I'm flying back out tomorrow to prepare for a show down south. Can I come by after your Senior Night match?"

The snow had stopped falling outside. We'd have school today. And the match later. I'd wrestle up after watching Sebastian wrestle my weight class. And then hear Rebecca's verdict on my art.

I might need more sleep after all.

CHAPTER 42

FOR YEARS, I'D ATTENDED SENIOR NIGHT CEREMONIES for family, friends, and teammates, watching them march across the gym with balloons and signs, their arms around family members and boyfriends or girlfriends. I'd known I'd be there one day. I'd expected it. But so much about my Senior Night was beyond the realm of my expectations.

The obvious—I'd lost my weight class. Instead, Sebastian's name was called for it. He crossed the gym with Christopher, who was holding a bundle of purple, green, and black balloons. The announcer read Sebastian's responses to a list of questions. How long he'd been wrestling, what other activities and teams he'd joined in high school, his academic success and his favorite memory. My mind flashed to when I'd finally given in to my feelings for him, and we'd kissed.

He turned away from the crowd and found me among the team. His eyes told me he'd been thinking exactly what I had. Then the announcer said, "Throwing up during conditioning in ninth grade."

Dutifully, people in the stands and a few of the guys on the team laughed, but Sebastian nodded at me. That would never be his favorite memory.

Ashley squeezed my arm. "You okay?"

"Yep. Just waiting my turn."

The announcer called my name, and the scene repeated. Ashley and I walked across the gym, through the archway of balloons, posed for photos, listened to the answers to my questions. "Enjoy this, Lise," Ashley whispered.

I took a deep breath and smiled. At Dom. At my mom in the stands hiding behind her camera. At my coach and teammates who had cheered me on for years. At the fans who'd embraced me as a girl on this team.

I smiled for all of my wins and my losses. All of the moments on the mat that had made me. I even smiled at the other team with their polite clapping. And then my eyes fell on one person.

Trevor Jacoby.

"What's he doing here?" I muttered.

"Who?" Ashley asked.

I didn't answer because how would she know. Trevor caught me looking at him and waved with little wiggly fingers and a confident grin. Gross. How could boys be so pompous? Wait! He must have heard that Sebastian beat me out for the weight, and he'd get to wrestle him, not me. He'd dodged me again.

For a second, I considered asking Sebastian to swap me spots, so I could take Trevor down once and for all, but I couldn't do that to him, and he couldn't do that for me. He needed this for the college coach he wanted to impress. That was more important than my ego.

Unfortunately.

"You okay?" Dom asked when we huddled up.

"When did Trevor Jacoby start wrestling for them?" I asked pointing in our opponents' direction.

"I don't know. Maybe it's a co-op thing. You finally get your chance, though!" It took a few seconds for him to work through the change in my weight class at which point he closed his eyes and grimaced. "Sorry."

"Me too."

We lined up, taking our turn at polite claps, while the announcer read the list of wrestlers we'd face off against that night. I held my breath when they got to my usual weight class, but Trevor's name wasn't announced. Instead, they announced his name for 132.

Dom grabbed my arm.

"Did they say Trevor's wrestling 132?"

"They did." Dom's smile could have lit the whole gym. "I bet he offered to wrestle up to avoid you."

I gasped. "You think?"

"Without knowing it, Sebastian gave you an end-of-season—hell end-of-career, gift."

"I'm wrestling Trevor Jacoby?"

"Yeah, you are. You have to win."

I smirked at my best friend. "You know it."

***

TREVOR'S ATTEMPT TO AVOID ME BY WRESTLING UP was pure speculation.

Until the horror on his face when the announcer called my name for 132 proved our theory. I barely watched Sebastian's match, expecting him to dominate. Instead, I jumped and paced in the corner, running the steps of my takedowns through my mind. I worked through the moves I wanted to hit when we were on the mat. I wouldn't leave anything to chance.

I wouldn't make mistakes.

I'd wrestle smart.

We shook hands, and at the whistle, we circled. After a few seconds of hand fighting, I saw my opportunity. I lowered my level and shot for an ankle pick. He couldn't counter and landed on the mat with a thud.

"Good for you," he muttered. "You got a takedown. Enjoy it because it won't happen again."

His words activated molten heat at my core. "Wanna bet?"

I let him stand to face me again, his eyes wide. I'd willingly given him an escape point. We both knew it. I'd had him on the mat with a 2-0 lead but letting him escape changed the score to 2-1.

I heard Sebastian in the mix of voices coming from our bench and smiled. No better time to use that double leg takedown than on a boy who thought I couldn't manage it. Although the look of terror in Trevor's eyes showed me he thought I could do just about anything.

We circled in our stances. He forcefully smacked his right hand to my neck for a collar tie, but I seized an opportunity again, hitting an elbow pass, lowering my level and taking another shot, this time, a double. He grunted when I pressed my head into his side. He attempted to get heavy with a sprawl, but I cut the corner and lifted him, scoring another takedown and two more points.

This time I didn't let him escape. Instead, I stayed on top, trying to apply smothering pressure. The ref eventually signaled the end of the first period with me winning 4-1. In the second, he had the choice. He chose top. I actually laughed. I mean, I guess on the one hand, I got it. Maybe his coaches thought he could turn me and earn three back points, tying it up. Or even better, turn me and get a pin to end the match.

But let's be real.

No way he was turning me.

Expecting him to push as hard as he could, I decided to go for a reversal instead of an escape. He didn't disappoint. Off the whistle, he wasted no time in draping his head and body over mine, trying to force a cradle. He dropped his head too far to the side, allowing me to grab it and his arm with both hands and hip down hard enough to hit a headlock and roll him onto the mat. After a few seconds, the ref slapped his hand against the ground, and it was over.

I won.

I'd pinned Trevor Jacoby.

Dom grabbed me when I stepped off the mat and spun me around.

"Let me breathe," I joked.

"They're be time for that later! I'm so proud of you, Lise. You crushed him."

I had. Trevor draped his T-shirt over his lowered head on the bench. I couldn't feel bad for him. He was the epitome of my time as a wrestler. He'd pinned me early in our rivalry, and every time, he'd done it with something smart to say. When I'd scored points on him for the first time, he pulled my hair and pressed my face into the mat. As I progressed in my skill, he progressed in his aggression. I'd worked for this moment. I deserved it.

And so did he.

***

REBECCA MOVED FROM ONE PAINTING TO THE NEXT, studying each carefully, taking in the story.

I hoped.

I fought the urge to tap my toes on the cement of the garage floor.

Or hold my breath. Wait. Was that a smile? I looked at the ground, afraid to see her reactions. *No. How often do you have an actual artist review your work? Lift up your head and watch, for better or worse.*

When she reached the final painting, she sighed and nodded. That had to be a good sign.

"Annalise," she said. "Wow."

"Wow?"

She laughed. "Yes. Wow. I challenged you to tell a story, to share your voice, and wow."

"Thank you."

"The story is rich in every aspect. The color. The clarity. The content. Your use of blurry imagery next to these crisp visuals is gorgeous. The arc of the story builds with the clarity and the color. This final image of two fierce, competitive, girls wrestling with all of the color and emotion and passion. I'm impressed."

"Thank you, Rebecca."

"You're welcome. And you're submitting for the gallery's art show?"

"The deadline was last week. I submitted my fall series because I couldn't think of anything else at the time. I developed these in the last two days."

Her eyes widened. "You painted this in two days?"

"Yes."

"Okay. Wow, again."

We both laughed.

"Can I write you a letter of recommendation to accompany your submission? I can't make any promises, but maybe if they have an opening still, they might accept it."

"You would do that?"

"Of course! I'm not exaggerating my love for this. It's the kind of social activism that's prominent in galleries now."

I wanted to say yes. And thank you. And let it be.

But part of me wondered if her kindness and generosity had anything to do with Sebastian. She adored him. He'd always said I was honest to a fault. Could I risk this opportunity to ask an honest question?

"Annalise, are you okay?"

"Yes. I…"

She nodded. "Want to know if my enthusiasm has anything to do with your relationship with my nephew?"

I groaned. "Yes."

"I respect you for wanting to know. It's an admirable trait to earn opportunities on your own. I see a lot of potential in you. We may have met because of Bash, but we don't have to continue our friendship because of him. We can continue it because of each other."

That made sense.

"And if I heard right, he may have put a dent in your relationship recently."

"That's one way to put it."

"I get it. Look, that's completely separate from us and from the show."

"Okay. Then, yes, please. I would be honored if you'd write a recommendation letter for me."

"I'll have it to you by tomorrow. And if you don't get into this show, we'll get you into another one."

Sounded like a plan to me.

CHAPTER 43

I WOKE UP FRIDAY SMILING.

I'd pinned Trevor Jacoby. Rebecca loved my paintings, and I didn't have to see Sebastian. He'd congratulated me the night before, but then we'd parted ways in the gym, both looking over our shoulders, but still parting.

We'd never officially spoken the words that we'd broken up, but a break too big to ignore was between us. Ashley had spent the night with Mom and me, eating dinner and playing games, but she'd checked her phone every few minutes. After everything, we were all back to that awkward space.

Despite the feelings that still existed between us, I wondered if Sebastian felt being together was too complicated. I wondered if we could ever smooth over that massive break. I got why he had to compete against me. In a way, I didn't even blame him for it.

Maybe it was aversion to vulnerability creeping back in, but like everything had felt so right on the dance floor at the winter formal, everything between Sebastian and me now felt so wrong. I couldn't ignore that.

Coach Joseph gave us the afternoon off from practice "provided we still get some training in." I'd already trained that morning, so I napped after school and then appreciated my own personal gallery in the garage, studying each painting for the slightest flaw until my phone rang with a number I didn't recognize. Normally I wouldn't answer, but what if someone was calling about my gallery application. I pressed accept and lifted the phone to my ear, eager for good news.

"Annalise! It's Christopher."

Christopher? Christopher Love?

"My mom's in a pinch," he went on without taking a breath, "and she won't let me stay home alone. Save me from a boring night out with old people, please. Want to come over for a Nerf battle at 7?"

I checked the time. Six p.m.

"Hey, Christopher. Um, let me check real quick. Okay?"

Christopher rambled about his mom's event and how going would ruin his life forever while I searched the house for my sister. I found her curled up in bed with a book. I hit mute and asked, "Is Sebastian away at that tournament today, do you know?"

"Yeah," she said, looking suspicious. "He and Nick both went. There's a dinner after, and they're getting back late tonight."

In other words, later than Christopher's mom, so if I watched his little brother, I wouldn't have to see him.

"Why?" Ashley asked.

"Christopher Love needs a babysitter."

"And you don't want to run into Bash?"

"Basically."

I unmuted the phone. "How long would your mom need me?"

"No later than ten, she said. Probably earlier."

Ashley nodded and whispered, "I think you should be okay."

"Okay," I said. "I'll be there by seven."

*　*　*

ARMED WITH A DUFFEL BAG FILLED WITH NERF GUNS and prayers that Mr. Love would not be home, I knocked on the Love's front door. Mrs. Love answered.

"Thank you for coming, Annalise. You are so sweet to spend time with Chris."

I wondered if she had wanted to finish that sentence with something like, "Given what his older brother—or worse, my husband—

did to you."

"Christopher's great. We'll have fun."

"Annalise!" Christopher plowed through the doorway and into the cold to hug me.

"Let's get inside, buddy. It's too cold out here."

He took my hand and led me to the family room where his armory awaited.

"Please don't break anything, Chris."

"Wouldn't dare, Mom."

Mrs. Love raised an eyebrow at me, telling me what I already knew—neither of us believed him.

"I wrote my cell on a tablet in the kitchen. He's already eaten, so it's playing and getting him ready for bed. Please make sure he brushes his teeth. He's sneaky about that."

"No, I'm not, Mom."

"I'll take care of it," I promised.

"Great. I'll be home by 9 or 10 at the latest. I'm having dinner at a friend's house. Mr. Love is out of town, and as you know, Sebastian won't be home until much later tonight."

As I know? Did she think Sebastian and I were still…together?

"Sounds great," I managed. "Have fun."

Christopher didn't waste time. After I walked his mom to the garage and listened to every detail she wanted me to know, I came back to the living room to face a one-man firing squad. He pelted me with bullets before I could dive out of the way and retrieve my duffel in the entry hall. I scooped it up and ran up the stairs, keeping my head low.

"You can't hide," he called, but I did. In *his* bedroom this time. I suited up and loaded all of my weaponry before opening the door a crack. I expected he'd be ready, which is why I used a mirror from his room to reflect the view of the hallway and the stairs.

Good thing. A stream of bullets flew through the opening, but I saw Christopher's reflection and fired back, hitting him a few times. He dramatically rolled down the steps. I took my position on higher ground and unleashed more foam on him until he reached the bottom and took cover.

Needing to reload, I had no choice but to duck into Sebastian's room and lock the door.

"You have to keep moving," Christopher yelled from downstairs. "Those are the rules."

"I'm moving around the room while I reload, so you better be long gone when I'm ready."

The shifting light under the door and the sound of his footsteps told me he'd run through the hallway but was back downstairs. A couple bullets had found their way into the room when I'd tried to hit Christopher on the stairs. I bent down to pick them up, and a picture next to Sebastian's bed stopped my heart.

Us at the winter formal. Smiling. Arms around each other. I remembered the moment it had been taken. The electricity shocking every part of my body. How I'd melted into the way he looked at me, and the feel of his fingertips on my skin. How fierce I'd felt in that dress. How confident I'd been that the worst was behind us.

How full my heart had been from friendship, from Sebastian, maybe even from love.

Believing it could never end.

That I wouldn't let it.

As if I'd had any control over that.

I sat on Sebastian's bed, breaking Christopher's rules about constantly moving, and picked up the frame. I got lost in the happiness of the two people staring back at me. Christopher's small feet ran past the room again, bringing me back to the moment. And the fact that I shouldn't be in this room, touching this picture. I should be with my charge, shooting him with Nerf bullets, making him popcorn, watching a movie.

Fully loaded, I scanned Sebastian's room once more, vowing not to come back in here no matter what. I cocked my pistol and reached for the doorknob, ready for Christopher to strike. I opened it slowly and startled to find a face staring back at me. But it wasn't Christopher's.

It was Sebastian's.

I pulled the trigger, and the foam bullet bounced off his face.

"Shit, Annalise!"

"Oh my gosh. I'm so sorry."

He covered his nose and continued swearing under his breath.

When he pulled his hand away, blood poured everywhere. Oh no.

"Come with me." I led him to the bathroom and wet a washcloth. He pressed it against his nose and looked at me over it.

"Hi," I said.

He waved a bloodied hand.

"You're probably wondering what I'm doing here. In your room." That got a nod.

"I'm watching Christopher." As if on cue, he ran down the hallway, firing bullets into the bathroom. I returned fire.

"You're standing still," he yelled. "That's against the rules."

"Injury timeout," I said, still firing.

"Denied."

I kicked the door shut and locked it. "That was a pretty good demonstration of why I was in your room."

He pulled the washcloth away. "Taking cover."

I nodded. "I can't believe a foam bullet gave you a bloody nose."

"I smashed it off the mat at the tournament, and it wouldn't stop bleeding all day. Until about an hour ago."

"Oh. Oops."

He checked out his injury in the mirror. It looked as if the blood had stopped, but he still had some on his cheeks.

"Here," I said. "Let me help you." I took the towel from his hands and wiped away any remnants of blood. By the time I finished, Sebastian's gaze had melted. I looked away, but he nudged my chin until I reluctantly made eye contact.

"When I saw your car outside, I thought…"

"What?"

He lowered his gaze. "You were here for me."

"Then I shot you in the face."

That got him to grin. "I bet that felt good."

I laughed. "It was a reaction."

"Come out with your hands up," Christopher shouted. "I'm arresting you for breaking the rules."

The small bathroom warmed with the two of us in it. Too close to each other. Too much unsaid. We kept expanding until every space was full, and every breath was taken.

"Are you training with the team for states next week?" he asked.

"No. I'm actually participating in the girls' tournament, so Coach Joseph released me to work out at the club."

His bright eyes widened. "That's cool. Fallon is, too."

"Yeah. Mrs. Errico encouraged all the girls to support the sanction movement by participating in the tournament." I wiped the water from my hands on the towel hanging by the door. "Besides, I think I'm done wrestling boys."

"Trevor Jacoby. That was a good one."

Yeah. Because it was only Trevor I meant.

"You should stay in my—our—the 132-pound weight class. Sorry I didn't mean anything by that. You did well yesterday."

"Thanks. I should go," I said. "Now that you're home, you can keep an eye on Christopher, right?"

He busied himself with rinsing the washcloth. "Sure. Unless you want to stay? Watch a movie like last time?"

When I'd fallen asleep on his couch until his mother woke us, and the sight of his mussed hair endeared me to him even more. And the cinnamon gum in the kitchen.

And what followed the cinnamon gum.

"I can't, Sebastian," I whispered.

"You know how sorry I am."

"I don't think I'm ready to know yet."

He lowered his head, and I thought he might stay like that until I left.

"Will you tell me?" he finally said.

"Tell you what?"

"When you're ready to know."

I nodded.

With soft hands brushing mine and sending sparks up my arms, he took one of my pistols and a handful of bullets. "I'll cover you."

My heart split wide open over two realities—comfort when he had my back and the times he most definitely hadn't.

CHAPTER 44

TO AVOID STARING AT MY PHONE ALL SATURDAY morning, waiting for a call from the gallery that probably wouldn't come, I drove to the Keystone Club to work on freestyle techniques with Fallon. The Nerf guns piled on the passenger seat of my car reminded me of shooting Sebastian in the face, making me cringe and giggle at the same time. But thinking about the photo of us next to his bed and his eyes softening in the bathroom when I'd helped him clean up—I shook those thoughts away.

When I pushed through the front door of the Keystone Club, four middle school boys hovered over Fallon while she stretched on the mat. Instinctively, I understood the situation. Intimidation. Heat blared through me. I scanned the room for one of the coaches, but the five of them were alone. Hanging back by the door, I watched and listened.

Fallon did her best to ignore the boys, but they wouldn't shut up. They wanted a shot at wrestling her, teasing her about whether she'd been touched off the mat like they'd touched her on it.

When they laughed and started with the hand gestures, I intervened.

By knocking them all on their asses.

Stunned, they gazed at me from the ground with wide eyes.

"Oh hey, guys. Did I misunderstand, or were you asking to wrestle a girl?"

None of them spoke. Probably a good choice.

"Who's first?"

Again, silence. A sideways glance at Fallon rewarded me with a smile.

"No volunteers?"

The boys slowly stood, backing away from me as they did. Coach Law appeared from his office and read the room in seconds. "What's going on?"

Fallon didn't answer. I assumed that meant she didn't want to out the boys. I didn't have any problem doing it for her. "I came to work with Fallon, but these boys wanted to wrestle a girl. They wouldn't stop running their mouths about it."

Coach crossed his arms. If there was any coach at the club who refused to put up with misogynist bullshit, it was him. "I see. Do you all want to give me more specifics, or should you start running now?"

They lowered their heads. Whether from honest guilt or not, I couldn't tell.

"Running it is then. Followed by 200 pushups and pull ups. Pick your combination."

A couple of them groaned.

"How about we give that a go and chat afterward?"

"Yes, Coach," they said and ran toward the indoor track.

"Five miles," Coach called after them. Once the boys were out of earshot, he asked Fallon, "Are you okay?"

"Yes, Coach."

"Not that I don't take words seriously. I do. Everyone should feel safe in this club, but can you tell me if anything physical happened?"

"Just words."

"Okay. But again, I have expectations about the kinds of words my wrestlers use. Their parents will be informed, and one way or another, they'll learn that behavior isn't tolerated at my club."

"Thanks, Coach," I said.

He followed after the boys, and I sat next to Fallon. "Are you okay that I did that?"

She smiled tentatively. "Yeah. We can't let them get away with that kind of stuff, but part of me wonders if it will help. If they think it's okay to do it once, they probably think it's okay to do it again."

I actually laughed at her statement.

"What?"

"I thought the same thing. I never gave anyone the chance to change, but truth be told, your brother convinced me otherwise."

Her eyes widened. "Did he…?"

"Yep. He was one of those boys in middle school, but he did change. Probably because of you."

Wait. Because of Fallon. Nick had seen Fallon's struggles and changed. My paintings could show people the progression of the sport for girls, but to convince them, to cause change, I'd need more.

I needed stories like Fallon's and mine and all the other girls' who loved this sport.

"Are you okay?"

"I had an epiphany."

"A what?"

"Would you mind helping me with something today? After we work out?"

"Sure, but can I ask you something?"

"Okay."

"Did Bash do something stupid?"

Good question. He'd taken an opportunity that he had every right to take—objectively speaking. Subjectively speaking, my rights felt a little trampled.

"I ask because you two clearly belong together, but you weren't at the tournament yesterday. And he seemed kind of wrecked."

That was a lot to unpack.

"Maybe we should work now, and chat about it another time."

"That's grown up talk for we're not talking about this ever again."

I laughed. "Smart girl. Let's go."

I couldn't detangle the mess of emotions where Sebastian was concerned—yet another Jackson Pollock masterpiece.

Ideas for how to help the sanction movement tumbled in my mind while Fallon and I worked through the freestyle technique that would benefit her the most in the girls' unsanctioned post season. If my plan worked, though, by the time she was my age, she'd compete in a sanctioned post season tournament.

After the workout, we borrowed Coach Law's office. Fallon tapped into her contacts, and I tapped into mine. Teammates, opponents, coaches, relatives—anyone who'd supported our wrestling over the years. The Diner on Third agreed to let us use their back room to meet since it wasn't booked. I promised to encourage takeout orders to show our gratitude.

And then hoped someone—anyone would actually show up to help.

CHAPTER 45

PEOPLE SHOWED.

Lots of them. Fallon had managed to recruit ten friends who wrestled for different middle schools. Eight high school girls showed, including Zora and her friends from Pacific. To my surprise, our male teammates filtered in through the doors, too.

When Nick and Ashley pushed their way through the crowd, I couldn't help but search the space behind them for Sebastian's face. When I didn't see it, my stomach knotted.

I'd pushed him away.

I did that.

I'd have to own it.

Supporters filled the room, chatting to each other until Fallon called for everyone's attention and then nodded to me.

"Thank you all for being here," I said, as they quieted down and took whatever seats they could find. The chaos cleared, leaving me with a view of the doorway, where Sebastian and Christopher stood side-by-side. Fireworks of hope exploded inside me. I did my best not to show it. Christopher waved. I waved back and refocused on the people who'd come at a moment's notice to support girls' wrestling.

"I'm Annalise Fiori. I wrestled for Iron Valley High School. Wrestling is my sport. I dedicate my time and energy to it all year round.

The problem is, it's not an officially sanctioned girls' sport in our state. Despite other states sanctioning the sport, our state officials haven't. They haven't because they want schools to sponsor teams, but schools don't want to sponsor teams when there isn't sanctioned competition. You see the dilemma."

I took a deep breath and studied the faces around the room looking at me, not their phones or each other. They were listening.

People were listening.

"I need your help to change that. We have middle school girls here today that love wrestling, too. When I was in middle school, everyone told me that girls' wrestling was the fastest growing sport in the country. I expected some day to be able to attend a sanctioned girls' tournament. Or to compete in a state championship against other girls, but we're still working toward both of those goals.

"Girls are at a disadvantage, and not in the ways people might think. We have to wrestle in different styles. We have to develop flawless technique. We face sexual harassment more times than we can count. But this isn't all about wrestling against boys. It's about creating opportunities for girls. Girls have shown they want to compete in this sport, and it's time we have that chance."

The room erupted in applause, bringing a smile to my lips.

"For the younger girls in this room, we owe this to you. We want to create this change now, so you can benefit from it these next few years. Our task is to convince Iron Valley's athletic director to start a girls' wrestling team. Now."

Zora stood. "I agree with everything Annalise has said, but more than that, I want to see the sport made official at Pacific, too."

Wrestlers from other schools stood. They wanted official teams, and they were willing to work for them.

"I love it!" I called over the chatter until everyone quieted again. "If we work together, we can develop a plan to use at all of our schools. We can convince the coaches, athletic directors, and school boards to approve teams for girls."

Molly Mattola raised her hand. "My aunt's on the school board. She can help us build convincing arguments."

"Perfect, Molly. Thank you. We have to leverage all of our connections and resources." I explained what I thought we needed to make that happen. Commitments from girls who wanted to compete, including girls who didn't currently wrestle but would if they had the chance to wrestle girls instead of boys. A willing coach. A petition from community members supporting—no, *demanding* the school district create a girls' team.

Everyone divided into teams to brainstorm ideas and connections they could leverage. From the front of the room, I watched them scrape chairs against the floor and move tables to get close enough to tackle the task. Notebooks came out. Pens, too. Plans developed.

It was happening.

Finally.

"Hey," Sebastian whispered, and I jumped. "Sorry."

"It's fine," I said. "I was caught up in the moment."

Sebastian surveyed the room, too. "It's pretty great."

I exhaled. "It is."

"I had an idea, though. There's something that speaks louder than anything."

The answer came to me immediately. "Money."

He showed me his notebook with numbers scratched next to a list of items. "The way I figure it, we'd need to pay a coach and referees. We'd need bus transportation to away meets, singlets, and maybe some other cash flow for the coaches to use as they see fit. We could talk with Coach Joseph about using the current wrestling facilities, so that would save us a huge expense on new mats."

The way Sebastian kept saying "we" convinced me he was all in, and I didn't even want to admit to myself what that did to the kernel of hope I'd clung to without even realizing it. The crushing weight on my chest reminded me that he'd apologized, but I hadn't been ready to hear it in his bathroom the night before.

When I realized Sebastian had stopped talking, I snapped back to the present. "What does all that come to?"

"I think fifteen thousand should cover it comfortably, but twenty could be very persuasive."

Wow. That was a lot of money. I scanned the room again, nervous about asking everyone for even more work.

"I think I know someone who could sponsor the team."

"Sponsor the whole thing?"

He smiled. Oh gosh. Look away.

"The company my dad works for," he said. "They're always giving to charitable organizations. They could write it off."

Sebastian's dad? The man who insisted he wrestle his girlfriend to take away her spot? We were going to ask him to support a girls' wrestling team? Good thing I hadn't eaten anything yet.

"How about you give me a day or two to talk to him about it," Sebastian went on, "and if he can't do it, then we can start looking for other sponsors. We could even start a crowd-sourcing campaign."

Part of me wanted to go immediately to the crowd sourcing to avoid Mr. Love. Those things raised tons of cash. But everyone in the room had plans and tasks already. Adding to them to satisfy my own pride wasn't the best leadership. "Thanks for thinking of it," I managed, humbling myself. "You're right. It would boost our proposal."

"Excellent. Consider it done."

Christopher chose that moment to sneak up behind me and wrap his arm around my waist.

"Hey, buddy."

"Can you be my girlfriend now?"

I glanced at Sebastian whose cheeks resembled the same color as when I'd shot him in the face with a Nerf bullet. "I'm not sure what you mean, Christopher."

He pointed to Sebastian. "I heard what this dope did." He eyed his brother with contempt and shook his head. "And I thought now maybe I have a shot."

I bit my bottom lip. Oh, Christopher Love. So cute. So young. So wrong.

"I think I'm gonna stay single for a while, bud. You know? Work on this project."

His shoulders slumped. "I knew it was a long shot. I'm keeping my heart open though."

I literally had to urge myself not to laugh. Christopher found his way to the table with the middle school girls. They scooted to the side to make space for him.

"That may have been the best offer I've ever had," I said seriously, and Sebastian snorted.

"You're brutal."

I sighed. "Maybe we should steer this conversation to other topics."

"Probably right." He flipped his notebook closed and adopted his most formal persona. "How are we presenting this?"

"Hopefully, in a super public venue with paintings on the wall to support it."

His grin returned. "The gallery?"

"My submission was late, but your aunt gave me a letter of recommendation."

He whistled. "That will carry some weight. Good luck."

"Thanks," I said, feeling shy all of a sudden. "If I don't get in, we can find a different venue. Throw a party or something."

"Don't waste your energy on that. You'll get in."

His confidence made my body tingle, and despite everything, as if it were the most natural thing in the world, my hand wanted to rise up to his cheek. My chest wanted to press against his. My feet wanted to bring our bodies closer.

My brain told all of my other parts to stand down.

"I should check on the groups."

"Sure. I'll let you know about my dad."

"Thanks."

"You're welcome, Annalise."

As I walked away from him, I couldn't ignore my disappointment that he'd called me by my full name. I'd asked him to, but part of me wondered if I'd ever hear him say *Lise* again.

CHAPTER 46

THE TEAMS WORKED EVERY SPARE MOMENT—AN
even bigger challenge with state championships only weeks away.
Fallon's friends built a list of fifteen middle school girls from Iron
Valley and Forest Run who'd wrestle on a girls' team. At Pacific Middle, the wrestlers recruited ten girls, and Riverport recruited eight.
Neither would have a full roster, but it was enough to compete, and
once the team was in place, the wrestlers who committed could recruit
classmates to join them.

The high school numbers surpassed the middle schools' with fifty
girls in all four schools showing interest. *Fifty* girls. I shook my head
at the number. That many girls wanted to wrestle, yet all these years
I'd competed alone.

Recruiting had been the first step of our plan. Next, the groups
attended events all over the valley over the next week, seeking signatures of community members who supported developing girls'
wrestling teams. Students, parents, and other community members
signed the petitions–seven thousand, three hundred, and twenty-five
to be exact.

And the icing on the cake, Sebastian pulled me aside before one
of our club practices with a huge smile on his face. "Done."

"Done?"

He handed me a check for twenty thousand dollars. "They were looking for a tax-deductible opportunity. It was perfect timing."

The tiny piece of paper could have fluttered away in the breeze, yet it held infinite power. I checked the number three times, which was harder when my eyes filled with tears.

"You okay?"

I nodded.

"This is a good thing, Li...Annalise."

I swiped the tears from my cheeks. "Everyone's worked so hard on this. It means everything to me."

My eyes found his—greener today under the lights. I knew if I stepped closer, I'd see the specks of blue, too. But closer and Sebastian were two words that had burned me before.

Twice.

"I scheduled us an appointment with the athletic director."

My breath caught. "When?"

"Tomorrow."

"I'm not prepared."

"Bring your speech from our first meeting. That should do the trick. And the petition, the roster, and the check. Hard to argue with that package."

I lowered my head and wished I could have a moment to myself, so he couldn't see my vulnerability. I also wished I could crumble into his arms and let him rebuild the broken parts of me.

"Do you want me to come with you?" he asked quietly.

"I do, actually," I said surprising myself.

He tried to hide his smile but didn't quite get there. "Okay. Let's do this, then."

***

ARMED WITH THE PETITION, THE ROSTER, AND THE check, we appealed to Mr. Charles, the athletic director, to create a girls' wrestling team the next academic year. When he said that would be great, but we'd need girls to fill it, we laid the roster on his desk. It had names and grade levels for every girl from sixth to eleventh grade who wanted to wrestle.

His eyebrows raised at that. "Impressive. I'll also have to look into possible competitions. Not many schools in our area have teams."

"The female students at Pacific and Riverport are appealing to their athletic directors in the next week or so with rosters, so they'll be primed for your call," I said, and he smiled.

"Impressive again."

And we hadn't even shown him the check yet.

"We also have significant community support," Sebastian said, passing him our petition.

Mr. Charles looked over the paperwork. "You've worked hard on this."

"Our whole team has. Girls want to wrestle, and they want to wrestle girls. We have every reason here for you to say yes to our request, and no reason to deny it."

He nodded. "It's persuasive, but there's one point we haven't discussed."

Sebastian glanced sideways, that smirk that always shook me playing at his lips.

"Funding?" I suggested.

"Yes. Unfortunately."

"We realize how difficult and important that can be," I said.

Mr. Charles pressed his lips together in that way grownups did when they wanted to soften disappointing news. "I can look at the budget."

"No need," I said and made a production of pulling the check from my bag and handing it to him. I'm not sure I've ever seen anyone's eyeballs that large before.

"Let me guess," Sebastian said. "Impressive?"

"Beyond," Mr. Charles said with a laugh. "You've thought of everything. I'll run this by the principal and superintendent. We'll have to coordinate with the boys' team for gym time, so I'll talk to your coach. I don't anticipate any friction there."

I didn't either. Coach Joseph knew about our plans, and he supported them, even adding that if necessary, he'd coach both teams.

When we left the office, neither of us could temper our grins.

"That was incredible," I said.

"Did you see his eyes when you showed him the check?"

"The check *you* got for us?"

Sebastian cleared his throat. "We, uh, make a good team."

True.

"Annalise?"

"Yeah?" Something told me to hold my breath when he asked the next question.

"You said you'd tell me when you were ready."

I exhaled, wishing what I was about to say wasn't the truth. "I'm not. Not yet."

He chewed his lip.

"But thank you for your help today."

"Any time."

CHAPTER 47

LATER THAT WEEK, MR. CHARLES CALLED TO SAY THE school district was moving forward with forming a girls' wrestling team. Phone calls from administrators from Pacific and Riverport followed, and before I knew it, everyone who'd fought for this change showed up at my house. Even Mrs. Errico called to congratulate us.

I would have liked to sweep the bracket—victories in the art show application, in the romance department, and in the move to form a girls' wrestling team at Iron Valley. I guess I'd have to accept my singular win.

It was a big one.

In my living room, Zora, wearing an adorable, short jean skirt, and an off-the-shoulder sweater, chatted with Sebastian close enough to see the glorious color of his eyes.

"You did a good thing," Ashley said, distracting me from my obvious jealousy.

"Thank you," Nick added. "This is going to be amazing for Fallon."

I smiled at the thought. In front of the fireplace, Fallon and her middle school friends laughed and made plans for their new team.

"Yes, it will," my sister said and held up an envelope. "And *this* is going to be amazing for you."

She laid the white envelope with my name on it in my hands. The return address read the gallery's location. I'd heard from another artist I'd gone to summer art camp with that she'd received an invitation to participate days earlier. And the list of artists in the show had gone live on the gallery's web site that day.

Obviously, the letter was another rejection.

"Thanks," I said and tossed it in a drawer.

"You're not opening it," Nick said loud enough to draw Sebastian's attention.

"I didn't get in. If they wanted me, they would have reached out before now."

"You don't know that." Ashley retrieved the envelope, and the three of them stood around me. "You're not going to open it?"

"Here," Nick said, taking it. "I got this."

"You're wasting your time," I insisted.

"Are we hoping for a yes or a no?" Nick said.

Ashley groaned, and I ripped the letter from his hands.

"I told you, but since you won't listen," I said, reading the letter aloud. "Dear Ms. Fiori, we are pleased to offer you a space in our winter art show…" But the rest of the words faded. Ashley tackled me, and Nick cheered. I got in. My work was going to be on exhibit at an actual gallery. How was that possible?

"But it doesn't make sense," I said.

"Let me see," Ashley said and took the paper from me. "Although your submission was late and at that point our roster already full, one of our artists is no longer able to participate. Because of the impressive nature of your series, we'd love for you to serve as her replacement."

"I got in?"

"You got in!" Ashley yelled, and everyone in the room clapped.

A real show. Wow.

"Lise, I'm so proud of you."

"Thanks."

"Congratulations," Nick said.

I hugged him, too. "Thank you."

Sebastian stepped toward me next, holding his arms open. "Congratulations, Annalise."

I fell into them and pressed my head against his shoulder. As everyone in the room celebrated and cheered, I stayed in Sebastian's arms. He made no attempt to pull away. Neither did I.

Until Nick said, "Wow. Okay. It's time for breakfast."

I glared at him, and he smirked.

Why shouldn't I celebrate with Sebastian? He loved art. I loved art. He loved the gallery. I loved the gallery.

The gallery!

"I have to go," I said.

"Where?" Nick asked.

"I have to check on my paintings. Make sure everything's right with them."

"No need," Ashley called from the doorway holding a stack of canvases.

"Careful!"

She recruited Fallon to help her prop the canvases on the window-sills. "You all are in for a treat. Our own Annalise Fiori was accepted to her first art show. You're about to see why."

My friends awed at the paintings. They asked questions. They congratulated me.

And they came up with a plan to take our girls' wrestling initiative to the next level courtesy of the art show, turning our celebration into another round of work.

***

TIME TICKED AWAY OVER THE NEXT COUPLE OF WEEKS. The guys worked out with Coach Joseph at school, prepping for regionals and then eventually states. Fallon, Zora, and I worked out with other local girls at the Keystone Club where Coach Law had set aside girls only mat time for us to prep for our own state tournament. Without seeing Sebastian every day, my heart started to heal, leaving only the good memories.

The more time that passed, the more I missed him. And the more I wondered if he still felt anything for me or had moved on.

And there was one other thing. One other glorious thing.

My art show.

The day of the show, I arrived at the gallery early. Okay, way early. The owner greeted me with balloons and hugs, congratulating me on my first show.

My first show!

Was dancing appropriate at an art gallery?

I took a deep breath and climbed the stairs to the second floor. Every step across the gallery felt like this momentous occasion. I wanted to remember every sound and smell and emotion, but the moments slipped through my fingers like intangible things did. I couldn't hold them in my hands, but I could feel it in every part of my body especially when the first paintings came into view. All the way to my toes. My eyes clouded with tears, and my throat thickened. With the wrestling progression beginning in bland colors on my left and ending in the most vibrant hues on my right, I collapsed onto the floor, letting it hold my weight.

My art. Bright and bold. On the white walls. Telling a story of passion from my soul.

Achieving something I'd wanted so long—I shook my head. How did it feel so normal and so surreal at the same time? I trailed my protagonist's story from beginning to end over and over, looking for brush strokes I might change or revisions I'd make.

There were none.

These images were ready for the world to see.

"Annalise," Rebecca said, "what are you doing on the floor?"

I stood and dusted myself off. "Thought it best to go down voluntarily instead of fainting."

She laughed and hugged me. "The exhibit is perfect."

"Thank you."

"People are lining up outside. More young people than I think we've ever had for an opening," she said. "The owners are thrilled. Are you ready?"

I scanned my paintings waiting to greet the world one last time.

"I'm ready."

CHAPTER 48

"HELLO, EVERYONE. THANK YOU FOR COMING. MY NAME
is Annalise Fiori. I'm an artist and a wrestler. In this exhibit, I com-
bined those two passions."

The crowd transitioned from muffled chatting to complete silence
as I introduced myself. Their faces offered me full attention and
interest. I recognized many of them. My friends, family, teammates,
and coaches. My speech varied slightly from the one I'd given when
my friends and their friends had banded together to change the landscape of girls' wrestling. I shared my experiences and downfalls and
challenges in the sport.

"Girls need to stop blurring into the background of this sport,"
I argued. "Ask any girl wrestler what they face every day. In fact,
ask them today. They're here as a sort of living exhibit, an extension
of the paintings on the walls. As you walk through the progression,
you'll notice the girl wrestler is blurry, not a part of the full image.
This represents her outsider status in the sport. The last painting symbolizes my hope for the future of the sport—our hope for the sport's
future. Thank you for being here and for supporting girls' wrestling."

The room erupted in applause, maybe a little more suited to a
sporting event than an art gallery, but given the audience, what could
we expect? The group shifted to the next artist's demonstration, and

someone tapped me on the shoulder.

"Excuse me? Annalise?"

"Hello," I said cautiously before recognizing Rand Denton, the sports reporter from the Pittsburgh Herald. "Mr. Denton. Thank you for coming!"

"Thanks for the invitation. As a sports reporter, this isn't my usual scene, but it's a great story. I'd love an interview if you have a few minutes."

"Absolutely."

Rand and I moved toward the corner of the room, near the final painting in the progression.

"This is quite an accomplishment," he said. "Is this your first art show?"

"It is and thank you."

"What inspired you to paint so many wrestling scenes?"

"It's a progression of the same moment," I said. The words tumbled out of me. Stories about my love for wrestling and how boys had reacted to that love over the years. How girls have been on the periphery of the sport and states other than Pennsylvania have sanctioned it and are building their programs while our state falls behind, despite its superior reputation for competitive wrestling. I talked about having to wrestle in two different styles and two different brackets to remain competitive.

"Eventually, and hopefully sooner rather than later, the state officials will sanction girls' wrestling as an official sport. When they do, it will be vibrant like the final painting. It will honor tough competitors like the girls you see here. But, for that to happen, we need people in positions of power, especially athletic directors and coaches across the state to build girls' wrestling programs. That will push the state toward sanctioning the sport and other schools to follow."

"Well said. Thank you so much. And you have states coming up, right?"

"I'm not competing in states, actually, not officially."

He squinted at me. "It's your senior season."

"I know, but the reality is girls have to wrestle boys for state titles. We don't have our own sanctioned tournament. The sanction movement, though, is hosting an unsanctioned state championship for girls. If I want to help grow the sport, then that's where I need to be."

"That makes sense," Denton said. "Good luck to you."

"Thank you."

"I'd like to take a closer look at the paintings. Is it okay if I find you later with any more questions?"

"Yes. Definitely. Thank you again for being here."

As soon as he walked away, Fallon practically tackled me. "I'm so proud of you, Lise. The paintings are gorgeous."

"Thank you. I couldn't have done this without you. You know that?"

She blushed. "Thanks, but without you, we wouldn't have a girls' team next year."

"I'm so happy for you! And it's about time."

Fallon glanced toward the stairwell. "Yeah, about it being time. Did you see Sebastian was here?"

"Good lead in. Did he ask you to talk to me for him? That's very middle school."

"Hey! I'm practically in high school now."

"That you are," I said with a laugh.

She leaned forward and whispered, "I saw him hiding out in the back of the room during your speech. He probably didn't want to distract you."

"He's altruistic like that," I said, sarcasm dripping from my words like the wet paint on a canvas.

"Do you miss him?"

I sighed. "I…"

Yes, you idiot.

"Better figure out what you want to say," Fallon said. "He's on his way over."

She rushed into the crowd like being close to Sebastian and me was similar to holding a grenade in her hand.

"Hey," he said.

I took a deep breath. "Hey. Did you ever notice that's kind of our thing?"

"The weighted 'hey'?"

I nodded.

"I did notice that, but we had some other 'things' too." He grinned.

"Is it okay that I'm here?"

"It's a public place."

"You know that's not what I mean, Annalise."

I'd told him to call me Annalise, but my full name on his lips felt even more like a personal attack after he'd secured a twenty-thousand-dollar donation from his father's company to start the school's girls' wrestling program. And that hug we'd had in my living room after the art show letter had arrived. Hard to say we weren't friends after those things.

"It's fine," I said quietly. "I'm glad, actually."

"Yeah?"

"Yeah."

He rewarded my lack of sarcasm with that bright smile of his. "Your paintings are beautiful. The story you tell is so full of passion."

"Thank you."

He turned toward the gallery wall. I did, too. I could stand here day and night and not tire from seeing my paintings on display in an actual gallery with people milling around, experiencing them, talking about them.

"I think it's interesting because they're kind of like you," Sebastian said.

"How do you mean?"

"People hear your name and they think of you as the girl wrestler. Like you're this one thing. They don't realize how dynamic and passionate and versatile you are. You are this progression of a person. Different moments and experiences. You're so much more than one thing, and so is the sport of girls' wrestling."

My mouth went completely dry. He'd understood my work better than I'd hope anyone could. Somehow, he understood me even more.

"Thanks," I whispered.

He opened his mouth but closed it again. Giving him the chance to formulate whatever thought he was working on, I waited, but he looked away for several seconds before trying again, "I…"

"What?" I asked.

Before Sebastian could answer, though, Dom swooped in front of me, wrapped his arms around my waist, and spun me around. "Lise, this is impressive!"

"Thank you."

Dom pulled back from the hug but kept his arm around my shoulders with an oddly protective closeness. "Seriously. All the things we've talked about over the years, you put them perfectly in these paintings. You're crazy talented."

When Dom kissed my cheek and grazed his fingers under my chin, Sebastian's cheeks flamed red, and confusion settled in my stomach.

"I'll let you two go," Sebastian said. "Congratulations, Annalise."

He walked away, looking over his shoulder once.

"Look at me," Dom said.

I did, and he leaned his forehead against mine.

"What are you doing?"

"Making him wicked jealous."

"You are ruthless, and here I thought for a second you'd fallen hopelessly in love with me."

"Everyone said it would happen eventually," he teased. "Besides, what's not to love?"

"Do you really like them?"

"Joking aside, I'm impressed."

"Thank you."

"Is this what you needed for your college applications?"

"I'm still talking to a few wrestling coaches. I think more will attend the girls' state championships. After that, I'll see what my options are and choose whatever school has the best art program."

Dom glanced in Sebastian's direction. "He's staring at us."

"Can't imagine why."

"Do you miss him?" he asked.

"A ton."

"Oh, Lise. I'm sorry."

"Do you think I'm stupid for holding onto this grudge?"

"I think you should feel whatever you feel and not judge yourself for it, but I do have a question."

"What's that?"

"I know that him wrestling you for your spot felt like a huge betrayal at the time, but with some distance, does it still feel that way?"

"Honestly? Not really. He needed the position to impress a college coach, and I had the opportunity to wrestle Trevor Jacoby."

"And kick his ass."

"Truth."

"And…" Dom pointed to my paintings on the wall. "It may have inspired you to something greater."

"True again," I said.

"So what's the issue then?"

"How many times does it take to stand too close to the fire before you realize you're going to get burned. What if next time it's even worse?"

"What if you enjoy the warmth until your dying day?"

I punched his gut. "When did you get so romantic?"

"I'm always romantic." He held out his arm. "Let me show you."

I took it and laughed. "At least I have good friends."

"The best friends."

I rested my head on his shoulder as we climbed the staircase Sebastian had showed me months earlier. I inhaled the fresh, cool air. Dom told stories about drilling with Nick at practice until I couldn't stop laughing. A couple minutes later, footsteps sounded on the stairs, and Sebastian appeared, hands in his pockets, a determined look on his face.

"Hey, Dom," he said.

"Bash."

"Can I talk to Annalise alone for a minute, please?"

Dom glanced at me, and I nodded.

He left us alone, and I gave Sebastian a confused look.

"Hey." Sebastian crept up next to me and leaned against the railing.

"Hey," I said.

"Your show's a hit. I heard some of the gallery groupies talking."

"Really?"

"Yeah. They don't usually feature sports either, so the exhibit brought in a new audience, which is great."

My exhibit. My audience.

Wow.

"You're smiling."

"I'm happy."

Sebastian looked away, and the thought struck me that I may have said something wrong without realizing it. "Are you happy because of the exhibit or because of…Dom?"

"Dom?"

"Yeah. I saw you two downstairs."

"He was trying to torture you."

"Torture me?"

"Make you jealous."

He groaned.

"Which I realize operates on the assumption you care enough to be tortured by me being with someone else."

"Oh, I do."

My tongue stuck in my throat.

"Say something," Sebastian said.

My mind was devoid of words.

"Are you okay?"

I swallowed, blinked, and tried to reset my brain. "Sorry. Um, I thought you said that you care enough about me to be jealous. And that set off confusion in my head. I think I forgot how to speak."

"And if that is what I said?"

My mind toggled between a warm blanket and a terrifying, blazing fire. Both metaphors had applied to Sebastian in the past. The problem was deciding which one fit him best in the future.

"I wasn't lying when I said I was crazy about you," he said. "I know why things ended, but I guess I…I don't know."

"I get why it all went down, but it still stung."

He stepped closer. "Losing you after wanting to be with you for so long wrecked me,

Lise."

My breath caught at the sound of *Lise* rolling off his lips.

"Sorry," he said. "Annalise."

"No," I said, leaning against the warmth of his chest. "Hearing you call me Annalise these last few weeks broke my heart."

He brushed my hair back from my cheeks. "I don't want to break your heart." His blue-green eyes consumed me, and I let the love melting in them warm me in the night cold. "I'm sorry."

"Me too," I whispered.

He pressed his forehead against mine. "Can you forgive me?"

Loving climactic sports moments, I wish I could say I debated my response, but the answer came to me as quickly as a first-period pin.

"Yes."

Sebastian wrapped his arms around my waist. I fell into him, nothing feeling more natural in the world.

"Third time's a charm, right?" I whispered.

"Or maybe we needed three periods to get it right," Sebastian suggested.

"You think we can go the distance?"

The twinkle lights reflected in those blue-green eyes I adored, and a smirk pulled at his lips. "Definitely."

Me too.

ACKNOWLEDGEMENTS

This is book three in the Iron Valley Vikings series! It's gone by so fast and been such a blessing. I could not have done it without my wonderful people, who are always here to lift me up.

First, authenticity is everything to me. I did so much research for this book! I have never wrestled, but it didn't take me long to gain the most intense respect for all wrestlers, especially the young women who generously shared their time and expertise with me, so I could ensure Annalise Fiori's authenticity. Thank you to the young wrestlers who showed me such kindness, patience, and inside secrets: Juliet Alt, Chloe Ault, Gabrielle Bateman, Georgi Butch, Alaina Claassen, Bella DeVito, Ava Golding, Talea Guntrum, Violette Lasure, and Abbie Miles.

Parents, coaches, and male wrestlers shared their expertise, too, and I thank you: Bethany Alt, Tracey Ault, Destinee Chirafisi, Joe Chirafisi, Casey Claassen, Michele Claassen, Lukas Gratzmiller, Laura Guntrum, David Lacinski, and Brooke Zumas. Thanks also to The Mat Factory, Namaste Wrestling, and nutritionist, Hailey Wegner.

Beyond researching, several wrestling experts read the manuscript for authenticity, and I'm so grateful to them for doing so: Laura Guntrum, Talea Guntrum, Maria Hoover, and Brooke Zumas. Thank you also to my critique partners and beta readers: Abby G. Scheg, Caitlin

Lennon, Chelsea Bobulski, and Kathleen Heidecker. You've helped me make this story so much better!

The same can be said for the team at Wise Wolf Books. Thank you to Kristin Yahner, Jake Bray, Laura Sarrafan, Tracey Govender, Samantha Towns, and Jason Bates. I also want to thank librarians and independent bookstore owners, especially Tara Goldberg-De-Leo and Kristy Bodnar, owners of Mystery Lovers Bookshop. My appreciation also to my writing groups—PitchWars, Sisters in Crime, and PennWriters.

I also want to share my gratitude and admiration to our cousin, the late Frank Girardi, a state championship wrestler from Arizona who, later, positively influenced so many young lives through his coaching. When I was working through final edits of this book, Frank passed away in a tragic accident. He was an example of how the power of sports connects and empowers people. We will forever remember him and miss him.

Thank you to my natural family and my found family for always lifting me up—my siblings, cousins, aunts, uncles, friends, and in-laws. My children are my biggest fans, and they humble me with their support every day. I'm so grateful to be sharing this journey with you and your dad.

I want to wish the best to the SanctionPA movement! Girls' wrestling is the fastest growing sport in the country. Girls want to wrestle in sanctioned tournaments and seasons, but at the time of this writing, girls' high school wrestling is not a sanctioned sport in my state. I'm so amazed by the coaches, parents, and wrestlers working to change that. You are a true inspiration!

Finally, thank you to my readers. Keep buying or borrowing books, please! Review them and share on social media. You make this world of pretending possible, and writers the world over cannot thank you enough. I hope these stories empower and inspire you. One of life's greatest pleasures is getting lost in a book. Best wishes on getting lost in this one!

A LOOK AT BOOK FOUR:
SHOT TROUGH THE HEART

From author Tamara Girardi comes an emotionally engaging story in the fourth book of the Iron Valley series.

Archery champion Elle Corwin spends her senior year focused on her romance with the friendly, football star Josh Brighton—until he moves away forcing them into a long distance relationship. As a distraction, Elle immerses herself in shooting and teaching archery lessons, biding her time until Josh returns to Iron Valley for college. Her perfect plan falls apart when Josh breaks up with her on prom night—by Express Mail—and she experiences the elusive but debilitating "target panic" at her first summer shoot.

If she has any hope of saving the money she needs for college expenses, archery equipment, and a trip to the other side of the state to convince Josh he made a mistake, Elle needs the best summer job ever—one that doesn't interfere with her shooting schedule. Her only option is Camp Good Grief, a summer camp for kids struggling with loss. Elle is all set to teach the campers archery, all the while avoiding her own grief.

Just as she accepts the breakup and creates a new vision for her life, Josh comes back into it in a way she never expected, leaving her at risk of missing her big shot—in more ways than one.

AVAILABLE NOVEMBER 2022

ABOUT THE AUTHOR

Tamara Girardi grew up playing sports with the neighborhood kids. Often the only girl, she loved nothing more than smashing a home run at the opportune moment or stealing the basketball from one of the guys and scoring two on a breakaway. In high school, she fell in love with the quarterback and played football in the back yard with him and his two quarterback brothers. Watching them play, she wondered, "What would it be like if they'd had a baby sister? Would she play quarterback, too?" And just like that, the idea for Gridiron Girl was born.

Also an academic, Tamara is an Associate Professor of English at HACC, Central Pennsylvania's Community College where she teaches creative writing, technical writing, composition, and literature online. She has a PhD in English from Indiana University of Pennsylvania and studied fiction at the University of St. Andrews in Scotland. Tamara also writes picture books.

She lives in a suburb of Pittsburgh, Pennsylvania with her husband and four adorably rambunctious children.

CPSIA information can be obtained
at www.ICGtesting.com
Printed in the USA
LVHW082121310822
727313LV00011B/99/J